April 2023

The Way to Hornsey Rise

An Autobiographical Novel

Jeremy Worman

Jeremy Worman

Holland Park Press London

Published by Holland Park Press 2023
Copyright © Jeremy Worman 2023

First Edition

The moral right of Jeremy Worman to be identified as the
author of this work has been asserted by him in accordance
with the Copyright, Designs and Patents Act of 1988.

British Library Cataloguing-in-Publication Data
A catalogue record for this book is available from the British Library

ISBN 978-1-907320-98-9

Cover designed by Reactive Graphics

Printed and bound by
CPI Group (UK) Ltd, Croydon CR0 4YY

www.hollandparkpress.co.uk

To Myfanwy

Lord it's time; the wine is already fermenting.
The time has come to have a home,
Or to remain for a long time without one.
The time has come not to be alone,
Or else we will stay alone for a long time.
We will consume the hours over books,
Or in writing letters to distant places,
Long letters from our solitude.
And we will go back and forth through the streets,
Restless, while the leaves fall.

Primo Levi, 'After R.M. Rilke'

CONTENTS

PROLOGUE
DECEMBER 1996: WINDLESHAM PARISH CHURCH, SURREY

Ma's coffin was lowered into the earth by the undertakers and I exhaled a sigh of relief. Soon she would be covered for ever. I was shaking and peered down in case she was rising again like Dracula. The grey helmet of sky enclosed the scene like a black-and-white film. I stepped back in line with the group of mourners as we made a thin square around the grave. Then the four undertakers walked away and the one at the front gave me a kind, professional smile. I looked down at my polished black shoes and thought about the next stage of the morning: I would be leading the way by car to Great Fosters Hotel, Egham, where a table had been booked for lunch.

My fellow mourners began to turn towards their cars, and to step heavily and slowly with that grave tread reserved for funerals. My oldest friend, Giles Summerhays, touched my shoulder.

'Okay, Worm?'

'Fine. Thanks. Fine.'

He walked away. I looked again into her grave.

'Darling,' Ma said in her lovely voice, 'Pass me down one last Sobranie Black Russian cigarette before I go.'

Of course, I almost said, and checked the knot of my tie.

I had been born a few miles away in the Windlesham Maternity Hospital on 2 March 1954. That morning it had snowed.

Ma and I both loved snow, and all kinds of weather. My father was rather sickly and needed plenty of rest; Ma and I spent a lot of time tootling along country lanes in her car.

On a June day all those years ago, when I was about eight years old, we drove in her open-topped yellow Triumph Herald to Chobham and stopped in one of our favourite lanes. She jumped out. 'Come on, slow coach,' she said. I caught her up. Beech and elm trees lined the road, and the sun filtered through in streams of light.

We turned into the entrance to Windlow Farm. Ma knew the farmer, Mr Dunlace, who had been surprised the previous year when she took up his challenge to milk a cow, and did it perfectly. 'You never forget old skills, Mr Dunlace. I told you I was once a proper country girl. I used to love helping out at a local farm in Burscough, Lancashire, although it seemed to annoy the dairymaids.'

Today, no one was about; we walked through the well-kept farmyard and stood by the four-bar wooden gate that opened to a meadow. Blues, greens and yellows blurred in a summer haze. I knew for the first time that I loved nature and the feeling of joy it gave me. Ma squeezed my hand. 'Look,' she said. 'That sturdy little horse, a cob, isn't he perfect.' The brown and white cob stood by the far gate, which led to other fields where the low evening sun spread its red glow. 'He's in a harness,' she said. 'Mr Dunlace must be about to connect his little cart to it.' I said, 'Oh, Mummy that would be so lovely.' I knew that we both saw ourselves in the cart as we drove through sunny fields to the ends of Surrey. 'You and I would be so happy living in real country, wouldn't we, darling? Surrey is getting so built up.' She hugged me and her tear fell on my cheek. 'I'm just happy, Jeremy, really. Hold on to these moments that seem to last for ever – "ever moments" I call them – and then in sad times they always come back to you...'

Despite many troubles between us, her advice has often sustained me...

Engines were starting up.

'Just coming.'

I looked for the last time at Ma's coffin.

CHAPTER ONE
DIANA DORS SAYS HELLO

Mummy was late. I sat by the classroom window and looked at the badge of my school blazer: 'V.W.J.S': Virginia Water Junior School or Very Wet Jam Sandwiches. All my friends had gone home. The dapply sun came through the beech trees and made the stone bird bath glow in the front garden.

Our paintings were all over the classroom walls. This was my last term and then I had to leave for prep school. Charlie was going to Papplewick, Rory to St Piran's and my best friend Giles to St George's, Windsor to be a choirboy. We were not quite sure where I was going. We had shortbread and custard for pudding today. Oh, where was she? Our headteacher, Miss Fish, was a Quaker and Daddy said she set a very good example. I wiped my eyes.

Honk, honk.

'Mummy!'

I stood up. She did a racing stop and waved. Her new yellow Triumph Herald convertible looked fantastic with the roof down.

I rushed to the front steps.

Miss Fish came out of her study and stood behind me.

Mummy walked up the path. She rearranged the blue silk scarf with blobs of horses' heads on it.

'Not like you to be late, Mrs Worman. I was about to phone.'

'So sorry. I was delayed at the butcher's.'

Mummy took off her dark glasses with white fin frames.

'Not to worry. We'll miss him when he goes. Only three weeks' left!' Miss Fish gave me a wrinkly smile and her short white hair stayed still. 'That William Blake poem you recited so beautifully last week in assembly; may I hear the first verse again?'

I stepped back a few paces:

My mother groan'd! my father wept,
Into the dangerous world I leapt:
Helpless, naked, piping loud:
Like a fiend hid in a cloud.

Miss Fish hugged me. 'What a lovely little fiend!'
'He's been very happy here. He doesn't want to leave.
Thank you so much. Goodbye.'
I ran down the path and sat in the passenger seat.
Mummy vroomed the engine. She turned to me. 'Have
you been crying?'
'No; well, a bit. You were late, and I don't want to go
to prep school.'
She squeezed my leg. 'You'll make lots of new friends.'
She twirled her wrist in the air as if encouraging a horse
with a gentle whip.
We whooshed off.
'You drive faster than Daddy.'
'Keeps me young, darling. Actually, I was delayed
because that awful Mrs Robinson jumped in front of the
car, near the chemist's. Ever since I said to her last year,
at the Women's Institute bazaar, that her recent batch of
marmalade was a little tart, she takes every chance to
annoy me. Anyway, I had tooted politely as she hurtled
into the road – she just glared. You would have thought I'd
run off with her husband, silly little man that he is. I wish
I hadn't stopped but her large frame would have dented the
wing. I pulled over and had words with her.'
'Did you shout?'
'Nothing so crude, darling. But she knew the game was
up. I could see it in her eyes. Funnily enough, that new tall
dark-haired local bobby, the one with the cheeky grin who
looks like a rugby three-quarter, had observed the scene
from the other side of the road. As I drove off, he smiled.'

Mummy always took away my fears with her stories.

We stopped at the junction on Gorse Hill Road. On the left was Coronation Playing Field where we played rounders, using rusty cast-iron discs as markers. On the other side of the road was our doctor's house, Dr Eric Taylor. There was a big boat in the garden. He used to be in the Royal Navy and had a beard.

'Eric bought that as a plot years ago,' Mummy said, 'and then had the house built; your father could have done the same thing, next to the Forbes's place, but he said it cost too much. And he calls himself a businessman!'

Mummy wanted to live here, on the Wentworth Estate, and often said how Daddy had 'missed his chance'.

'I put your swimming togs in the boot. We'll go to Great Fosters. It feels like the beginning of summer.'

'Great.'

Mummy touched 50mph down the steep narrow hill at the side of Holloway Sanatorium, but then slowed up. Last month she was stopped for speeding. The policeman, who wore a white cap, had got out of the black Ford Zodiac police car and walked towards us with a notebook in his hand and a fierce face; Mummy apologised and said she had been worrying about what to cook for supper tonight. She told him, 'I love you speed cops for making the roads safer.' He laughed: 'No more driving like Stirling Moss, Madam. Next time you won't be so lucky.'

At the corner in Stroud Green I looked up the lane that led to an ancient farmhouse. Giles and I went on bike rides up that track, with fields of high grass on both sides, which cut off the noise from the main roads. There were lots of birds and butterflies, rabbits and dairy cows. A mile further on we turned into Great Fosters Hotel, which was an Elizabethan building, just outside Egham. There was a swimming pool for the guests and they allowed in a few season-ticket holders like us. The front gates were used as the entrance to the school in the children's television programme *Billy Bunter*. I got out and took my trunks and towel from the boot.

'Aren't you swimming today, Mummy?'

'I've had a lot of exercise; I'll just watch.'

But she told me this morning she was going to bake a cake and that isn't very energetic.

She did not bother to lock the car. We walked down the wobbly York stone path. The round blue fountain by the gate to the pool splashed us.

'Great to be back!' I said.

All the dark-wooden changing huts at the deep end had been creosoted and that smell mixed with a chloriney whiff. The surface of the blue water flickered with sun and my heart raced.

'Hello, Wormy.'

'Hello, Frank.'

Frank had been in charge of the swimming pool for years. In the winter he worked in the hotel gardens. He stood in front of his big-windowed little office, which was in the middle of the changing huts behind the diving boards. He was short, tattooed and barrel shaped. He had been a diver in the Royal Navy and could walk on the bottom of the pool with no one on his shoulders. Daddy used to say, 'All that barley wine gives him ballast.' It was only June but Frank looked suntanned already; perhaps his body was coloured by rum too, which was what he drank in the winter.

'Hello, Mrs Worman. You're looking younger than ever.'

'You old charmer, Frank.'

'Shall I book Jeremy in for a few diving lessons?'

'Good idea.'

'Did you hear that, darling?' She rubbed my ear.

Why had no one asked me? I didn't like diving even though I could do it off the springboard without making a splash. Last summer I went off the middle board as Susan

18

Duncan-Smith and Clare Rhodes watched. But I never wanted to go off the high board.

'You shoo off and change. I'll find a spot in the sun.' She gave me a push, then tugged me back. 'Darling, who's that waving at you?'

At the side of the pool by the old small-red-brick wall, a curvy blonde woman got up from her lounger.

'Gosh, it's Diana Dors. Go on.'

Mummy shuffled me forward as the woman called me over.

I stood in front of her.

'It's my lovely little cricketer!'

She grabbed me and held me to her bosom. I could not see or breathe until I bounced off.

Mummy stepped in front of me. 'I'm Barbara Worman,' she put out her hand. 'How do you know my little urchin?'

Diana shook Mummy's hand. 'He was playing with Liam the other week, the American boy of my next-door neighbours; their cricket ball came over the fence, and I handed it back.' Diana smiled at me. 'We had a chat and I learnt so much about cricket.' She reached out for me but luckily this time only patted my head. She pointed to a deckchair next to hers. 'Why don't you join me, Barbara?'

'I'd love to.'

'My pool is out of action; I come here in the weekdays. No one bothers me.'

I went off to change.

When I returned I jumped straight in and did a few lengths of my best breaststroke. 'He's like a little fish,' I heard Diana say. Soon after I got out of the freezing water. I sat in the deckchair at the other side of Diana. She rubbed suntan lotion over the top of her big breasts, and then between them. 'Want some?' She turned to me.

'No thank you.'

'Let me get us some tea and cakes,' Diana said.

'What a lovely idea,' Mummy said.

'They're very good to me here. Frank is an absolute angel.' She waved at him. 'Frank, Frank!'

He came over, his short legs moving like a crab. 'Don't tell me, Madam, you want to sign up for diving lessons.'

'I'm too top heavy to be a diver, but we'd love tea and cakes; Jeremy, would you prefer a Coke or Fanta?'

'Coke, please.'

'I'll sort that out,' Frank said.

'You lovely man; ask them to put it on my tab, please.'

'I will.'

'Just going to warm up,' I said.

'All right, darling.'

I ran off to the little field-like area set back from the pool. Down the side path from there, at the back of the hotel, were the beautiful gardens, where Elizabeth I used to have archery tournaments. I loved the secret rose garden, the maze and the fountain. We weren't really allowed in the gardens, but Giles and my other friends took no notice. I ran round the big patch of grass and felt warmer.

When I returned to Mummy and Diana, they were chatting away. 'Of course,' Mummy said, 'I know Irene Bosanquet.' And then they found they both knew a few other people who lived on the Wentworth Estate. At the side of the hotel the small red bricks on the chimney pots glowed. Diana handed me the glass of Coke. 'And those cakes have your name on them,' she said. The chocolate eclair and the Neapolitan slice were delicious. After, I closed my eyes and enjoyed the warm sun on my face.

'Here's my number,' Diana said to Mummy, 'let's keep in touch.'

'I will,' Mummy said as she scribbled her number on a scrap of paper, which she gave to Diana.

I went to get changed.

On my way back to them, Mummy stood up to leave and Diana said to her, 'I'm not working for the next month; you must come to lunch.'

'I'd love to,' Mummy said.

Diana leant forward on the lounger. 'See you soon, my lovely little cricketer.'

I stepped back quickly.

We waved to Frank on our way out.

'First diving lesson next Wednesday, after school. 4.30?' he called after us.

'We'll be there,' Mummy said.

In the car she beamed at me. 'Well done to you.' She tapped the steering wheel. 'You've learnt a great trick of life – how to impress people without trying – it's magic. You'd not believe the offers of holidays, horses and marriage I've had from just being myself.' She patted my arm. 'You get it from me. You marvellous boy. To think one can go from the pits of Mrs Robinson to the heights of Diana Dors in two hours – isn't life fun!'

Just before Egham station level crossing, we turned into our house, Inglewood. Daddy's Alvis wasn't there, although he often finished work early. He had decided the whole house was too big for us, and a few years ago had stairs put up the side: we lived on the top two floors and had a separate flat downstairs, with its own front door. For the last year Uncle Neville had lived there. He wasn't really my uncle but Mummy called him 'our oldest family friend' and said it would be very nice if I called him 'Uncle Neville'. He liked that and so did I. He had been in the Indian Army, and won medals, but did not have money. He was waiting for an annuity so he could buy himself a little house.

Mummy got out of the car. 'I don't need to put the roof up,' she said, 'it's not going to rain tonight.' She smiled. 'Come on my lovely little afterthought.'

She called me that because they had tried to have children for years, but nothing happened, and so they stopped thinking about it. Then I came along.

I charged up the stairs. She followed me and opened the door. I rushed up to my bedroom on the top floor. It was a small attic room with an angled roof and blue wallpaper with silver stars on it and my bed was under the slope. The window looked on to the back garden. By the door was a curtained-off partition that led to the long airing cupboard, where you could stand up. We kept our sheets and towels there on long thick shelves; there was a lovely scent from the fresh laundry. I changed into corduroy shorts, a jumper and put on plimsolls.

I said at the top of the stairs. 'Mummy. May I go and see Uncle Neville before supper?'

'Yes, but don't disturb him if he's busy; he has lots of papers to sort out.'

I ran from my bedroom to the first floor and then tiptoed down to his flat. These stairs were uncarpeted as we only used this as a utility area. There was a long row of hangers with jackets, coats and hats that no one wore; shelves of homemade jams, pickles and a huge can of Australian honey that Uncle Fred had sent from Adelaide; little tins with funny things in them like baby bees in sauce, seaweed in beans, and even fried insects. A Japanese client of Daddy's gave them to us once a year.

'Uncle Neville?' I tapped on the connecting door. Perhaps he had gone for his daily constitutional.

The big bolt slid back.

'Nice to see you, old boy. Good day on the front line?'

'The art class went on for ever; it's so boring. Will you teach me more cricket today?'

He put his hand on my shoulder and led me into his sitting room, which looked out through the French windows to our garden.

'Lovely smell,' I said.

'Trying to make a proper chicken korma. I mixed the spices this afternoon – it was a Mughal dish, as you probably knew.'

'Not really.'

He laughed. Uncle Neville was tall and bent down to collect the scruffy sheets of paper off the sofa. His tie, one

22

of his Army ones, waved about. 'An art lesson is better than filling in tax forms, so hold on to that thought.'

'All right.'

He piled the papers on a side table. His legs were springy and his hands flapped at his side as if he might start galloping at any minute. Mummy said he had 'the swinging gait of a born horseman'. They had met a long time ago when hunting with the Surrey Union but both of them had to stop because it was expensive. Daddy did not like horses and said to Mummy last year, 'Too many of those people are terrible snobs.' Daddy and Uncle Neville were the same in some ways because they always had polished shoes, except when they wore suede ones, and perfect creases in their trousers. Mummy said it was very nice living with two real gentlemen.

I looked at the silver-framed photograph on the mantelpiece of Uncle Neville's dark-haired daughter, Geraldine, in school uniform. She was about twelve, with short hair, but very pretty. Next to that was one of him and his wife, Dorinka, who was wearing a bright blue velvet gown, and he had on a bright yellow dress jacket of his regiment, 1st Duke of York's Own Skinner's Horse. He leant on the mantelpiece: 'That was Poona.' He traced his finger round the frame. I wanted to jump into the photograph with him. He was getting divorced. Dorinka and Geraldine were living in Bayswater. Geraldine was grown up now. She was at art college.

'Come on; let's sort out a few cricket shots. It will get you off to a good start at prep school.'

'I don't want to go to prep school.'

'You do. Can you put on your pads?'

I took them from behind the sofa, sat down, and turned my leg round to do up the straps. They were a present from Uncle Neville. The middle strap of the left one got twisted and he untangled it.

'I'm ready.' I stood on the tiled steps outside the French windows.

23

'Don't forget your gloves.' He handed them to me and I walked up our long garden and stood in front of the apple tree we used as stumps. 'Get ready,' he said. He put down an old jumper at the other end. 'Remember, we're not using a tennis ball anymore.'

He bowled with a real leather cricket ball and I hit it back.

'Very good, Jeremy. Your bat and pads were close together. That little crouch, as you came forward, I like that. You'll be the next Ken Barrington.'

He bowled me lots more balls. After a while I took a breather and sat against the apple tree.

'Mummy!'

She was standing by the window in his sitting room.

'Join us, Barbara. Your daisy cutters fool everyone.'

'Patronising bloody man!' She kissed his cheek.

'Do you want a bat, Uncle Neville?'

'Now your mother is here, perhaps we could play catch?' He wiped his brow with a white handkerchief.

'Lovely idea. I always beat you at that,' she said.

I took off my pads and gloves.

'Drink that, darling.' She handed me a glass of Rose's lime juice.

After I had gulped it down, Uncle Neville lifted me high and from the tree I picked an apple.

'Isn't the garden lovely this year?' She nodded at the new bed of nasturtiums by the rockery, which I had helped our gardener Bill Cranham put in. 'And those hollyhocks.' She pointed. 'Aren't they divine?'

I threw her the tennis ball, and she caught it. The three of us made a triangle. Uncle Neville surprised me by throwing an apple from behind his back. He had such blue eyes.

'Neville! Those apples have better things to do than be part of your magic tricks.'

We played one-arm, one leg etc. and chucked the ball around, trying to fool each other. I almost won, but Mummy actually won.

Uncle Neville tapped the face of his watch: '6.30. Gin-and-tonic time, Barbara?'

'Lovely idea, but no. I must cook. Lamb cutlets tonight. Before I go, you'll never guess who Jeremy chatted up at Great Fosters today.'

'Enlighten me.'

'Diana Dors. Jeremy met her a few weeks ago; she lives next door to a friend of his...'

'Not really "met", Mummy.'

'Don't interrupt, darling. Anyway, Diana is charming; we knew a few people in common; we swapped phone numbers.'

'How very glamorous. Good for you two. There's not much glamour in England for me these days. Now why not come down after dinner, Barbara? Isn't this Geoff's night at the Rotary Club?'

'It was a subcommittee meeting, actually; it's been cancelled.'

'Another time.'

'Yes. Soon.'

'Goodbye, Uncle Neville. Can we play cricket again tomorrow. Please?'

'Jeremy, don't bully the poor man.'

'Next week. I'm in town for the weekend.'

'Okay.'

I ran upstairs and turned on the television in our sitting room to watch *The Lone Ranger*, the best cowboy in the world. Five minutes later Mummy rushed up as the phone rang in the corridor.

'Hello...'

'Oh, really Geoff, so the cancelled meeting is uncancelled. Thank goodness I didn't prepare the lamb cutlets. See you later then. Bye.'

She put her head round the door. 'Did you get the gist of that? There's spag bol left over; shall we have supper watching *Coronation Street*?'

'Yes, please.'

'Then you can go straight to bed. After that I may keep Neville company; he's rather low.'

'Can I play with my soldiers first?'

'Of course.'

I went up to the playroom, next to my bedroom. It had a big window and the walls were cream. In the alcove under the eaves we kept an ottoman of all my baby clothes and other things I had grown out of, which Mummy did not want to throw away. The framed photo of the Surrey First XI that Uncle Neville had given me was above the fireplace. Mummy wanted me to put up more pictures but Daddy said, 'If Jeremy likes his playroom simple, leave it at that.'

Great-Aunt Em's Christmas present of a Confederate fort was in the middle of the floor. I kept sentries on each corner in case of attacks by Red Indians; behind the entrance gate there were a few cavalry soldiers on horseback ready to make a surprise attack. I was short of old-fashioned American soldiers and Red Indians, but I had loads of Second World War British and German troops. When I wanted a huge battle, I had to let all sorts of soldiers fight on the same side.

I always tried to make the Confederates win as they were underdogs (Uncle Neville told me that); I liked their pale-blue uniforms and the swirling hats of the cavalrymen. They looked like the Cavaliers of our own Civil War; Daddy had shown me pictures of them and they were better than the Roundheads. It was clear from my Ladybird history book that Cavaliers had more fun: they smiled while the Roundheads looked cross, as if about to hit you. Cavaliers had nicer clothes, like Daddy's and Uncle Neville's. Cavaliers liked parties, and dogs, which you often saw in their paintings. I was sure Roundheads beat their dogs. We used to have a mongrel black Labrador, Pedro, and I could not bear the thought of anyone hitting him. He had been put down last year because he was very old.

We had tried to buy more Confederate soldiers for my eighth birthday but the lady in the Caleys toy department told us 'there had been a run on them'. She did not know when they would be getting more. So today for my big battle I had to join all my soldiers together, and English commandos were fighting with the Confederates. I knew it didn't look quite right. 'Historical accuracy is quite important,' Uncle Neville told me last week. When I explained the problem, he said he would try to pop in to Hamleys next time he was in town.

It really didn't look at all right and now I was older it made me cross. I put all the Second World War soldiers back in their box. The Confederates were on their own. I had placed a group of Sioux Red Indians, most on horseback, just outside the main gates. I opened them – the small Confederate cavalry charged into the middle of the brave warriors, knocking over their horses and shooting the men. There were losses on our side too. But at the end, my hero sat bravely in the midst of the battle. Uncle Neville and I had come up with a name for him: Major Nathaniel Lee. He waved the Confederate flag, a blue-starred cross shape on a dark red background. I saluted him. A few days ago, when Uncle Neville had seen one of my victory scenes, he smiled; he also said that Major Nathaniel Lee was probably a long way from his farm and tobacco plantations in Kentucky and must be missing his wife and children. I had said, 'It's good to be on the side of the goodies.' Uncle Neville frowned: 'Well, in those days some Confederates had slaves to work on their land, but I'm sure Major Lee didn't.' Today, I stood up and saluted: 'I hope you get back home soon, Major Lee.' Major Lee would never have slaves. I hoped too that Uncle Neville would stay with us and not look for another home.

'Supper, darling,' Mummy called.

I ran down to the kitchen and we carried our trays to the sitting room. I turned on the television and we watched *Coronation Street*. Mummy said it brought back memories of her Lancashire roots, but I didn't think her life was like Ena Sharples's. Mummy was brought up in a huge house, and her grandmother had a chauffeur. But I know her family had been poor once. During the interlude Mummy got me a piece of strawberry flan. I quite liked the programme but I wished Ena Sharples wasn't so bad-tempered.

I yawned. 'Goodnight, Mummy.'

'Goodnight, darling.' She gave me a squelchy kiss on the cheek.

After brushing my teeth, I got straight into bed and read *The Beano*. Just as I was getting off to sleep, I heard Mummy tiptoe down the wooden stairs.

CHAPTER TWO
ESCAPE

My name had been down for Caldicott, but then my parents decided it was not the right one, so we had to look again. Perhaps it was too late and maybe I could have a tutor instead.

One early Saturday morning we visited Wallop School in Weybridge. The headmaster, all whiskers and red face, sat me with a book at a high wooden desk while he showed my parents round. He was very unfriendly. We did not stay long as there was another school to visit.

As we drove away, Daddy said, 'He was a bit like Wackford Squeers.' He opened the window and flicked ash from his Capstan. He drove quite fast to the next school, which was near Windsor. The leathery smell of the red seats at the back of the Alvis was nice. Daddy's hair was white and his neck wrinkly. A few weeks ago, when he came to Sports Day, Paula Day said to me, 'Your grandfather looks really sweet.' I didn't say anything back, and never told anyone what she had said.

From the corner of my seat, I peered at the side of Daddy's face, which looked almost young. He was wearing the suit that was Mummy's favourite, his light-brown houndstooth one. He wore tortoiseshell bifocals, which Mummy had chosen for him. It did not take long to get there. Daddy turned into the drive. I read the sign out loud: 'Haileybury and ISC (Imperial Service College) Junior School.'

'Sounds impressive, doesn't it?' Daddy said.

'S'pose so.'

'What a marvellous building,' Mummy said, 'the oldest part must be the original Clewer Manor, which was Elizabethan.' She tapped Daddy on the shoulder, 'Remember the pamphlet the school sent us: the headmaster is Cheltenham and Oxford; far more than we can say for that scoutmaster at the last place.' We parked outside the main entrance. The headmaster walked down the stone steps and opened the car door for Mummy; his moustache twitched and the brass buttons on his blazer glinted.

'I'm Mr Beckwith.'

'Barbara Worman. How do you do.'

Daddy came round to Mummy's side of the car and shook Mr Beckwith's hand.

The headmaster looked down at me. His hair was silvery at the sides and bald on top. 'Hello; welcome to our school.'

'Thank you, sir.'

'Perhaps we should start with the dormitories; parents often worry about those.'

'Jeremy will be a day boy to start with,' Daddy said, 'but we'd like him to board after a few years.'

No one had told me.

We followed Mr Beckwith into the huge, high hallway, like a baron's court in a story book, and up the shiny polished stairs.

'This is Dorm 9, for the older boys. It's kitted out for about ten.'

He looked at me. 'Try a bed; reassure your parents.'

'Thank you, sir.'

I was dressed in my Virginia Water Junior School blazer, tie, short grey trousers, long socks and polished black shoes. What should I do? Take my shoes off as if I was going to bed, or keep them on, which might mark the bed and get me into trouble.

'Go on, old chap,' Daddy said.

Mr Beckwith tapped my shoulder. 'Jump on; your shoes look very clean; don't tell Matron.'

The mattress was thin but the beds were the sort that soldiers slept on and I liked that idea. 'Very nice, sir. Thank you.'

We followed him downstairs and then stood by the dining room where the long window looked onto a spacious lawn. The House names glowed in gold letters on the thick wooden bookshelves – Dewar; Athlone; McCormick-Goodhart; Alexander. Then the headmaster led us through the changing rooms: rows of double basins extended in the middle of the red-tiled floor. In an alcove at the end, a short man with a shining bald dome and Brylcreem on the sides of what remained of his dark hair, sat on a stool dubbining rugby boots.

'You look busy, Boots,' Mr Beckwith said.

'Almost there, sir.' He looked up.

Mummy leant towards him. 'Hope you'll get the chance for some fresh air today; it's lovely out there.'

'Oh, yes, Madam, it's my afternoon orff; I'm goin' into town.'

'That's good.'

Mr Beckwith talked about the 'brilliant First XV we have this year'. Out of nowhere a boy came to a skidding stop at the headmaster's feet.

'Walker. You know we never run in the corridors and especially not in the shower rooms.'

'Sorry, sir. I've had permission to phone my parents.'

'They'll still be there if you don't run. Didn't you see us?'

'I was thinking of other things, sir.'

'Well,' Mummy said, 'How very nice that he wants to phone his parents.'

Mr Beckwith laughed: 'Save your speed for the match this afternoon.' The boy walked off.

The headmaster took us at a whizzy pace into the new part of the school, which contained the classrooms and art room. After seeing the playing fields, we walked round to the front entrance, where he said goodbye.

As we drove away Mummy said, 'That is a proper prep school.'

'I liked the headmaster,' Daddy said.

'I hope it's good for cricket; the pitch looks fantastic,' I said.

When we got home, I ran upstairs and changed into jeans and a checked shirt. From the window I watched Bill Cranham mowing the grass. I wanted to tell Uncle Neville all about today but he was in London.

Downstairs, Bill and Daddy were sitting in the dining room, drinking beer from tankards.

'I know Mrs Worman loves her gladioli, but they just won't do it in our garden, Mr Worman. The fuchsia has come back beautiful and that will please her.'

'Perhaps it's snails,' Daddy said.

'They certainly don't help.' He turned to me. 'Hello, young man; your father tells me there's a new school on the horizon.'

'I think so; they have a great cricket pitch.'

'Is Colonel Prideaux still giving you lessons?'

'He is. My forward defensive is much better.'

Bill's stiff hairs bristled on his nose and ears like a cat's whiskers. 'You couldn't have a better teacher; he played for his regiment, but as he's such a modest man, I had to squeeze that out of him.'

I stood in front of Daddy.

'Would you like a shandy, old chap?' Daddy said.

'Yes please.'

He picked up the big bottle of Whitbread Pale Ale, poured a little into my silver tankard and topped it up with ginger beer.

'Sit on my knee.'

I did. They were very bony; he put his long thin arms round me.

'Cheers,' I said.

Daddy's face was blotchy; when I stared through his bifocals, his eyes were hollow and their rims like the craters of an extinct volcano. Bill and Daddy chatted about vegetables. I looked out of the window. Sometimes when Mummy and I went out with Daddy it was nice. The week before we had lunch at the Red Lion in the High Street and the landlord treated us very well. 'Shall I bring out your drinks, Mr Worman? I'll put it all on your tab.' Daddy was a chartered surveyor and senior partner with Gale and Power. Lots of people knew him. When we went out, I did not worry so much that he was old and had a bad cough from smoking. But we did not do it often as he needed extra sleep in the afternoon at weekends. He was thirteen years older than Mummy. Yesterday, she said on the phone to Great-Aunt Em that she worried how much longer he could carry on working...

'You're very quiet, old chap.'

'Thinking about his new school, most like,' Bill said.

Mummy stood at the door and looked at the trug by Bill's chair. 'What a lovely selection – the lettuces look perfect. And I think I'll make a potato salad tonight with the charlottes; those tomatoes are so ripe.'

'We're going to have a good season, Mrs Worman; I'm optimistic about the strawberries too.' Bill stood up. 'Would you like a few overs, young man, before I go to the Red Lion to meet my brother?'

'Yes, please.'

On Sunday morning Giles and I went for a bike ride to Prune Hill. He was my best friend from school and he lived next door to us. We had to get back quickly as Giles was going sailing with his brother.

Mummy had cooked roast beef, Lancashire pudding, roast potatoes, vegetables and gravy. She was such a good cook. After lunch, I helped to wash up; Daddy had a rest. Mummy had to write letters and went upstairs to her bedroom. Giles was busy all afternoon. I watched a Norman Wisdom film on television but found him silly. Around teatime I had a glass of milk and ate a digestive biscuit in the kitchen. I heard Uncle Neville's front door open. He must be back from London. I waited as long as I could.

'It's unlocked,' he said.

'How did you know?'

'I left it open for your mother; we were going to have a cup of tea.'

'What are you doing?'

'Well…'

Mummy came down. 'You got here quickly, Jeremy.'

'No; I tiptoed slowly.'

Uncle Neville laughed. 'Now we are here together, I shall tell you my news.'

Mummy flopped on to the sofa. 'Why are you taking your books off the shelf?'

'I've just spent the weekend at Rosalyn and Hugo's.' He looked at me. 'They are Dorinka's sister and brother-in-law.'

'Get on with it,' Mummy said.

'As I was trying to say, at their place in South Kensington. Dorinka came for dinner on Saturday. We had a long, long talk, which we continued on Sunday morning.'

'So she stayed the night too?'

'The upshot is, Barbara, that we are having a reconciliation. I will try to buy a small place, possibly in Old Windsor…'

'Planned it all out, then,' Mummy said. Her fingers bent into a fist and the knuckles went white.

'No. This has come as a great surprise.' He scratched his head.

'Can we still play cricket?' I said.

'Often.'

'I may go to prep school in Windsor; Mummy and I can drop in.'

'Anytime at all. Let me make a pot of tea; I came back with a good chocolate cake from a patisserie.'

'Aren't we the lucky ones,' Mummy said.

34

When he went out she squeezed my hand. Her cheeks were flushed and she twiddled the wedding ring on her finger. He came back with a big tray and put it on the side table. He handed round the plates and we helped ourselves to a slice of cake. After pouring tea, he sat in his armchair opposite the sofa where we were sitting.

'I'm going upstairs,' she said.

He asked if I wanted to play cricket but I had to tidy my bedroom and went up too.

The rest of the summer was all about my new school. Caleys in Windsor was the most important shop in Mummy's world, and now it was mentioned every day as we had to get my school clothes, and lots of other things, very quickly: uniforms, shoes, name tabs, games clothes, socks, and even garters, though Mummy was not sure about them. On the first Wednesday of the school holidays we set off for Caleys.

'Can we put the hood down?' I asked.

'Not today; you know it blows Em around too much.'

I sat in the passenger seat. Mummy turned the ignition switch.

'I'm pleased Em is coming,' Mummy said, 'she was rather low yesterday on the phone. This will cheer her up.'

We set off.

'Why was she sad?'

'She would have loved a husband and she gets lonely.'

'Couldn't she get one?'

'There weren't enough men to go round after the First World War.'

Mummy was whizzing past Great Fosters.

'You said she had a boyfriend who you called a "lounge lizard".'

'Yes, a charming ex-officer from the Royal Flying Corps who conned her out of a lot of money so now she gets much less from the Piggott Trust Fund, set up by your great-grandfather for his children.'

'Watch out for speed cops, Mummy.'

I knew that whenever Em's Dividends, or perhaps it was Annuities, arrived, there was always a cheque for Mummy. One of Em's sisters, my great-aunt Alice, who lived in Droitwich and had someone to look after her, did not trust men – 'Deceivers all, Barbara,' she said to Mummy last time she stayed with us. The third of Em's sisters, great-aunt Bertha, married a defrocked Lancashire vicar and she died young from a disease. I never met her except through Em's sleep-talking when she stayed with us: 'Bertha, Bertha,' she whimpered, and the words came up the stairs like ghosts to my bedroom.

Last summer Em had fainted outside Caleys, 'a touch of the vapours' as she put it. A shop assistant came out with a chair. And a kind gentleman gave her a nip of brandy from his hip flask. That taught her a lesson: never leave home without medicine. Since then, wherever she went she took her own supply of brandy in a tiny sterling-silver flask covered in crocodile leather, with a slit of glass down the middle, to show how much was left.

When we got to Virginia Water, Em was waiting on the pavement outside her flat. I hopped into the back seat, and made sure the front window was down, as the combination of perfume and floating powder from her well made-up face made me cough.

'And how is my little Jeremy? Prep school, prep school; I can't believe it.' Her body was small and slender and her face like a pretty apricot stone; her grey eyes shone out. She patted a brown patent handbag: 'Always keep a little medicine, Barbara; you never know.'

'Quite right,' Mummy said.

We took the country route to Windsor and parked in the Castle Hotel car park. Em insisted, 'We fortify ourselves with a glass of sherry.' We sat at our usual place in the foyer of thick carpets and chandeliers. As they gossiped, I drank a Coke, nibbled peanuts and watched people go by outside. After their second sherry, Em said, 'Best be on our way.'

I followed them into Caleys. The brass handles and fingerplates were very well polished as the doors sprung open to welcome us to Gloves and Perfume. We went down the wide curving stairs to Menswear. School badges were behind the counter: I was not going to any old school but one with a plaque, as if I was a sort of by Royal Appointment schoolboy. Caleys had been by Royal Appointment to Queen Victoria and her seal of approval, the Royal Warrant, was on display as you went up the side stairs to the hat department. Mummy and Em led the charge to the Menswear counter.

'Good afternoon, Mr Ferris; are we there with the sports kit?' Mummy said.

He nodded. She always found a shop assistant who gave her extra attention. Mr Ferris had on a two-piece dark-blue suit, glasses, and a middle parting in his brown hair flecked with grey. A few weeks ago, Mr Ferris had said to Mummy that he 'would take personal responsibility for my uniform'. He blinked a lot and you thought something was worrying him, but when he stopped, good news always came out of his mouth: 'The shoes you wanted for the young man arrived today'; 'The name tags look very smart'; 'We can deliver next week.' He made Mummy very relaxed. Today he checked the list and said, 'The other orders are on their way.' I tried on the shoes and we decided to take them with us.

After her two Amontillados, Em was a bit distracted by the men's jumpers: 'Lovely colours, Barbara, and a good weight, not too heavy. A little treat for Geoff?' She gazed at the well-dressed manikins.

Mr Ferris ticked off most of the items on the list: 'Don't worry about a thing, Madam.'

Em suggested a light lunch at Fullers. We bagged a table seat upstairs overlooking Castle Street and the mighty walls of Windsor Castle. I had toad-in-the-hole; they enjoyed smoked salmon and scrambled eggs. 'Haileybury prep school, isn't it wonderful?' Em said as if she had just won a prize for her jam at the Women's Institute in Egham. After our meal they bought macaroons, Em's favourite, from the downstairs counter. She was staying the night and I wondered if I would learn more about great-aunt Bertha.

***

Daddy wasn't feeling well over the summer and could not come on holiday. Instead, he went to London to see another specialist about his wobbly legs. And his cough was really bad these days; one morning his face went a bit blue; we helped him to his chair in the dining room. Mummy and I went to Swanage for a week. While we were away, Uncle Neville moved to his new house in Old Windsor. I knew where it was because Mummy and I often took the back road to Windsor, where they were building a row of little box-like houses. Uncle Neville had bought the one on the corner. A week after we returned from holiday Caleys delivered everything we had ordered for my school uniform. All was present and correct. I hoped Uncle Neville might drop in to wish me luck, or phone, or send me a postcard. I wanted to ask Mummy how he was getting on, but the last time I mentioned him she shrugged and went into the garden.

***

In my bedroom on the first morning of prep school, Mummy watched as I struggled with my royal-blue Dewar House tie. She fiddled with the knot.

After breakfast she drove me there and parked near the modern classrooms. As we walked towards them, she reached for my hand but I took it away before anyone saw.

38

I marched on ahead. I was in Form 9 at the end of the block. I opened the door into a small room with the bottom half of the walls all lumpy, as if someone had thrown blobs of grey concrete at them. Three columns of desks were in very straight lines. The top parts of the walls were glossy cream with no paintings at all. The wooden floor was dark with cracked varnish. I wanted to turn round and go somewhere else. How could they have chosen this school for me? You could never have happy thoughts in this room. In the old part of the school, in that large fairytale entrance hall, when we visited for the first time, I had imagined all sorts of magic that might happen there – adventures with friends, learning new things, sliding down the banisters – but Form 9 looked like a gaol. A teacher walked towards us from the back of the class. 'I'm Mr Madden,' he said with an Australian accent. His skin was tinged yellow. Mummy nudged me forward. He pointed to a desk at the front and I sat down. There were five or six boys already in their places. Mr Madden followed Mummy out of the room. A boy behind me whispered, 'His nickname is Yellow Dog Dingo. He's had jaundice. My brother told me.' Mr Madden returned. His face was as pock-marked as the walls. 'Your form teacher will be here soon. I teach Maths. I look forward to seeing you all again tomorrow. Goodbye.'

Five minutes later our form teacher walked in.

'I'm Miss Shaw.'

She wore a dark grey two-piece suit and her hair was shaped tightly round her head. She tried to smile but her makeup was so thick it made it difficult to move her mouth.

'There are twelve of you. You need to know each other's names.' She looked at a boy in the second row, right behind my desk. 'Hello Rogerson; you look like your brother.'

'Poor you,' said the boy sitting next to him.

We laughed.

'Silence. And what is your name?' she asked that boy.

'Bailey, Miss Shaw.'

She went round everyone and got to me last.

'Worman, Miss Shaw.'

'You will soon all get to know your way around the school. Now, I always begin with a little test, to see what's what.' She looked at me. 'Worman, hand these out.'

'Yes, Miss Shaw.'

I gave everyone an exam sheet.

'You must try to answer all the questions,' she said.

We never did this sort of thing at Virginia Water Junior School.

I sat back in my place.

'No one begin until I say. You have half an hour to answer as many questions as you can.' She looked at the clock on the wall: 'Begin.'

There was a short passage to read. It was the first few pages of a story, about two children, Billy and Marian, who were putting up a tent in the garden, which collapsed, and then Marian cried. It was the most boring opening I had ever read, and the questions were stupid, and you had to say what certain words meant, so I did some of those, and then I added a few lines to the story to make it more interesting. After that, some of the sums were okay, but there were lots with shapes and squiggles in them...

I put up my hand. 'Miss Shaw; what does this mean...?'

'Silence, Worman. We're here to find out what *you* know.'

There were many sums I could not do. Soon the half hour was up.

'Rogerson. Please collect the papers.'

'Yes, Miss Shaw.'

I looked round as he picked up the tests from the other boys. He put them on Miss Shaw's desk. After that she gave us a timetable of what we would be doing each day, told us a bit more about the school, and said we were growing up and had to 'get used to a different kind of school'. I looked round and some boys were nodding in agreement. But why had Miss Shaw not asked anyone about themselves, or their old schools, or what they liked doing, and then let us introduce ourselves to one another? Miss Fish always did that sort of thing.

At break, Miss Shaw led us to a little open quad at the end of the long corridor, where small milk bottles with straws in them were set out on a long table; there were slices of buttered bread, which looked disgusting, on big plates next to the milk. A boy from my class knocked into me.

'Sorry,' he said, 'I'm Simpson. How do you do.'

'I'm Worman.' We shook hands.

'I'm a boarder; my parents are in Dubai.'

His hair was white-sand fair and cut in a pudding-basin shape; he was a little tubby, and his legs were quite short, which made him look squashed up. He had rosy cheeks.

'I'm a dayboy.' I felt guilty. I didn't have to sleep in a dorm and I had home-cooked food.

'It's not that bad. Both my brothers are here: Simpson I is in the top form and Simpson II is in form 4.'

The bell went and we followed the others back to class. No teacher was there so we went on chatting. Bailey came over and squeezed Simpson's shoulder.

'Owh,' Simpson said.

Bailey said, 'Simpson I is a good friend of my brother's. So I'm going to see you're all right.'

'I am; thank you,' Simpson said and rubbed his shoulder.

'Come and meet Rogerson,' Bailey said to Simpson.

I sat alone at my desk.

For the next few days we got used to things. Mr Madden took us for Maths and told us about how his car hit a kangaroo on an Australian outback road. He was not frightening and made sums interesting. The food at lunchtime was quite nice. On Wednesday afternoon we had football. Rogerson and Bailey were on the other team, and tried to tackle me really hard, but I got past, and scored. I grinned at them on my way back to the centre spot. On Thursday we had a house meeting in Form 4, which was next to the art room and smelt of oil paints. Mr Benson was our housemaster. He was tall and thin and had a voice like a big drum. He was sports master too. He told the House that he knew everyone would welcome the new boys (there were four of us in Dewar House) but no one did.

On Friday morning Miss Shaw sat stiffly at the front. Her dark skirt, black lace-up shoes, and white top buttoned to the neck made her look very strict. Miss Fish used to wear more floaty clothes

'I've looked at all your tests,' she said. 'You can get on with reading the first ten pages of our history book, *The Battle of Hastings.* She called boys out one by one to sit beside her, beginning at the back of the class. Smythe was the first; she told him it was quite good but 'do try not to smudge your work'. Blenkinsopp was next; he was a large, pudgy boy with skew-whiff black hair that seemed to pull his head to one side. He smelt, a peculiar mix of Marmite and bottoms, and I was quite pleased when she told him, 'You will have to change gear. You're at prep school now.' Luckily, she was not too flattering to the rest of the boys, except Rogerson: 'What a good start. If you carry on like this, you might follow your brother on a scholarship to Harrow.' Simpson was the only one she smiled at. Anyway, I thought the pressure was off me. I was the last to be called up.

'Where did you go to school before this?' She straightened the two sheets of my answers.

'Virginia Water Junior School, Miss Shaw.'

'Never heard of it.' She pointed at my work with a pen and told me I should have to do extra work on my handwriting and on maths. 'And your spelling isn't very good, is it?'

Bailey and Rogerson laughed behind their hands as I was sent back to my desk. My eyes were stinging as I looked at her red pen all over my work.

After lunch, Simpson was telling me a joke on the steps outside the old part of the school when Rogerson came over and told him, 'Simpson I has something important to tell you,' and tugged him away. I looked for other boys to play with in the grounds at the back of the school but could find no one. Then a master rang a bell, 'All in, all in,' and I ran back to class for the Scripture class. Miss Shaw took it and made Jesus seem like a boring bank manager.

By the time Mummy picked me up, I longed to be back at Virginia Water Junior School, with all those paintings on the bright classroom walls, and lots of friends. As she drove away up the drive, Mummy said, 'You'll never guess who phoned.'

'Uncle Neville?'

'No, no. Diana Dors. She asked me for lunch next week, with Irene Bosanquet, and a few others.'

'Why did you ever send me to this school? How could you?'

Every morning before school, I had stomach ache.

I felt lonely sitting at the front of the class. Between lessons, Rogerson blew paper pellets at me through a Biro tube and the others sniggered. One afternoon, Mr Benson picked Bailey and Rogerson to be captains of the football teams, but neither of them picked me until the very end, even though I was one of the best players. After the game, when I was walking to the showers with Simpson, he stepped ahead and talked to someone else. In the big changing room we took off our clothes; I was the last to get into the showers. If I went in before that, Rogerson or Bailey always tried to trip me up.

On the Monday of the third week, before lessons, I was standing outside our classroom by the wooden stairs that led up to the senior forms. Boys were leaning on the thick old pine handrails, rubbed clean of grey paint, as they joked with each other. I walked back into the day boys' changing room. Our blue winter coats hung on pegs and bulged out. Two boys from my class were chatting but took no notice of me. I waited in the corner and half hid behind the coats. All the others had gone into class and no one was bothering me. Soon there was no sound from boys or masters.

I peeked outside and saw the metal railings that stopped us running onto the busy path. Sun glowed on the October frost. The older of the two Davidson brothers glanced at me, and then headed towards the gym. I took my chance and walked round the edge of the playing field and along the right side of the curving drive where the trees gave me cover. It was far enough away from the headmaster's study, where he often looked out through the full-length window.

I passed Windsor Girls' School and at the Clewar traffic lights turned left, took off my blazer, and went up a side road, keeping my eyes on the pavement until I came out at Brigidine Convent School on King's Road. I crossed the Long Walk with Windsor Castle on my left. On the right, at the end of the Long Walk in Windsor Great Park, was the Copper Horse, a statue of King George III: the sculptor had forgotten to put on the last stirrup, which upset him, and he jumped off and killed himself. It was a long narrow road to Old Windsor and drivers had time to notice me, but no one stopped to ask what I was doing. After the roundabout, I turned off the main road and was halfway along it when I realised that Uncle Neville lived round the next corner. Peeping from behind a tree, I stared at his miserable end-of-terrace house. Perhaps he would pop outside and I could say, 'Uncle Neville, I'm in a spot of bother.' He always said to do that and we could sort things out. The Morris was not in the drive. Perhaps it was in the garage, and he was studying the racing pages of the *Telegraph* or he might have a new job or been left annuities so he could live somewhere nicer than this little box.

I edged along the pavement and squatted behind a bush for camouflage. He might glance out at his front window as he blew away cigar smells. After five minutes there was still no sign of him. But I saw a woman – Dorinka – through the side glass in the porch. She recognised me. Her face was motionless and she turned away. Her light-brown silk scarf was dotted with horses' heads, the sort of scarf Mummy used to wear. Had she gone inside to tell Uncle Neville I was here? Perhaps he would come out with orange juice and a biscuit for me. No one appeared. I ran away up the road and cried. At the The Bells of Ouzely pub I turned right up Cooper's Hill past Beaumont College, a public school, 'which likes to think it is the Catholic Eton,' Daddy used to say. The fields of Cooper's Hill flowed down to the Thames. I stood by the footpath gate for a breather. I loved the old trees and the rolling green of the land. No one was bothering me and I enjoyed my thoughts. Further along the river was Staines and beyond that London. Daddy had been reading me *Oliver Twist* at bedtime. I felt like Oliver who, after he had left the Sowerberrys, was excited when he saw London because nobody could find him in that vast place, not even Mr Bumble. I wanted to stay here and live in a tent, cooking sausages and bacon on a Calor Gaz stove, and reading *The Beano* and *Valiant* all day long.

I carried on through Englefield Green, down Prune Hill, and along Whitehall Lane until I arrived at my house. Mummy's car was not there; I hid in the outhouse, behind the garage, where we kept coal and paraffin. Grime stuck to the broken windowpanes.

After a while, the Herald turned into the drive. Mummy drove straight into the garage and I ducked as the car door opened. 'I'm sure he'll turn up; he always does,' she said and another woman's voice replied, 'We don't need to panic or phone the police just yet.'

The police! For the first time since my adventure began I did not know what to do and the petrol fumes made me feel sick. I wanted to run away again. A policeman might take me away in a police car with the blue light flashing... Through a gap in the fence I saw Mrs Summerhays sweeping up leaves from under their apple tree. Giles would never run away.

If I rang on the front-door bell Mummy would tell me off and what would I say? Who was the other person with her? I pulled up my socks and darted across the back lawn to Uncle Neville's old sitting room. I pushed the handle of the French windows and the damp wood unstuck with a thump-crack. Had they heard me upstairs? I stood stock still in front of the large mirror: 'Please help me, Uncle Neville. I don't know why I did it. Don't let me get into trouble.' I chucked my blazer on the floor and rubbed my foot over the school badge. Mummy's clear voice rose through the floorboards; I lay on the Indian rug, with its vivid patterns of red and green. After ten minutes, I tiptoed upstairs and gripped the flower-patterned china doorknob of the sitting room.

'Hello,' I said.

Mummy jumped up. 'What have you done?'

From the corner chair in the bay window, the other woman, in a black skirt and a white blouse, said, 'I'm Mrs Rawlinson, the school secretary. We were terribly worried. What made you run away?'

'I just did... I hate that school.'

'Your mother rushed to the school the moment we knew you were missing.' She looked at me. 'Well, I think I should be off. You will have a lot to talk about. May I phone for a taxi?'

'Let me do that,' Mummy said.

They went into the hallway where they whispered. A little later the doorbell rang. I recognised the voice of Mr Ranicar, the ancient taxi driver. Mrs Rawlinson said goodbye in a sing-song voice, as if she was thanking Mummy for a nice party.

Mummy came along the corridor and stared at me from the sitting-room door. I wanted to ask if I should change out of my school uniform but I knew that was not the right thing to say.

'You must be hungry after your journey.' She hugged me. 'Go into the dining room and I'll bring you something to eat.'

I sat at my place. She soon came back and sat opposite me as I ate beans on toast with an egg on top. After that I went upstairs and flicked through a comic.

Mummy called up, 'There is someone to see you.'

'Coming.'

In the sitting room, Dr Eric, who had been our family doctor for years, was standing by the window. He turned round: 'Hello, Jeremy. Let's get to the bottom of this.' He smiled through his beard and half glasses twitched on his nose. 'If you are ever worried about things, you can always talk to me, you know.'

'Thank you.'

'I mean it. I think you should come to tea one day. I'll show you how I'm getting on with building my boat!'

'That would be nice.'

'Were you being bullied?' He put his arm round my shoulder.

'No... yes... a bit.' I started to cry.

'That's better. I'll mention that to your parents and we can go forward from there.' He handed me a clean white handkerchief.

The day after the running away Mummy drove me back to school.

We walked through the main entrance and up the grand staircase. We knocked on the headmaster's study.

'Come in.'

He was sitting at his walnut desk, wearing a sports jacket and yellow tie. He shook hands with Mummy. We sat on the leather sofa, while he picked up a black Parker fountain pen, which hovered over a blank sheet of paper. He looked at me: 'You worried us all very much. This must not happen again.'

'No, sir.'

'I need to talk to your mother. If you could wait outside.'

I stood on the wide landing. What was Mr Beckwith going to write on the paper? Was he going to say something bad about me? Would he send it to the police? This part of the school was beautiful; if only the teachers allowed us to have more fun, and to explore things for ourselves, which was what Miss Fish believed in, I should be happy. A few minutes later the door opened and Mummy kissed me goodbye and whispered, 'Don't worry.'

Mr Beckwith came out after her. 'All right; let's try again. Follow me.'

We walked downstairs and along the corridor. Lined up on both sides were the kitchen staff, Matron, the two sub matrons, Mr Reynolds the geography teacher, and Boots, who smiled at me. Matron sneered; the tall chef, Cookie, examined me as if I was a tender lamb chop he would grill later. I followed Mr Beckwith to my classroom. He opened the door for me and then walked away.

The boys were seated at their desks and lowered their heads as I took my place at the front. Bailey looked away. Rogerson gave me a sideways sneer. They all wanted to pretend I wasn't there. No one spoke. A few minutes later the door opened: Mr Benson, my housemaster, perched on the edge of my desk: 'That was rather silly, wasn't it? Next time you come and see me first. All right?' He stood up. 'Now all of you get on with your work until Miss Shaw comes in.'

I did not run away again but often had days off school. When Dr Eric dropped in to see Daddy, I heard him tell Mummy that it might be a good idea if I saw a child psychologist but she said, 'Really, Eric, we haven't got to that point yet.'

During the rest of the term life got a bit better.

On Saturdays even Miss Shaw had a tinge of weekend cheer and sometimes brought in her two dachshunds, which sniffed around the classroom. She smiled at them more than she had ever smiled at me. On Saturday afternoons there were rugby matches and, although I was too young to be in a team, I gazed out at the playing fields with yearning. At 12.30 teaching stopped: we lounged on desks; the boarders discussed their plans for the rest of the weekend; we swapped jokes. Older boys dropped in and told us who they were playing against in the First XV match, or gossiped about the teachers, their next dorm feast or the sub-matrons. One of those boys, Daniels, was four years older than us; we got on well. 'Hello, Worman; things looking up?' he would always ask me. His dark hair was soft, smooth and neatly shaped round his well-defined features. His eyes were deep-set and the colour of chestnuts. If I agreed with everything he said I would never be afraid, and no one else would hurt me. I smiled and became anything he liked. I was free.

After that I managed to survive by being a blob of amoeba in a big sea of school. No one took much interest in me, but no one ate me either. Time passed. One thing I liked was helping Boots clean the rugby boots in the small closed-off alcove at the end of the changing rooms. 'Two toffees for each pair; make sure you scrape off all the mud.' He once told me, 'I'm a proper Cockney. London, Poplar, you wouldn't believe how nice it was; we was all good neighbours, and the fun we had. Then I went off to the war.' He was very short and I could not imagine him fighting. Perhaps he was in the Catering Corps. On Saturday lunchtimes he would get dressed up in a smart camel-hair overcoat, pressed dark trousers, tie and a red spotty silk scarf. 'I'm going into town,' he'd say. But one day Rogerson ran past and shouted at me, 'How is Boots's boyfriend getting on?' I didn't spend so much time with Boots after that.

At home, we decided that I was too grown up now to call them 'Mummy' and 'Daddy'. We decided on 'Ma' and 'Pa'. My parents told me that Uncle Neville had split up again with Dorinka: he was living in Malta in the house of an old army friend. Twenty years later, at a dinner party in Valetta, I asked an ancient brigadier if he had ever known a Neville Prideaux. He had not.

After the first few weeks of homesickness I liked boarding. At twelve, I'd finally settled at school and was ready for it. I enjoyed the camaraderie of the dorms, of the steady routine of school life, of getting to know better a few of the masters. I noticed Miss Gibbs, one of the sub-matrons, with a new interest. She was pretty and smiled at me. I liked the way her body moved under her white coat when she walked. At school I no longer had to worry about my father's bad health or the whispering secrets of my parents. I made people laugh in dorm at night by making up ridiculous stories about the masters, telling them for instance that I had seen Mr Madden, holding a long lead tied to his pet kangaroo, giving it exercise behind the copse. Some of the boys believed me at first, and everyone chuckled. People began to like me more.

One afternoon at the beginning of March, there was a mock General Election at school. Two older boys from Form 1, the common-entrance class, stood: Dutton for the Conservatives and Reynolds-Forbes for the Liberals. Mr Boardman told us in the French class that no one wanted to stand for Labour. 'I will, sir.' I did not know what made me say it. Boys jeered. Rogerson pointed at me. 'Worman is a socialist...'

'Quiet,' Mr Boardman said. 'There is nothing in the rules to say it has to be a boy in Form 1 – and as there is no one else.'

The next day at break we had hustings on the upstairs landing. We three stood on crates and I was in the middle, shorter than the other two. Dutton began in his clipped colonial accent, 'This country will go to the dogs if we risk the economy to a Wilson government that gives money away to those who don't work.' He rambled on and was asked pat-a-cake questions to which he replied with such answers as 'Quite right' or 'I agree'. Reynolds-Forbes made a case for more freedom 'for every man, woman and child to choose their own life', and then it was my go. I said, 'It's funny that Dutton is worried about this country going to the dogs when he's Rhodesian and does not even live here – what about Rhodesia going to the dogs?' I was not sure what I meant but got a loud cheer. Dutton, who was sensitive about his accent, went red in the face and his second-row-forward body swayed as if he had been hit by Henry Cooper.

'Rhodesia is the finest country in the world, thanks to the democracy taken there by the white settlers.'

'Are you saying there are too many black men in Africa?' I said.

The group of boys brayed and Mr Boardman said, 'Quieten down. Enough.'

'That is a disgusting thing to say, Worman.' Dutton wagged his porky forefinger. 'If this was Rhodesia...'

'What then? Would you hang me?'

Boys booed. Dutton wanted to hit me. Mr Boardman stood behind us: 'Only discuss British politics, please.'

'But he isn't British, sir,' I said.

Laughter drowned us out.

Dutton said more about the 'hideousness' of Harold Wilson.

I said, 'There is nothing hideous about a Labour government which wants fairness and equality for all.'

Parmiter called out from the back of the group, 'You'd better give away your five-star Stuart Surridge bat to someone poor and deserving, Worman!'

Everyone laughed, including me, but I couldn't think of a good reply.

The vote, a secret ballot, was taken. Mr Boardman stood in the corner and counted the slips of paper. A few minutes later he announced the result: Conservatives, 7; Liberals,

1; Labour, 4. I had won a great victory, even though I had lost. In that moment I knew that most of those boys would never change their views throughout their lives.

'Bloody hell, Worman did well,' Avery said.

A week later, the history teacher, Mr Ansell, who wore bright ties, long sideboards and had been to Oxford, said, 'And of course if we want an alternative point of view, we have a communist in the class, don't we, Worman? We can ask him.' I smiled. 'I'm Labour actually, sir.' The class heckled pleasantly and Mr Ansell bowed: 'I stand corrected by my learned friend.'

He was the only teacher with any wit and he left at the end of term to work at a school in London.

At the beginning of the Easter holidays, Ma had told me it would be a good idea if I wrote a letter to Uncle Fred in Australia, as he hoped to stay with us next year. 'Why don't you make a good impression on him?'

Pa was at work and Ma was having a coffee with friends on the Wentworth Estate. I was bored. On a whim, I went upstairs to her bedroom and started rummaging around in her writing bureau, looking for paper. One of the side drawers was locked, but I found the key in the long, dusty bottom drawer. Inside were many folded letters, stiff and old. I read two of them, from a boyfriend, before the war: he sounded soppy to me. I took out other letters, and a Bible, which was a bishop's confirmation gift to Ma, when she was at boarding school in Whitby.

At the very back of the drawer, scrunched up tight, was a less yellowed newspaper cutting. I sat at the desk and unfolded it: the *Daily Mail*, November 1964. 'Army hero Lieutenant-Colonel Neville Prideaux OBE commits suicide on Chobham Common.' He had shot himself in the head with his army pistol as he sat in his green Morris Minor on the Army tank training area at Chobham Common. It had happened two years ago.

53

Sometime later, I did not notice Ma come in.

'What's the matter with you?' she said.

I flapped the paper in her face – 'Uncle Neville killed himself.'

'We didn't want to upset you.'

'You said he was living in Malta.'

'He was for a time...'

'Why did he do it?'

I pulled her wrist but she held my shoulder and folded me in her arms. 'His marriage went wrong, he had no money, and he missed the army – any of those reasons, darling, or all of them – we'll never know.'

All my bad feelings slipped away as she stroked my back.

'What were you doing in my writing cabinet?'

'Looking for notepaper for my Uncle Fred letter.'

She switched on the dressing-room light and asked me help her choose a pair of shoes for the evening.

I followed her into the dressing room. It was like a cocoon: shoes at the bottom, a shelf for bags, another for jumpers and scarves. The top shelf was devoted to hats, of every style and shape, colour and size. The place was a lavender-scented cave. I snuggled my face into the jumpers. I became no particular age, and no particular person.

We chose green Bally slip-ons, which she was to wear with a grey two-piece for a concert at the Literary Institute in Egham. She was going with Mr Osborne, a family friend. 'You should have told me about Uncle Neville,' I said, but wasn't cross. I wanted to live in her dressing room because I was hers and she loved me and when she was upset at night I slept in the twin bed beside her. Pa was a restless sleeper and had his own bedroom on the middle floor.

'Come on,' she said, 'let's see what's growing in the garden.'

I followed her down and we stood in Uncle Neville's musty sitting room.

'It needs a good airing; open the French windows, darling.'

I pushed them open. 'Aren't you coming then?'

'In a minute; I've got something to tell you.'

I propped myself on the edge of the sofa.

'No more secrets, darling.' She sat in the armchair. 'Well, last week I had my last session with a psychiatrist in London; I was feeling terribly stressed. Dr Eric put me on to this wonderful man in Harley Street.'

'Oh, no; you mustn't get ill too, Ma.'

'I'm a new person. Dr Kuster helped me understand a lot of things about my past, my childhood, and trauma – he was hot on that. Such a wise man. I'll never look back now.' She stood up and ogled the mirror. 'I'm not sure if that lipstick is the right shade.'

She kissed me on the forehead and in that instant we both glanced at the mantelpiece, which Uncle Neville used to lean on as he puffed a cigar – the air was filled with the aroma of Romeo y Julieta No. 3s – and we both smelt it.

'What a good omen,' she said. 'Neville's come to welcome me back.'

We wanted to cry.

'Come on,' she said, 'I'll show you my googly; I've been practising. Get you ready for the cricket season.'

I picked up the cricket bat from behind the sofa and handed her my practice composite ball. A ray of sun moved along the white hollyhocks like an officer checking his troops. We did not have Uncle Neville but we had each other. I took guard and the garden fences seemed to dissolve as I ran into the green open space of my future.

Although I was happier at school, I remained in the bottom half of the class for most subjects, except English and Latin, which were taught by Mr Blundell, who gave me encouragement. He used to wear light-colour jackets, boring ties, and square glasses, but when I sat at his desk to go over my Latin homework he was never cross or shouty.

His dark, Brylcreemed hair stayed in place as he explained the order of a Latin sentence, and how useful it was to learn declensions. I began to get the idea. Mr Blundell would often ask me to collect the weekly tests on our Latin primer, *First Steps in Latin*, or *First Steps in Eating* as we rewrote the cover. I would then follow him up the corridor to the masters' common room with the tests under my arm. I was pleased when other boys passed us and noticed me. By the end of term I was near the top of the class, along with two good friends, Mitchell and Dunn-Wooding.

Many of the other teachers had been in the Second World War and did not believe in class discussion; Mr Benson was younger and had been in the Korean War but he had also learnt how to frighten boys. In our history class, for instance, there could be no dissent that historical figure X did A, B and C – no other possibilities were allowed. I dared to ask, 'What would have happened if Hitler had not attacked Russia and invaded us instead?' and I was put in my place by Mr Davidson – 'Stop wasting our time with irrelevances.' He was broad and tweedy with dark bushy eyebrows, a ruddy complexion and a throaty voice enhanced by roll-ups. He did not like me. He taught maths too, but only told you rules; if you could not follow you were lost.

***

I took my common entrance in the summer of 1967 but did not do well. I had to stay for an extra term to retake. The upside was becoming a prefect: we could make our own toast with long tongs in front of the gas fire; there was a prefects' common room with a record player, secret supplies of biscuits and a kettle. And I began to find freedom on the playing fields. I was captain of the First XI football team: short, nimble, fast – 'Twinkletoes' – and I got past anyone. To run, to catch, to shoot, to bowl, to bat was to live. I was in the First XI cricket team. I was also scrum half in the First XV but my glittering advance was stopped by an undropped testicle. I had wondered where it was, or if it was only half there, for about six months. The school doctor said I needed an operation.

In November, the night before I went into hospital, the boys in my dorm sang affectionately: 'Worman, he's only got one ball, the other is in the Albert Hall.' I was admitted to a men's ward of the King Edward VII hospital in Windsor and put next to a nice, friendly man, Robert Myers, who reminded me of Uncle Neville and whose mother knew mine.

It was not too embarrassing until the morning of the operation when a young dark-haired nurse with a lovely smile picked up the clipboard on the end of my bed: 'What are you in for then?' I blushed and stuttered. She read the notes: 'Ah, well that's nothing to worry about then.'

By the afternoon of 18 November it was over and I was drowsy but awake, reading a James Bond book, *Dr No*, which Robert had lent me. I was groggy but not in pain and from my position at the end of the ward I had a good view. It was like being in dorm but with much older boys. I put in my earphones and tuned to the Home Service. There was a special broadcast by Harold Wilson. I felt he was speaking to me personally. He said the pound was being devalued but 'that doesn't mean, of course, that the pound here in Britain, in your pocket or purse or in your bank, has been devalued'. There were guffaws from Robert, who was also listening to the radio: 'Stupid bloody man.' It was not the right moment to say I had stood as a Labour candidate. Anyway, I was a little concerned I was on the losing side. But what did it mean to devalue the pound? I thought about it logically and had a brainwave: the pound had only been devalued for foreigners. I was okay. We, the English, could go on buying fish and chips, chocolate, LPs, flared jeans, cricket bats, and nothing was changed. I was much relieved and then winced. My left testicle ached.

Something to do with the connection between 'pound', 'pocket', 'pocket billiards' and testicles had unsettled it.

At visiting time, Ma dropped in with a home-made chocolate cake and grapes. She was wearing a new two-piece suit, as if going out to an expensive lunch. The eyes of the ward followed her to my bed. She hugged me keenly. 'Well done, darling. You'll never look back now.'

'Ma!'

'You know what I mean.' She turned to Robert. 'So sorry about your hernia; your mother told me all about it.'

'Ah,' he said.

Ma entertained us for the next fifteen minutes and then the royal visit was over. She blew me a kiss and her Blue Grass perfume was like incense and made me sad as I realised how much I needed her love.

Two days later the headmaster picked me up. I hobbled to his Jaguar in the car park. He opened the passenger door and the smell of leather dissolved the antiseptic aroma of the ward. Buses, pigeons, women with shopping bags, cyclists, a Mars bar wrapper caught against the wheel of a grey Austin 1100, two uniformed soldiers on their way to barracks: how good to be alive and in the outside world again.

'Everything, er, all right?' Mr Beckwith said as the engine hummed.

'Oh, yes, sir. It's nice to be here.'

'Chocolate fudge in the glove compartment.'

'Thank you.'

I took a chunk from the packet. We turned into the drive and the fine old school building felt like home. I looked forward to seeing my friends again. Mr Beckwith stopped in front of the main entrance.

'Wait in the hall for a minute; I'll put the car in the garage.'

'All right, sir.'

'Don't look so worried; it's not a caning; we're pleased you're back; I'll walk you down to class.'

I went in. A few minutes later the headmaster came through the main door.

'Come on,' he said.

I followed him. The wide floorboards had been polished and I traced the knots and gnarls in the old wood. As we passed the overflow dining room, used at lunchtimes to accommodate the extra number of day boys, I noticed feet on either side of the corridor. When I looked up there were Cookie, Matron, Miss Gibbs, Mr Benson and some boys from my class. By the time we reached the changing rooms someone cheered, and then everyone clapped. Once I had been lonely and bullied. I had not really changed but the attitude of the boys and masters had. It struck me that I could always slip back to being someone to kick. I was really popular now but they could change their minds.

After three weeks I was playing rugby again but dropped down to captain the second XV, which pleased me: you did not have to tackle so often and as scrum-half I scored more tries on the blind side as the opposition scrums were slow and agricultural. Ma watched a match against Papplewick and afterwards gave me the single 'Hole in My Shoe' by Traffic. We prefects played it all the time in our common room. The psychedelic lyrics made no rational sense but opened a world of vision. I wanted a flowery shirt like Steve Winwood, long hair and a pretty girlfriend.

Friendships became intense. 'We'll keep in touch,' Mitchell said, 'I'll get my parents to ask you up to Cheshire.' We knelt and pushed the toast against the gas fire. I looked at the top table. 'I'll miss old Becky,' I said as I watched the headmaster drink tea. I would see him forever in a spot of time on this cold frost-glow of a winter's afternoon. In the dining hall we were a band of *Beowulf* warriors huddling against a dark world. In the last week I asked Cookie at breakfast, as I had every week, 'Can I have another fish finger?' and he said 'Not blooming likely' but gave me two extra. In the final rugby match against Thorpe House I left my mark, running and jiggling the length of the pitch before scoring between the posts. And so to the last rites, 'The headmaster's talk', when the facts of life were revealed, as we clutched mugs of cocoa in his drawing room.

On the way back to dorm, I thought about what he had left out: he never mentioned 'masturbation', only 'self-abuse', and warned us not to sleep on our stomachs so we did not 'excite ourselves'. He said he was sure 'we all understood, er, about women's periods, probably from chats with your sisters'. What if you didn't have a sister? And what about the masturbatory sex life of girls? How did they do it? When we were adjacent to Matron's sitting room, Wilkinson illustrated this point for us as he rubbed his finger between his legs and made an orgasmic face. We exploded with laughter and Matron stood at her door – 'What are you doing, Wilkinson; do I need to get out the straightjacket?' We laughed again as this was the only joke Matron had ever made. As I stepped into the dorm I was aware of my throbbing erection. This had happened a lot to my penis in the last month, especially if it was in the vicinity of Miss Gibbs.

The next morning in our final assembly the headmaster handed me an old boys' tie; he turned me round to face the assembly: 'Worman is a fine example of the proverb, "Try, try and try again".' He patted my shoulder, 'And his results this time in the common entrance exam were excellent. He will be leaving to start at the senior school in January.' Everyone clapped.

By late morning all our trunks and tuckboxes were stacked up near the front entrance to the school. At midday Ma arrived with Mr Marshall in his black Humber Hawk. As Pa was finding it hard to drive, he had a chauffeur, who took him to and from work, and Mr Marshall had been doing that for the past six months. Ma had a cream MGB convertible now, a present last month 'for being a perfect wife', but the boot was not big enough for my trunk, so Mr Marshall drove her. She had told me he sometimes helped her when she had shopping to do. He wore a dark-blue suit and chauffeur's hat; he stood by the car and kept looking at his watch. As his lips moved up and down, two front teeth protruded like a hungry rabbit. The school porter, Jim, helped to put the trunk and tuckbox in the boot. Ma and I sat in the back as we drove away up the winding drive. When we got home, I helped Mr Marshall carry the trunk and tuckbox up to my bedroom.

'Thank you,' I said and closed the door.

I unlocked my tuckbox. I took out a pack of cards; a diver's watch with a broken rubber strap; an unused tube of balsa-wood glue; my almost complete collection of James Bond bubble-gum cards; pens and pencils; geometry sets in various stages of breakage; a Corgi James Bond Aston Martin DB5; three small rubber super balls; a Slinky; four *Valiants*; a blue Parker fountain pen; a pot each of black, turquoise and green ink; a leather cricket ball; tennis balls; a pen knife and a sheath knife; two Mars bars, a Crunchie and a packet of fruit Polos. Stale toffees were stuck to the bottom surface and I shut the lid. Ten minutes later I heard Mr Marshall say 'Goodbye' to Ma.

Soon after that she called me for lunch and I sat in the dining room. Through the open hatch to the kitchen I could smell fried food. A pan crashed on the stove. Smoke puffed through the serving hatch. She came in with a plate of two burnt beef burgers, baked beans, a slice of white bread, and shoved the plate in front of me; she sat opposite with a tumbler of dark sherry. Thin red lines flared on her face.

'What's the matter?' I said.

'As if you care.'

'Of course I do.' I put down my knife and fork. 'What's wrong? You can tell me.' I touched her hand but she pulled away. I realised I was taller than her now and felt less petrified.

'Eat your food. I went to all the trouble of cooking it.'

I cut a piece of the hard burger. The table was smeared with polish. Her fair hair was turned up at the shoulders so that when she flicked her head it swung in an arc, and veins throbbed in her neck. I remembered our country walks when I was young; we loved the fields and lanes. Yes, I thought, *that* is my mother and I must bring her back. As she held the tumbler at eye level an arrow of light through the crystal cut-glass made crazy pavings of her eyes. She might hate me for ever.

'Why are you drinking?'

'Wouldn't you like to know.'

'Do you remember last Easter, after your final session with Dr Kuster? We played cricket and then went for afternoon tea in Chobham? You said you were a new person.'

'So what?' She gripped her glass.

'I'm home now; it can be like that again.'

Her green eyes were glazed over, and her lips curled down.

I put out my hand. 'Come on.'

She sat motionless. The pulse beat in my neck. She stared into her empty glass and stepped back. Her arm swept across the table and knocked my plate. 'My darling boy, I didn't want to upset you, I never mean to upset you. It's so hard; your father is getting worse, and I feel alone. We must stick together. Mr Marshall has been so helpful.' Her face changed from a death mask to smiles. I pushed away my burnt food.

'Would you like a cup of tea?' I asked.

'Thank you, darling.'

'Won't be a minute.'

As the kettle boiled I looked at my school uniform, blue shirt and house tie, blue jumper, long trousers and black shoes. I would never wear them again. I hated the idea of going on to Haileybury. Ma had better not be like this all holidays, I thought, and slammed the fridge door. I set out a tray for her and took it to the dining room.

She was standing by the window: 'It's brightening up.' That other person inside her had gone away, that strange person who spoke through her, and could take away all I was by not loving me anymore.

'When does Pa get back?'

'About 5.30.' She stroked my hand. 'We'll have a lovely Christmas.'

Upstairs, I changed into blue jeans and a checked cowboy shirt; I tossed my school uniform in the dirty washing bin on the landing. Long ago, ages before I was born, Pa had a fitted wardrobe constructed on one side of the landing. I opened all the doors. I loved the organisation: small drawers, with tiny ivory-like labels, engraved with black lettering, beneath each drawer, 'Socks', 'Underwear', 'Studs / Cufflinks', and so on; larger open drawers of 'Shirts', white and striped, all laundered, many without collars. Next to them, in the long vertical section, numerous suits, business ones, weekend ones; sports jackets; a waterfall of ties on a thin mahogany rail. On the bottom shelf, a variety of shoes, black, brown, tan, a pair of dark-brown brogues (my favourites), all shoe-horned, all polished; suede shoes and tan slip-ons. I liked the father revealed inside his wardrobe: smart, confident, successful. When I thought of that father I thought less about Uncle Neville.

Downstairs, Ma was asleep in the sitting room.

I'm going to see Giles,' I said.

She smiled.

I bundled up in my blue fisherman's jumper as it was icy outside and went next door. I usually walked up to the tradesman's entrance but the path had been dug up; York stone paving slabs were piled against the fence waiting to be put down. I ran across the garden and knocked on the front door.

'Hello, Jeremy,' his mother said, 'how lovely to see you.'

'Hello, Mrs Summerhays.'

Her voice, coiffured hair and film-star features, were so perfect that I always shrank a little on first meeting her after a break.

'You go and find Giles.'

She went off to the kitchen while I went into the hallway and peeped into their sitting room where the sky-blue walls enhanced the light through the French windows. On the white marble mantelpiece was a family photograph in a silver frame. They were standing in a line, their hands on one another's shoulders: Father, Mother, Joanna, Susanna, Soames, Virginia, Giles, Sorrel. I counted the children in the photograph, six of them, all touching. I sat on the sofa and looked at the photograph of Giles as head chorister at St George's, which was used on the front cover of the *Radio Times* last Christmas.

'Hello, Worm. Great to see you.'

'Hello, Giles.'

We were best friends and there was neither excitement nor anxiety about meeting again. His mother brought in orange juice and biscuits. I sat on the sofa and Giles in an armchair. He told me about his first term at Gordonstoun (Soames was already there and in the same year as Prince Charles). Giles said that boys swam a lot in the Moray Firth and ran up mountains in blizzards. It seemed to me there was not much time left for lessons, but it was not a school for brainboxes.

Giles had a nature magazine in his hand, always a bad sign. I did not share his excitement for bugs and wildlife. He turned to a diagram of beetles, rather than holding the latest Beatles LP.

'You've got to watch this,' he said, 'Soames got it last week.' He drew the curtains and turned on a reel-to-reel film about lions in South Africa. The projector was on a table in the corner. He focused it on the blank wall and drew the curtains. The lions yawned, stroked their cubs, yawned again and, oh the excitement, ran across the dry veld. It went on for ages when we could have been outside having fun. After Mummy Lion gave a final tickle to her pride and joys the film ended.

Mrs Summerhays stood at the door: 'Giles, I need some help lifting down some boxes from the store room.' She smiled at me.

I got up. Very nice to see you again, Mrs Summerhays.'

'See you soon,' Giles said.

At home, Ma was sober again; she was making a ham and mushroom soufflé in the kitchen and singing 'Keep the Aspidistra Flying' in a Gracie Fields voice.

'Your father will be home any minute,' she said, 'he's longing to see you.'

'I'm going to get out my Scalextric.' I ran up to the playroom.

Fifteen minutes later I heard Ma say, 'Hello, Ken.'

I watched from the landing. My father hobbled in with Mr Marshall – Ken! – supporting him from behind. I came down. Pa's face was flushed and his legs jerked out like a broken Action Man doll. His tie flapped and there was a coffee stain on his collar. He looked at me, and then away. It was the face of an old man. He hobbled to the dining room, where he almost dropped into his chair. Mr Marshall stood in front of him, without his chauffeur's hat, which he had put on the hall table. Once dark haired, he was going bald but tried to disguise it with an Elvis Presley quiff. He smiled at me from the bubble of his large, greasy face. I glanced at my father but dared not look properly for fear of revealing my private thoughts. He looked at the whisky bottle, its silver optic glinting, as he waited for his six-o'clock medicine. His shirt was crumpled and the chalk-stripes on his dark suit looked faded. The father I needed would always be inside his wardrobe, not here.

'Perhaps you'd like me to take you and your mother out for tea out, Jeremy,' Mr Marshall said. 'Give you a break.'

'No thank you; I'm just sorting out my Scalextric. See you later, Pa.'

I listened from the upstairs landing. A few minutes later Marshall told Ma a joke in the corridor; they laughed and then there was silence; she closed the front door softly as he left. Sitting on my bed, I wondered if that ghastly Mr Marshall could ever be Ma's boyfriend. Surely not as they had nothing in common, unlike her and Uncle Neville. How could I ever go out with Marshall and Ma – strangers may think he's my father? No, Ma would never do that. Luckily, Ma is a terrible snob, but pretends she isn't. She used to say to me, 'There were no snobs in Lancashire, darling; we all mucked in.' But in the next sentence she would tell me a story about Collins, my grandmother's chauffeur, and how, when Ma was a teenager, he would drive her around to the poorest houses where she would deliver food parcels. And Ma always called Collins 'Collins' as if he did not own a first name. Surely Ma could therefore never go out with my father's chauffeur, 'Marshall'.

Later, we had a pleasant supper, and Pa went to bed straight after that. I helped Ma wash up and went to bed too.

***

Em arrived by taxi on Christmas morning.

'I can't help but love Christmas,' she said and gave me a powdery kiss. She was small, thin, bony, but her eyes were full of life and mischief.

In contrast, as Pa made a champagne toast over the first course of smoked salmon and quails' eggs, I felt as if I was looking at a ghost. He was going to die and my role was to be a kind son until he had gone. There was nothing he could do for me. I was sitting next to him and after our plates were filled with turkey, vegetables and gravy he touched my arm: 'We must have a good talk, old chap. On

Boxing Day? We need to discuss pocket money and so on. It's probably time for a rise.'

'Okay,' I shrugged.

'Em laughed. 'I wish I was getting a bit of extra money as easily from those miserable blighters, the Piggott trustees.'

'There, there,' Ma said, 'We'll write to them again after Christmas.'

We pulled crackers and put on our silly hats.

After our feast, Ma and I carried the dishes to the kitchen.

'Come out with Ken and me; he's been so helpful; he's become a very dear friend.'

'He's horrible.'

I ran up to my bedroom.

The days after Christmas were grey. I set up my Scalextric in Uncle Neville's sitting room, and then spoke to him in the mirror: 'I wish you were here to put Marshall in his place; he's a slug.' I rubbed the mirror: if I looked hard enough, I might receive a sign from Uncle Neville, a smell of his cigars or the aroma of his curries, to let me know his genie spirit was here to destroy my enemies. 'God bless you. Kill Marshall, please.'

For the next week I avoided my parents as much as possible. Every night they would drink, from about 5.30 onwards. In the dining room one night I dared to ask, 'Isn't there anything to eat tonight?' and I was ignored by Ma. 'It will come soon, old chap, don't worry,' Pa said as he shuffled to the bathroom with his walking frame.

Then she turned to me, 'Do you think I'm afraid of you and your bullying?'

'Of course not,' I said as she picked up the steak knife and jiggled it like a cut-throat razor in front of me. I stared at her. She put it back in its place.

Pa returned to work on 2 January.

Ma did not speak to me all day but I had a peaceful time reading upstairs. Pa came back at about 5.30pm with Mr Marshall walking behind him. I crept onto the landing; when Marshall was leaving I peeped round the corner. He and Ma kissed at the front door, on the lips. In the background, the last track of The Beatles' *Magical Mystery Tour* was playing in my bedroom: I tiptoed back to my bedroom. Ten minutes later Ma came upstairs, with a glass of sherry in her hand, and stood at my bedroom door. 'I'm going for a drive with Ken, Master Cromwell.'

'It's disgusting, Ma; he's horrible. You've got a husband.'

'You little shit.'

She threw her glass at the wall above my head, then moved towards me. I jumped off the bed and backed towards the little fireplace. Her fingers were slashing out and I could retreat no further, so lifted my hands to protect my face – the emerald ring on her middle finger pushed through and grazed my left cheek, drawing blood. I opened my mouth to speak but no words came out.

'Don't tell me how to live my life.' She walked out.

My hands were shaking but I managed to put on *Sgt. Pepper's Lonely Hearts Club Band*. The songs on *Sgt. Pepper's* cut away my dread. I dabbed my bleeding cheek with a handkerchief; I would tell people a gorse bush had scratched me. Ma did not love me and I wanted to hate her: only love hurts but hate sets you free. I shouted down to Pa, 'I'm really tired; I don't want any supper.'

The next morning she knocked on my bedroom door; I pulled the bedclothes over my head. 'Darling, you need some new clothes for school; you're allowed to wear sports jackets at Haileybury; isn't that grown up? Let's go up to Harrods, then on to Fortnum's. Their spring hats are always the best. We must stick together. We need a treat before you start your new school.' She put a tray on my bedside table, sat on the bed and poured tea; her Blue

Grass perfume was sweet and she loved me again. My heart pumped with happiness.

She got up. 'I'll leave you to enjoy your breakfast,' she said, 'but I want you to do one small thing for me, please. I need a treat. Well, Ken, Mr Marshall, knows I love The Compleat Angler, and wants to take us for lunch tomorrow. He's very fond of our family.'

'I'll think about it.'

That was the pattern of my life. I would do anything for her love. But I wanted to stop being a puppet she could bring to life at will. I had to be more like a soldier, more like Uncle Neville. I was fighting on a psychological battlefield; I had different scars, and needed a different courage, from those who fight in combat.

Early the next morning I ate toast and honey in the dining room. Ma was in bed; Pa was in bed too as he was working at home today and did not need to get up. What should I do about Ma's request? The Compleat Angler was a special hotel where our family went for treats or afternoon tea. The place had nothing to do with greasy-hair rabbit-teeth Marshall. But if I did this for Ma, she might treat me better; she would know that I loved her.

I made breakfast for her and carried it upstairs. My hand sweated on the blue-flowered doorknob of her bedroom. *Sgt. Pepper's Lonely Hearts Club Band* blared out.

'Morning, Ma.'

I bent down and adjusted some of the items on the tray: china tea in the Mason's green dragon pot, toast and marmalade. The door was ajar and I went in. The lamp made shadows across her thrown-on-the-floor clothes; I put the tray on the bedside table and a packet of St Moritz menthol cigarettes fell off the bed.

'I'll draw the curtains, Ma.'

'Do you have to?'

I swished them back and sun blazed in and the frost-hard lawn shone.

'Okay, I'll come to lunch, but I want my Beatles record back.'

'It's so cheerful. I love it.' She poured tea.

'It was the first LP I bought. It's mine. Not for your generation.'

'I'm with it, darling. The Sixties are me.' She shook her head as if she was dancing under disco lights.

I sat on the bed and she stroked my hair, working her fingers from the parting to the back of my neck, as she did when I was very young.

'It's still blond from the summer. Have you seen Suzie Fitzgerald this holiday?'

'You can see I've dressed nicely for today – proper trousers, new psychedelic shirt, and I'll wear my blazer.'

'Don't change the subject, and don't blush. You're growing up; you're almost fourteen, and Suzie is so pretty.'

The record had reached the end of 'With a Little Help From My Friends'.

'Shall I turn it off?'

'No.'

'You put the stylus on by hand, not on automatic, and you haven't put the arm across, so you need to lift it off or the needle goes on turning in the smooth vinyl.'

'Worry-guts. When I get up. We'll leave at 11.30.'

'I think I'll read *Diamonds are Forever* until then.'

Downstairs, Pa was hobbling to the bathroom. 'Will you go to lunch with your mother?'

'With Marshall, you mean. Yes.'

'Look, old chap, it's for the best.' He took a five-pound note from his dressing-gown pocket. 'A gentleman should always be prepared.'

'I'm going to read.' I snatched the note.

At 11.30 Ma came down in a black linen dress with a low neckline. Looking in the hall mirror, she put a horse-patterned silk scarf over her hair and tied a knot under her neck. The buckles of the red patent shoes sparkled. Pa shuffled out of the dining room and kissed her cheek; she pushed him away.

'Let's go,' she said to me.

I followed her out. She reversed the MGB from the garage into the drive.

'I know it's cold, darling, but what a beautiful day! Let's put the hood down.'

'Yes!'

We folded it back. I jumped into the passenger seat and we zoomed off.

'Light me a cigarette,' she said as we reached Englefield Green.

I pressed in the car lighter and then took a puff before handing it to her. I put the heater on high and the warm air blew out in the floor wells by our feet.

As we passed Windsor Racecourse, I remembered our picnic three years ago when I won ten pounds on an each-way double – it would have been more but at the last stride Rough Streak was pipped into second place. Salmon sandwiches, champagne and strawberries; parents laughing on the blue-tartan rug, their feet touching. We felt like a family that day... When we reached Furze Platt, beyond Maidenhead, the countryside expanded. The brown stubble field was flecked frost white. I closed my eyes and tried to stitch together the bright spots of my life but they were covered by wheat fields burning.

'Don't bite your lip, darling; I'll be a good mummy from now on. Ken and I are just good friends. I need a bit of attention, that's all.'

'Ma!' The car veered towards the white line.

She corrected it and we snaked down the leafy road into Bisham and, just before Marlow Bridge, turned right into The Compleat Angler. I looked at Marlow Suspension Bridge, which had been opened in 1832; it was designed by the civil engineer Charles Tierney Clark. Pa told me all that. I liked it when he gave me historical nuggets; it made me feel more secure about the world; it made me feel that I had a real dad.

'Wasn't that a fun drive, dreamy? It's a beautiful bridge, isn't it?'

Ma parked the car. 'I don't think we need to put the hood up, do you?'

'No, it's not going to rain.'

Ma checked her watch. 'It's almost midday. Ken will be here soon. Let's have a coffee and sit outside.'

We went over to a corner of the terrace, near one of the paraffin heaters the hotel put out in winter. I noticed that Ricardo, our favourite waiter, was on duty. I wondered what he would make of Ken Marshall: a family friend; Ma's boyfriend; an accountant advising Ma at a business lunch (Marshall did not look like that sort of person)? She stared at the swirling foam around the weir: 'That's gushing from the rain last week – Oh, God, I never turned off the record player; those poor little Beatles are working overtime.'

'It's not like that, Ma. The needle turns in the smooth bit until we get home.'

Behind me, footsteps got closer. I turned round as rabbit teeth nibbled his lip.

'Hello, Mr Marshall.'

'Bit cold for cricket, eh Jeremy?'

'Oh, yes.'

'Hello, Barbara.' His red-and-white striped Polyester tie glowed between the lapels of his shiny light-grey suit. He touched my shoulder. 'You must be excited about your new school?'

'Bit nervous. Are your wife and children well, Mr Marshall?'

He gave me a crocodile smile and sat down with his back to the river. One nil, I thought.

Ma leant on the balcony. 'We're here to cheer ourselves up. No quarrelling, boys. This is a beautiful day, a special day.'

Marshall adjusted the poorly tied knot of his tie.

'This is my treat; I insist,' she said and patted Marshall's hand. 'Let's begin with a cocktail. It will charge us up. I know what Ken likes.'

'Why not have a sherry, Ma?'

Ricardo came over. 'Hello, Signora Worman; Jeremy. How nice to see you both again.'

He was young, tall, dark and thin. He looked like an actor or an artist. Marshall should swap places with Ricardo.

'Two Manhattans and a Coke and ice for master Oliver Cromwell, please Ricardo. And this is Ken Marshall, an old family friend.'

Marshall almost swooned.

'How do you do,' Ricardo said.

'Just going to the gents,' I said.

As I came back Ricardo was putting the fiery cocktail glasses in front of them. Ma said, 'We'll have champagne with lunch, the nice bottle, you know, with the yellow label, Veuve Clicquot, is it?'

'That's the one, Mrs Worman.'

Ma put her hand on my neck and whispered, 'My way, darling, my way.'

Although it was a cold day, the paraffin heater worked well. And the glass roof of the terrace kept in some of the heat. The special Wednesday fish menu came, and we usually went for that. It was decorated with images of prawns and halibut, lobsters and crabs. Ma and Marshall chatted about West End musicals, and the engineering apprenticeship that his son, Jason, had just started at Petters in Staines.

Twenty minutes later the wine waiter showed the champagne bottle to Ma.

'Lovely,' she said. 'Give Jeremy a little; we are celebrating a chapter of our lives.' Golden bubbles fizzed as we studied our scallops; Ma said, 'I am so happy,' and lifted the glass above her head. I savoured the sea taste, mixing white mussel with orange meat and cheesy-potato-sauce.

For our main course we went for Dover Sole. The wine waiter stood with the second champagne bottle and popped the cork, muffling the sound with his white linen cloth. I whispered, 'Slow down, Ma,' and Marshall said loudly, 'You really know how to enjoy yourself, Barbara!' A slither of Sole wriggled on his bottom lip. They were getting drunk. Ma scowled at me. They tilted their heads and champagne poisoned their bloodstreams; their talk circled like an endless record. No one wanted pudding.

'Isn't this wonderful, darling?' She wound her napkin into a ball and spoke more slowly. 'Waiter! Creme-de-menthe frappé for me and Rémy Martin for Mr Marshall. Coffees all round.' I sensed the eyes of other diners on us.

A few minutes later Ricardo brought the drinks. 'Everything all right, Signora Worman?'

'Marvellous!' She raised her glass and her eye turned green through the liquid.

Knives, forks and spoons were silenced as people at other tables examined the three of us, especially my drunken mother. I felt the audience waiting for my move.

I stood up. 'Excuse me, lovely lunch.'

'Of coourrrse, darling.'

I leant towards her, 'I'll just have a walk by the river, and please stop drinking.'

She stood up and swigged champagne. 'I'll do what I bloody well like.' She lifted the glass level with her eyes and squinted through it at the next table. 'Don't stare. We're having fun. Cheers.'

I ran down the gravel path and the weir's rushing water sluiced through me: if only I could leave, if only I were eighteen with money in the bank and my own car. I would drive to John Hearson's parents near Taunton. They were kind and knew Ma had problems. Perhaps they would know a cottage where Ma and I could stay. We could walk across fields without fences and she would get well again. 'Holy Mary, I pray you are watching over Ma and directing her towards Pa and me. Amen.' I kicked off the heads of red carnations. I lay behind a laurel bush, made up stories about clouds, and shivered.

'Jeremy!' Ricardo stood over me. 'I'm glad I found you.'

'I'm fine.'

'I keep an eye on your mother. See you later?' He stepped away, then turned round: 'Sometimes women in Italy, sensitive, beautiful women, like your mother, go through a bad time. It will pass.'

He walked off. I stayed there for another ten minutes and worried about starting my new school, and the state Ma was in. I made my way back to the terrace.

'Ma!'

At a table by the river, beyond the terrace, she lay with her head in her arms; her white handkerchief was smudged with mascara; one of her red shoes was stuck in the flowerbed, its heel pointing up.

'You've ruined it all, bully boy, vile boy.'

'What about you? You're drunk.'

Diners peered over the terrace at us.

'Trust you to think about yourself.'

'Please don't, Ma. I'll help you. Where is Mr Marshall?'

'As if you don't know.'

'Has he gone?'

'He said he had "a special client to collect at Heathrow", and went off without another word, or a thank you.'

I held up her shoe. 'Let's go for a walk.'

'Darling boy, I'm so sorry, sorry.'

We managed to get across Marlow Bridge with my arm round her, so she didn't look too shaky if people gawped. At the other side I wedged her on a seat in the public gardens. 'Have a fag, Ma.' I pulled a bent St. Moritz from the bottom of her handbag. She lit a match, and wobbled it in front of her mouth, half-lit the cigarette and scorch marks browned the sides.

'Little bastard.'

An elderly lady in a mink coat stared as she went past as if we were down-and-outs on Waterloo Station.

'Excuse me,' I called, 'Is there a phone box near here?'

She stepped on and didn't answer. Please would she help me? but her feet trotted like a trained horse in blinkers.

Ma tottered and began to weave back to the hotel. One side of her hair stuck out horizontally, and I tried to brush it flat but she pushed me away. Cars passed slowly on the narrow bridge and the occupants gazed through their safe glass screens. She elbowed my chest, broke free. A green Triumph Stag veered. The driver had a nice face like a beery second-row forward. I waved but he did not stop. Ma dashed across and rested against the bridge. She faced me and her lips quivered in a smile that wasn't really.

'Hold on, Ma.'

As I began to cross she clawed at the iron fretwork, as her bag spilled lipstick, a comb and small change.

'Ma. Stop!'

She kicked off her red shoes; one dropped into the Thames, its buckle glinting. She spread her hands wide and pulled herself to the next section. Her foot got a hold in a round patterned iron gap of the bridge, her other leg flayed out. People watched. I rushed across and my arms just caught the top of her legs, but she kicked my chest. I fell back and saw Ricardo running out of the hotel gates. She had made another upwards footing.

'Signora Worman, please.'

He got his arms round her stomach. 'I help you down; we talk.'

Unmoving, Ma watched the river. Then she inched her way down. We put her between us and got her back to a corner table in the hotel garden. I ran to the lobby and phoned Pa. He told me to get a taxi back 'as soon as possible' and 'we'll sort out her car later'. It was odd that our chat was so brief, as if Pa was not really surprised by what had happened. I went back to Marlow Bridge and leaned over where the suspension chains were low. Why hadn't Pa been here? How could he have just left it to me as if I were a grown up? I took the five-pound note he had given me, tore it to bits, and threw them over. I walked slowly to the hotel. Ma was in the lobby, drinking coffee. Ricardo came over to me.

'I have to get back to work. The receptionist told me the taxi will be here soon. If your father permits it, I could drive her MGB back on my day off. I've put the hood up. Signora Worman gave me the keys.'

'Thank you very much, Ricardo.'

'Here is my home phone number. Get in touch soon. Bye, Jeremy.'

I stood in front of Ma. Already she seemed more sober. She looked out towards the weir as if I did not exist. The dark blue Zodiac taxi soon arrived. We sat in the back as the small, hunched, silver-haired driver took us to Egham. Dandruff flecked his black jacket. When we turned into Inglewood, Pa was on the doorstep, looking pale.

The next day Dr Eric came early and gave Ma an injection. By the time he returned in the evening she was in the sitting room flicking through the *Daily Mail* as if the events of yesterday were merely a story about someone else. In the years ahead whenever I drove over Marlow Bridge and glanced at the iron fretwork, I felt sick in the pit of my stomach.

On the last evening before starting at Haileybury, Em came for supper. Father stood up in the dining room and raised his glass of red Burgundy: 'Here is to a great future for my son.' There was a stain on his blue shirt. Em held up her Amontillado, and Ma her tumbler of tonic water. The dark oak dining-table drained the room of light. Em said, 'You'll soon be captain of football again.' A dribble of wine trickled down Pa's cheek. Ma stroked my hand. I worried that if I did not stay at home, the other Ma who lived inside her might take over. The rare beef and Lancashire pudding were delicious. So was the trifle.

At 9.30 Mr Ranikar the taxi driver knocked on the door. I saw Em out and she pressed a five-pound-note into my hand. 'You'll have a lovely life, my little Jeremy.'

I hugged her.

'I think I'll go to bed,' I said to my parents.

The next day after lunch Ma drove me to Hertford. On a road near Stevenage, I turned round for no reason. I wanted to see my house, my home, but of course it was not there, and neither in my imagination. Only a white space. We turned into the long drive of Haileybury and the dome of the chapel loomed up. It had been designed by the Victorian architect Sir John Blomfield, so Pa told me. We parked. In a car next to ours a tall dark-haired woman in a sheepskin coat stepped out of what Pa would refer to as 'a shooting-brake', and spoke to another mother in a tweed overcoat. They exchanged cheery remarks about their sons, who joked in the background.

A porter put my trunk and tuckbox on a trolley.

Ma hugged me but I did not hug her. She drove off as the quad glowed eerily.

'Follow me,' the porter said, 'it'll be all right.'

Lights from the school buildings and the old-fashioned gas lamps along the footpath glimmered in the twilight. At the other side of the quad, by the entrance to my House, Edmonstone, I met a few other 'new guvs', which is what they called new boys here. The housemaster, Mr Richards, tall and unsmiling, came out and led us into his study. He gave us a pep talk. The knot of his striped tie was tight on the neck of his starched collar.

He showed us round the big school and the grounds. We ended up in the large hall where everyone was sitting down for supper at the long tables; some of the older boys were dishing out the food. After the meal we were taken to our noisy House common room; soon after this a prefect took three of us new guvs to the dorm. It was a very long room where the whole House, about seventy boys, slept; beds were evenly spaced in small cubicles along both sides of the long walls. I was allocated a bed at the end. This room reminded me of photographs of Florence Nightingale in a ward full of injured soldiers during the Crimean War. Halfway down the long dorm there was a wide entrance to the left that led into the showers, baths and lavatories. I stood on the threshold with another new guv, Percy. In front of us an older boy wallowed in a large bath.

He looked up. 'Hello, new guvs; don't look so worried. You'll enjoy it quite soon.'

He turned away as a friend told him a joke. Rugby kit was scattered around; they must have just played a match. From the showers a dark-haired boy came out naked and steaming.

'Worman!'

'Hello, Stevenson.'

He had been two years above me at prep school, was likeable, told funny stories and was sociable with junior boys. He noticed the other new guv. 'Tomorrow, I'll give you both the lowdown on the House. Help you feel at home. See you then.' He went off to change.

Back in the main room, boys were getting ready for bed. Percy's bed was opposite mine. I hung up my clothes on the chair, got into my striped red pyjamas, sat up in bed, and opened a Hardy Boys adventure, *The Ghost at Skeleton Rock*. Two older boys, prefects I assumed, fully dressed, walked down the dorm from the senior end and chatted to some of us. They stood at the end of my bed. The tall one in the fancy waistcoat, his dark hair swept back, had matinee-idol good looks, as Ma would have put it: 'Any special skills – chess; debating, sport, that sort of thing?'

'I play chess, but not very well; I'm keen on politics, and I was captain of the First XI football team at prep school.'

From the door at this end of the dorm, a large, gangly boy with long reddish hair, pushed through, 'Stuff your bloody skills, Alexander!' he said as he lurched on.

'Don't talk to a prefect like that,' the matinee idol's second-in-command said, 'and get your hair cut.'

'Yeah, yeah.'

The gangly boy turned and looked at me, 'Don't take too much notice of them; they like to play the High Command.'

'Williamson!' they said in unison, 'you will be reported to Mr Richards.'

I looked down at my book. I felt suddenly less afraid. Thank you, Williamson, I thought.

'I've noted your point about football,' matinee idol said, 'good luck.' And the High Command walked up the middle of the dorm and stopped at Williamson's bed, which was towards the far end. Fifteen minutes later, the prefects called: 'Lights Out, Lights Out.' Coughs, sniggers, farts and chatter snaked around the dark long dorm.

I closed my eyes and thought of all the boys in their separate cubicles. We all had different skills; we were all different types in a public school that would make us a special collective type to rule the world. It was going to be hard to be a person here; already it was clear that most of the boys even spoke to each other as if they were already types; they talked as if they were in the public world and had polished their images for that. Of course, when I got to know people I might feel differently. No, really, we were being trained to be types. You could move this whole dorm, like a human ant hill, to any part of the world, and we would scatter there, from our little cubicles, well spoken, well dressed, worker human ants – the High Command of human ants – and arrange much larger groups of human ants to work for us in their cubicles of life, while we would enjoy our own separate human-ant-hill palace. I laughed to myself for the first time that day.

It would be pleasant not to worry about Ma for a while. When I saw her in my mind her image was constantly forming and deforming. I did not mind about not being able to pin down an image of Pa, as he had really gone anyway: he was not going to live very long. I tried again to imagine Ma, and being with her, but the image was of her raised hand scratching me. I touched my face. How could I trust her love when it came and went so swiftly?

This was a school for boys like Rogerson and Bailey. Boys from Haileybury had won loads of VCs and were very brave in that sort of way. When you were that sort of boy, and would become that sort of man, you were able to cut off your emotions so you had the courage not to feel too much in the heat of battle. But why did I have to be here? There was a new world coming but this was the world of Tom Brown's school days. And what would 'home' be like next time I was there? Would Pa be dead? Would Ma have run off with Mr Marshall? She would probably love his children more than me.

'Oh, I feel so homesick,' a boy shouted histrionically.

The whole dorm laughed.

'Smithson. Shut up. See me tomorrow,' a prefect said.

The next morning I managed to put on my detached collar and tie. I wore a sports jacket, a lovely brown Norfolk one, with four buttons on the front, a pleated back and side pockets. I smiled in the mirror. Worthington, another new guv said, 'Are you allowed to wear that?' My heart pounded as we walked to lessons across Quad. These were the walls of a prison. I thought of home but could see nothing. Forsyth, who had come up with me from the junior school, said hello and put his arm on my back but I was thinking about other things: if I were not at home to protect Ma, what would happen to her? I saw her pulled-down lips and the curled-up claw of a hand in front of my

81

face. It was a relief too not having to be terrified of her moods.

That evening, after supper, as we did prep in the library, which looked on to the frosty quad, bright under the tall lamps, the prefect-in-charge told us a joke about the geography teacher Mr Jackman and his pet ferrets. Perhaps I could be happy at this place. We got up and the prefect led us into chapel. The high dome drew up my anxiety where it popped. The chaplain welcomed us and said, 'Thomas Malthus was the first Master of Haileybury but not to worry as we are far from being overpopulated yet.' I glanced at the pews filled with boys, some of whom I recognised from prep school, and felt an entry into this new world. Perhaps I would soon be laughing and joking with them. We sang 'All Creatures of Our God and King' and I did not want the service to end. I liked being together but when everyone filtered out I became afraid because they all had something to do and people to talk to. I had no one. And no one to tell about what it was like at home.

As I walked back to the dorm, Daniels, the older boy who had been kind to me at prep school, tapped me on the shoulder. 'You'll be all right; you'll like it here soon.' He must have been sixteen and looked the same except for the bum fluff on his upper lip and spots on his forehead. He walked off to his house, Bartle Frere. In my dorm cubicle I undressed, put on pyjamas and peered through the long window where mist had descended on the quad.

Three weeks passed and we played rugby on the cold pitches. There were so many of them and the flat land stretched indefinitely under sky that was always grey. I was playing scrum half and the sports master was encouraging about 'my dashing blind-side tries'. Nothing lifted my spirits. In the raucous noise of a rugby game I felt terribly alone.

On Saturday I was allowed an exeat. A teacher drove three of us into town and I said, 'I think I'll explore on my own if you don't mind.' I bought sweets and thought about my grandfather, 'Pop' Worman, who had been born in Hertford; he had died of cancer nine months before I was born. Pa had told me about him last month when we were chatting over elevenses. Pop had lived in the downstairs flat before Uncle Neville lived there. Pop had been a bank manager and in 1953 had been about to take over the largest National Provincial bank in England, their City of London branch, but was too ill to do it. He had a lovely face, as did his wife who also died before I was born. At home we had a photograph of them in a country garden, with a cream hammock behind them swinging between two apple trees. I wanted to be a small boy in that hammock. My other grandmother was dead, and Ma had not seen her father since she was a schoolgirl, when he ran off with another woman. I sucked a Callard & Bowser toffee outside the shop. Uncle Bingo, my father's brother, was alive, but did not like children. Great-aunt Em was lovely but very old. My parents were falling to bits. My family was a scattering of names. It was a cold clear day and I wanted to begin again. There was no one around who knew me. A sign pointed 'Hertford East station'.

'Single to London, please.'

I bought the *Guardian* from the kiosk and waited on the platform. Both ends of the platform sloped down, as if I was on a floating pontoon which could sink at any minute; my legs felt unsteady. I had to go home and make it work there, even if people thought me a coward. A crackly announcement over the tannoy said there would be a ten-minute delay for the London train. I sat on a bench and hid behind the opened *Guardian*. What if the master from school was already searching for me?

The train arrived. We were soon speeding past masses of happy-family houses. When we reached King's Cross, I went to the taxi rank. From the station entrance a porter seemed to be following me but perhaps he was going to talk to someone else?

'What are you doing, son?'

He was squat with a large belly and red hair that billowed from under his cap.

'I'm on weekend leave from boarding school. I want a taxi to Waterloo. My parents live in Egham.'

He straightened his cap. 'I'm here to help. Harrow, is it?'

'Haileybury, actually.'

He ran to a cabbie parked away from the taxi rank. A few minutes later I was called over and bundled into a cab where two men and a blowsy woman like Diana Dors were sitting. I perched on a flip-up seat.

'And what takes you to Waterloo?' the woman leant forward.

'I'm going home for a night; I'm at boarding school.'

'Do you like it?'

'Very much. I boarded at prep school so it doesn't feel too bad.'

'We've come down from Leicester for a sales conference. Office equipment. These are my boys, my junior executives.'

She laughed. They looked sheepish. I rather liked the idea of being one of her 'boys', travelling round Britain with her.

The taxi dropped them off and took me on the high-number end of the station from where the Egham trains departed, platforms 19-21. The driver did not offer me any change from my ten-shilling note, whose silver strip glinted as he slipped it into his pocket.

The train from platform 21 soon departed and forty minutes later arrived at Egham Station.

I knocked on our front door.

'Jeremy! What on earth...' She shuffled me into the dining room.

'Hello old chap,' Pa said.

'I couldn't stand it... everything you did this summer... what did you expect...? I'm never going back.'

The room felt sticky.

***

I did go back but a few weeks later ran away again. When Ma returned me the second time it was agreed that if I was not going to stay they could not make me. My trunk and tuckbox would be sent on. A bundle was given to us, wash things, plimsolls. Someone had stolen a pair of my shoes. I had only been there for eight weeks but it felt as if a new kind of life had begun, and ended, in that time.

CHAPTER FOUR
LIMBO

It was an early spring morning in my bedroom as I looked out at the white and purple crocuses round the apple tree. Sun sparked on the mirror. On the mantelpiece was a framed photograph of the First XI cricket team from prep school: I was sitting at the end of the front row. Mitchell was next to me and Dunn-Wooding, the captain, in the middle. Wilkinson and Reed had been my friends too but what would they all think of me now? When they got together one of them might say: 'What about Worman; he funked it, didn't he?' I was no longer in their club so what could I be now? I tilted the photo and their mouths smirked at me. Last week, Mrs Reed had phoned and told Ma she looked forward to us visiting their new house in Rottingdean. Did she mean it?

I got up and turned the photo to the wall so they could not see me and then curled under the blankets as the worms of shame bore through my eyes and ears. At least I am clear about my reasons for leaving school: it was not the regime, which I could have got used to (it didn't seem any tougher than prep school). It really was the horror that Ma might go mad or try to kill herself; the more private horror was that she did not really love me. My father had spoken to the Master of Haileybury and they had come to an agreement about the payment of fees etc. My parents did not know what to do with me.

What would the neighbours think? The Timms' lived next door and Peter was at Eton on a choirboy scholarship. He could smirk at me too. I knew that Giles would stay friends. I had run away to save Ma but could I do it?

The doorbell rang.

'Morning, Ken,' she said.

'Won't be long,' Pa called out.

A few minutes later, his cigarette cough led him out of the house.

I dressed quickly and went downstairs. Ma was standing at the front door in a pale tweed skirt and brown suede blouson, holding the curved handle of the wicker shopping-basket.

'Steak for tonight, darling?'

'Yes please. Have you had breakfast?'

'Not yet.'

'I'll have toast and marmalade ready when you get back.'

'All right. And don't worry, as I've known worse things.' She blew me a kiss.

In the kitchen I cleaned the work surfaces and put away the pans. 'Please, God, let this mother stay, and don't let the mad one return.'

An hour later she came back and put two shopping bags on the kitchen floor.

'Breakfast is almost ready,' I said.

'You look better.' She inspected my blue jeans and cowboy shirt.

I loaded the tray with tea, toast, a pot of milk, marmalade and butter and she followed me to the dining room.

'It's so much brighter in here,' she said.

'I took down the lace curtains.'

'Your father won't like that.'

I poured her Earl Grey and she took it to her place at the end of the table. I slid the toast rack towards her and sat in Pa's chair. The single diamond glinted on her ring finger as she spread the marmalade. I sipped my instant coffee, and did not want to rush, because after breakfast I would worry again. Here we could do anything: Ma had transformed into her real self again.

I glanced at the drinks cupboard on the right. Painted gloss cream, it had round brass-knob handles. When my father came home the doors would open, a conjuror revealing his tricks, and he might say, 'Are you ready for a relaxer, Barbara?' and mix a gin and it for her and pour a Grants for himself; 'Much safer for me, old chap, Dr Eric told me that,' was his motto. Arthur, the delivery driver from Tylers, the wine-and-spirit merchants, came almost as often as the milkman, and was paid in cash. I looked at the side table on my left and there was a tantalus with three cut-glass decanters – 'Gin', 'Sherry', 'Rum' – announced on their hanging silver labels. Alcohol on both sides of the room and on both sides of the family. We were a booze house in stereo.

'Perfect toast, darling.' She buttered a second slice. 'Aren't you hungry?'

'Not really.'

'You should go for a walk. I'll put a brown bag over your head to keep you anonymous.'

'A psychedelic one, please. Why does Pa drink so much?'

'Why do we do anything?' She looked towards the garden.

'Can we live in the country? Please.'

'The Wentworth Estate is like the country, without tractors or pigs, but we'll never make that move now.'

'I want the real thing.'

'Poor old man.' She ruffled my hair. 'Have you thought that I may need a fresh start too?'

'What do you mean?'

'Your father can be frustrating. But I'd never leave you.'

'I must tidy my bedroom.' I slammed the door.

Five minutes later there were loud knocks on the front door.

'Ken. It's too early for Geoff to finish work.'

'There's been an accident.'

I tiptoed down and watched from the foot of the stairs as Pa hobbled in. His left foot and ankle had been bandaged. Mr Marshall guided him to the dining room and then joined us in the corridor.

'He fell over a stool in his office, and couldn't get up,' Marshall said.

'Did anyone see?' Ma asked.

'Only his secretary, Mrs Turvis; she helped him and then phoned me. She won't tell.'

'If everyone is all right, I've got a pick-up at Heathrow.' He gave me a surly look.

'You're so good to us, Ken.' Ma followed him out.

I went into the dining room. 'Want anything, Pa?'

'It's just a sprain, old chap.' Cigarette ash scattered from his shaking hand.

'Can I get you an aspirin?'

'In a manner of speaking: could you reach my whisky glass from the cupboard?'

'Of course.'

Pa poured a good measure from the decanter; he turned to that when the Grants bottle was empty. 'I'm tidying my bedroom,' I said.

'Good for you. See you later.'

He winced with pain.

I stood in front of my bedroom mirror. Did he feel so embarrassed by his decrepitude that he would never again look me in the eye? He was old but what was it like to actually look old? I pulled down my bottom lip and squished up my face; I brushed my hair back and made my face twitch; I puckered my eyes to give me wrinkles; I opened my mouth and chewed on one side; I hunched my back. For all my attempts I couldn't look old.

Ma closed the front door. 'I'll join you for a drink, Geoff. God knows, I need one.'

I lay down and fell asleep.

Ma's shout woke me: 'Come down and speak to your father.'

'What's happened?'

She ran up and pushed open my bedroom door.

'You know what. You're always crawling around.'

'I'm not.'

'Spying on us.'

'I don't.'

'We need to talk to you.'

I followed her to the dining room.

'Feeling better, Pa?'

'A little.'

His swollen foot rested on a stool and his toes were bruised purple.

It was 6 o'clock. He was hunched over with his right hand on the back of the chair, and a whisky and ginger in the other hand. His suit jacket hung limply on him, and the red braces were loose on his weedy chest. Ma sat at the other end of the table with her gin and it (she changed to whisky after dinner). We formed a triangle as I sat in my place at the side. He lit a Capstan and the smoke curled in the airless room and held its shape. His round tortoiseshell bifocals had slipped down his nose and as his head moved his cheeks went in and out of focus like sand dunes. In the dimly lit room, the blue and grey smoke was very still and I thought it might have a message for me: Pa was going to die and I was not afraid because he had only loved me up to a point and that was probably the best he could do.

'Blow a smoke ring,' I said.

'You haven't asked me that for years.'

He made an O shape with his lips and blew out a slow ring which bloomed as it rose, and then a second with stronger outlines. I liked these wispy vapours of him. I enjoyed the tranquil smoke until Ma slammed down her glass: I could almost hear the buzzing-wasp talk in her head, as if she had a private language to express her emotions. They caught each other's eye and looked away. The unsaid had been exposed. Pa said quickly, 'That new barrister, Peter Ward, came down this morning to talk about the Spelthorne planning appeal.' He looked again at her. 'He has a grip on the case, which is more than you can say for the opposition.' Pa was trying to convince himself he was the important senior partner of Gale & Power and not someone who could neither control his drinking nor stop his body's collapse.

'You've always picked good barristers, Geoff.'

They rubbed speech like Germolene over family wounds.

'Why did you put back the lace curtains?' I said.

'Privacy, old chap.'

'They're grey and miserable.'

Ma stood up. 'For God's sake, we must talk about Jeremy, not blow bloody smoke rings.'

'No need to be so sharp, Barbara. In the short term let's consider a tutor.'

'Why did he damn well run away in the first place?'

We looked at her.

'He's certainly not going to Strodes, Geoff. It's a grammar school.'

'A very good one.'

'When Mrs Randall did that charcoal sketch of me of last year,' she said, 'my anniversary present to you – did you really like it? – her two Strodes boys slouched on the sofa when I came in to the room – didn't get up, said nothing. No manners.'

'Jeremy has to go somewhere. And he needs friends.'

'He can play with the boys in the recreation ground. Colin Duncan-Smith's advice was very good: "As long as Jeremy brings them up to his level, and doesn't go down to theirs"...'

'Oh, Barbara. Please.'

'Someone needs a few ideas. Pour me another drink, Jeremy.'

'No. You've had enough.'

'How dare you!' She slapped my face.

'Barbara!'

'Don't touch me,' I said.

'Calm down, old chap.'

'I'm going upstairs.'

'Take a Coke with you,' he said.

I got one from the drinks cupboard and flicked off the cap with the bottle opener.

'And some crisps.'

I took a packet of cheese and onion.

'Pass me the bloody gin, Geoff,' she said as I left the room. 'Why don't I go to bed and you two can go on plotting against me?'

I took up my listening post on the landing.

'We have to eat even if that selfish little bastard doesn't.'

She walked heavily along the corridor. From the kitchen she banged around plates and pans. Five minutes later she shouted through the serving hatch: 'It's oxtail soup. I made it yesterday.' Anything could happen now. She might throw something; she might scream for a long time; she might run out and slam the door; she might go out and not come back for hours; she might be so quiet that I'd worry she had slashed her wrists.

The soup bowls jangled as she carried them on a tray to the dining room. The door was open and silence descended like smog. Between mouthfuls, their spoons grated on the china.

A little later: 'That was lovely, Barbara.'

Good one, Pa. She could be deflected by flattery that would, in the blink of a phrase, direct her along the charismatic Ma path where we had fun. Pa's 'That was lovely, Barbara' might prompt a response like: 'Oh, do you think so, Geoff?' or 'Simple but delicious' or 'Next week I want to try the Fanny Craddock fish pie recipe'. Then you knew you were safe for a while.

'Shall we listen to a programme?' she said.

'Good idea.'

The decanters tinkled as they were poured into cut-glass tumblers. I squidged my feet into the mottled-green carpet.

'We have to sort out Jeremy; we can't go on like this.'

'Don't start that again, Barbara.'

'As you aren't man enough to put Jeremy in his place, I shall.'

I ran to my bedroom, lay on the bed and turned off the light but kept the door open to warn me of enemy action. Pa did not often come up as the stairs were difficult for him. He was a going-to-die father, not one who played cricket or came to watch you play rugby. I wished he were pottering about in his workshop under the eaves where, when I was young, he made me a lovely little wooden chair. The next twenty minutes were quiet until Ma said loudly, 'I'm going to have a bath, Geoff. You always side with him.'

Well, baths were good for her and with luck she would pour in loads of bubble bath; she always came out of those soaks much happier. I turned on the light and started reading *From Russia with Love* as it was too early to sleep. I took a bite of Mars bar and washed it down with a swig of Coke. I got to page five.

'Ma!'

She stood at the door holding a tumbler of whisky. 'I can be very quiet when I want.'

'That's good.' I sat bolt upright. 'I thought you were having a relaxing bath.'

'Do you think you can slouch around for the rest of your life?'

'Do you think you can get drunk and frighten people and have vile boyfriends for the rest of yours?'

'Little bastard.'

'Leave me alone.'

She came for me with a clawed hand; I covered my face with outward palms. She stood back and gin flicked across my leg.

'You need to talk to a child psychologist. We'll arrange it.'

'Not before you've seen a psychiatrist.'

Her lips curled down, and she thrust her clawed hand at my cheek. She backed off and went to her bedroom.

'No quarrelling up there,' Pa called as he shuffled to his bedroom.

Ma stumbled into bed.

Half an hour later I tiptoed into the corridor and there was no light beneath her door. I was on the top floor of a crumbling house and wanted to live in the basement. Flicking on the sidelight, I gently pulled out three Scalextric boxes from under my bed. The grand-prix circuit would look great set up in Uncle Neville's sitting-room. Perhaps his spirit was watching. I hoped so. He had been brought up a Catholic, although he once told Ma, when she found a dusty rosary behind his sofa, 'It was all piffle'.

Touching the face-to-the-wall photo of my First XI teammates, I whispered: 'Our father who art in heaven hallowed be thy name. Amen.' I made the sign of the cross twice on the back of the photograph. 'Rest in peace and God bless.'

Ma was snoring.

I tiptoed downstairs with the first box of Scalextric as moonlight through the tall landing window gave me guidance. The last uncarpeted flight creaked slightly. On the last step something in the box rattled. But there was no response from my parents, so I slid the door bolt. In the cavernous hallway the patterned tiles were cold on my feet. I walked over the echoes of Uncle Neville and could almost smell curry spices from the kitchen. 'Good to see you again, old boy...' There were two large rooms on either side of the front door; the one on the left was his bedroom. 'Uncle Neville?' A rustling sound made my heart race. 'Uncle Neville?'

The brass headboard of his bed glowed from the small orange streetlight on Manorcrofts Road; on the wall facing the window was a chest of walnut drawers, 'the best in the house' Ma told him when he moved in. There seemed to be a lumpy shape beneath the green eiderdown: 'Uncle Neville?' I sensed him lying there and saw his face, which looked unready to be dead. Bare trees flickered on the road.

After a few minutes of reassuring silence, I made two more tense journeys to collect the other boxes from my bedroom and, finally, bolted the dividing door from my side. I turned on the sidelights in the sitting room and put the three boxes next to the fireplace. On the long curtains, patterned with a hunting scene, men in red coats were Tally Hoing on their horses across fields with hounds in chase of a single fox. The fox was never caught but, if you overlapped the curtain folds, you could make a hound bite his bum. Ma never liked the design, 'too much, darling', but they were the curtains Uncle Neville had chosen and paid for. 'Reminds me of England,' he had told me, 'but not the one I came back to.'

A few days before I had prepared the fire with kindling and logs, and now it lit first time. I took the blue picnic rug from the small corner chair and lay on the sofa. Last Sunday, Ma had been in the garden, just outside the French windows, in black wellies and a torn Barbour, collecting fallen branches from the pear tree; when I took her a mug of coffee she said, 'You don't light fires down here, do you?' 'No, of course not,' I said in a tone that really said You know I do and she responded, 'All right, then.'

Perhaps I could live down here. I picked up the bellows, blew into the ashes and kindling, which began to flicker and spark. I walked across the room and held the doorknob: solid glass with a cut-glass base; when the sun hit it rainbows danced on the walls. Uncle Neville had brought it with him: 'No logical reason, old boy,' he said, explaining why he had asked his landlord in South Kensington if he could possibly have it, 'but it lit up my gloomy sitting room. I imagined I was back in India under those strange huge skies I loved – well, we don't have to be rational all the time, do we? Now come on, I'll show you how to make a proper chicken korma, an old Mughal dish.' I was very young then but it lodged in my mind. He talked to me as if I were grown up. Ma used to say, 'Oh, he knows nothing about children; they sent Geraldine to boarding school when she was eight', but he knew a lot about me. In the fireplace the apple-tree logs began to glow. Did Ma and Neville ever have sex before I was born? Is it possible he was my father? Did Pa stop having sex after my birth? Was that the last time they did it (I couldn't imagine Pa having the energy)? Yuk! What creepy thoughts. Who would have been my favourite father? I blinked, not wanting to think about that, nor to be disloyal to Pa now he was dying.

Time for a cuppa. I had secret supplies in the 'scullery' as Ma called it: chocolate-digestives, a packet of Assam tea, milk, Cheddar cheese, Branston pickle, butter and a cucumber. I lit a hissy gas jet and put on the kettle. Inside the fridge the flickery light and hum-hum was like Dr Who's Tardis taken over by Daleks. I warmed the pot and put in two teaspoons of tea. When it had brewed, I put my big mug of tea on a tray alongside two digestive biscuits topped with butter and strawberry jam.

Tucked behind a cushion on the sitting-room sofa was Arthur Mee's *Book of Everlasting Things*, which I had borrowed from the dining room bookshelf. I turned to 'I Am' by John Clare, who died in a lunatic asylum in 1864, and read the first verse in front of the mirror:

I am! yet what I am who cares, or knows?
My friends forsake me, like a memory lost.
I am the self-consumer of my woes,
They rise and vanish, an oblivious host,
Shadows of life, whose very soul is lost,
And yet I am – I live – though I am toss'd.

Smoke curled up the chimney. Perhaps one day my adolescent attempts at writing poetry could turn into something good.

I shut the sitting-room door, said a prayer for Uncle Neville, and snuggled down on the sofa with my tea and snacks. On a scrap of paper I made a plan of the Scalextric circuit as flames lit up the red-marble fireplace, and an appley aroma filled the room. This was my perfect little world where I didn't have to worry about grown-up things, or about Ma. It even took my mind off its frantic thinking about naked girls doing all kinds of things. My Scalextrix was like a comfort blanket. Were there enough bridge-building blocks to ensure the incline was not too steep or the track links would get buggered up, which made the cars stutter? It took a while to design a really exciting circuit.

On the corner table was a record player and beneath it I kept a few of my favourites, *The Village Green Preservation Society* LP by the Kinks, the Beatles *Magical Mystery Tour*, which had been a surprise present from Em last month, 'I know how with-it you are, Jeremy,' she said, although I could hardly bear to listen to one beautiful track, 'Fool on the Hill', as it was the saddest song I had ever heard. I played *Sgt. Pepper's Lonely Hearts Club Band* a lot because that was about me in the future, *everything* I wanted to be when I grew up. The way the Beatles dressed on the inside cover – in exotic psychedelic military-style uniforms – took me beyond my troubles. Last summer I'd been allowed to go up to Carnaby Street on my own. In a shop called I Was Lord Kitchener's Valet they sold clothes like that, but I bought a pair of loons and a flowery shirt from Carnaby Kids. It had been a sunny Saturday with buskers playing Joni Mitchell songs. I had never seen so many beautiful girls in mini skirts and tight jumpers. They were so gorgeous that I nearly exploded. One of them, with long brown hair, a flower-child band round her head, a thin black V-neck jumper and leather sandals, said to her friend, 'Isn't he cute?' referring to me. They giggled and walked on.

As I opened the boxes, silver strips in the middle of the tracks gleamed: straight sections; curves; chicanes. Crash barriers, grandstands; hay bales and model figures. I kept the best for last: two rally cars, a Mini Cooper and a Ford Escort Mexico; two racing cars, a Lotus and a McLaren. I glanced at my plan of the circuit and then put the tracks in approximate positions round the room, following the curved shape of the French windows to make a sweeping bend followed by the long straight, and another curve to the rising up of the cross-over chicane bridge. 'What do you think, Uncle Neville?'

The grandstand looked just right by the first corner, with spectators sprinkled round the track; the man with binoculars, sports jacket and cavalry twills was scratched and I put him next to the woman with dark glasses and a horsey scarf – Ma and Uncle Neville together, coming to watch me race the Mini Cooper. I placed the cars in the four lanes next to the official with the starting flag by the 'Grand Prix' bridge, linked wires to the transformer and plugged in hand controls for each car. What a great circuit! I picked up two controllers: the Mini Cooper with my right hand, and Giles driving the Ford Escort Mexico with my left hand (I'm left-handed so this gave Giles an advantage). We were off, a slow first lap to check connections, and Giles stopped on the bridge. I reconnected that section of track. Off again, very smooth, with Giles skidding round the first corner, the back of his Mexico clipping the Mini Cooper's front wing – 'Any more driving like that, Giles, and I'll report you to the race marshal' – but I made up ground on the long straight as we competed our second lap. Ma blew me a kiss from her prime spot in front of the grandstand. After three laps Giles and I were evenly matched. I switched controllers and whoosh I was driving like a wizard. 'Goodbye Giles.' I pushed the throttle to full and the Mexico rolled over on the sweep of the non-crash barriered corner. Poor Giles came to Rest in Peace beneath a framed photograph of my parents at Royal Ascot.

The fire was burning down. I yawned.

'I've made a good start, Uncle Neville.'

In the corner was a small teak table, inlaid with ivory. Uncle Neville had left it when he moved out, along with his small oak rack of three pipes, which were always on the table's top. He usually smoked cigars, but sometimes the room would be filled with a Balkan Sobranie pipe mixture, whose exotic aroma made me think of a camel trail across the desert. The pipes and rack were always dusty, although the rest of our house was spotless, and this room was regularly cleaned. I might go for months and never notice the table or pipes and then they would catch my attention: it was like a tiny ancient ruin and just to have it there pleased me. Although Ma and I never said it, this was our shrine to Uncle Neville.

I had never touched the pipes: two were mid-coloured wooden ones of different sizes, but the third had a bowl in the shape of a lion's head and was made of an Indian wood. I stood close to the table, stretched out my finger and quickly touched the lion's head, as if it might give me an electric shock. I took the pipe from its stand, half expecting lightning to strike. It didn't, so I smoked the pipe – without tobacco. It still gave off a warm aromatic smell: I heard Uncle Neville speaking through me, 'One day soon, Jeremy, I'll take you to the Oval. You hold your bat so well, and your forward-defensive stroke is perfect.' I returned the pipe to its place, walked round the track, and chatted to the drivers. I put the two fire engines near the pits. It must be well past midnight so I turned off the light and lay down.

When I woke, the thick curtains had kept out the light.

The time by the scullery clock was 8.45. Pa would have gone to work and Ma was probably still blotto from last night. There was time for a cuppa and a cheese-and-pickle sandwich before I faced my upstairs world. Anyway, she would probably think I had gone for an early bike ride. In about ten minutes I could sneak out of the French windows, and return through our front door. I made tea and a sandwich in my Y-fronts.

'Where are you, Jeremy?' Ma banged on the dividing door.

Rushing into the sitting room, I put on my shirt and jeans, and drew the curtains.

99

'Is that you, Ma?'

'Who do you damn well think it is?'

A full confession might be the best policy and 'Come and see what I've done'. No, that would not work today. Wish me luck, Uncle Neville.

'I pulled back the bolt. 'Morning.'

Her crumpled cream silk nightdress was coffee-stained. 'Disobedient boy!' She pushed me aside and blasted me with her whisky breath.

Her legs wobbled.

'Watch the circuit!'

'Little bully boy. I am alone and get no support. You think you own this house, do you?' She jabbed a finger against my right cheek. 'I'm not going on with this... I'm not... this is no life for me... I'm a prisoner.'

'Please stop, Ma. We can talk it over at breakfast.'

'Think you can live down here? Think Uncle Neville will save you? Couldn't save himself, could he?' She put her face close to mine: 'You're going to be a failure, like your father.' She jabbed my arm and fell backwards. 'Now look what you've made me do.'

'I'll help you up.'

'Don't touch me!'

'Would you like a boiled egg?'

'Boiled bloody eggs!' She scuttled onto her knees and tottered up. 'Get all those baby toys out of here; take down the Scalextric.'

'No.'

'I'm leaving. See how you get on then.'

She kicked at the Ford Mexico but her foot went over the top.

'Please, Ma; stop now.'

'I'll stop all right. Good little Mummy. What then? What would you do without me, little bastard, always plotting with your father to get rid of me – I'll save you the trouble.' She picked up the Lotus – 'No, please, I love that car' – and threw it against the wall.

100

'Who cares? None of you cares about me.'

'Don't shout, Ma.'

'The neighbours! I'm going into the village for milk… the police can take me away… you'd like that… I'm leaving… no one will stop me.' Her bare foot trod on the Mini Cooper – 'Selfish boy. Get off… Get off me…'

I was nowhere near. She toppled over at the banked curve, got up on one knee and lurched at the French windows.

'You'd love me dead, wouldn't you? Ken will take me away if I ask him, and what will you do then… keeping me prisoner… I'm going now.' She shook the bolted French windows. 'How dare you lock me in.'

Her elbow heaved at the glass, and she hit the frame, but as she spun round her right fist smashed the glass.

'Ma!'

Her hand was trapped.

'Don't move,' I said.

I grabbed the fire poker and knocked out the splintered glass. Her arm was coated with blood, but at least it was not spurting. She fell back and I pulled her onto the sofa.

'Hold out your arm,' I said.

I took off my blue-flowered Carnaby Kids shirt to wrap round the gash, which had just missed a vein.

'Stay still,' I said.

I pulled out two thin shards of glass and wound my shirt round the wound.

'Stay there,' I said.

Her head flopped against the back of the sofa. I ran upstairs, found Dr Eric in the address book, and dialled his home number.

He answered at once.

'Dr Eric; it's Jeremy Worman. My mother has a badly cut arm, and she's drunk.'

'I was just leaving for the surgery. I'll be there in fifteen minutes. Wrap her arm tightly. If it keeps bleeding, phone an ambulance.'

'I've dressed the wound.'

'Well done. Stay with her.'

I went downstairs.

'What happened?' she said as the blood dried in snake patterns on her arm.

'Dr Eric is on his way.'

'Why?' She put her hand to her mouth and retched.

I ran to the utility room, got a tin bucket, and got back just before she puked into it. She sat up and held the bucket; her head dropped down and she puked again.

'I'll get you a glass of water.'

I put on the cold tap in the scullery. She had smashed two of my favourite cars, I thought. What a cow. There were no more puking sounds.

'Feeling any better?' I handed her the glass.

'Thank you.'

'I'm going to wait by the front door for Dr Eric.'

I stood on the porch and breathed in the fresh air of this clear day. I picked up a rancid tennis ball from the bottom of the hedge and threw it against the house over and over. A few minutes later Dr Eric's green Volvo estate turned into the drive. I ran over and opened the driver's door for him. He took his doctor's bag from the passenger seat.

'You've done well, Jeremy.' He ruffled my hair. 'Lead the way.'

She was sprawled on the sofa.

'Morning, Barbara. What's all this about then?' He sat down and took her pulse. He turned to me. 'Selfless of you to use such a special shirt, Jeremy.' He unwound it and examined her wound, 'That doesn't look too serious. I can't see any glass under the skin. You were lucky. I'll clean it up and put on iodine.' He looked at me. 'Could you empty the bucket?'

I took it to the downstairs lavatory and poured away her sick; I rinsed the bucket in the big scullery sink, and found Dettol, which I swilled round. I washed my hands and returned to the sitting room.

'Give me a few minutes alone with your mother. Wait outside and I'll come and get you.'

Five minutes later he called me in. 'Your mother is much calmer now. I gave her an injection.'

'I need to go to the bathroom,' she said.

'Watch the stairs, Barbara. When you come back, we'll all have a chat together. He squeezed my shoulder: 'What about you?'

'Oh, you know.'

'I see that two of the cars had a terrible crash.' He sat on the sofa.

My head dropped.

'Mother?'

I nodded.

'She needs some psychiatric help. There's a new man at Holloway Sanatorium, Dr Flack. I like him. I think he would be amenable to taking her in for a while. It will probably have to be a private bed at such short notice. He might get to the bottom of what makes her do these things. Your parents are in Bupa?'

'Yes. Not that I believe in it. Will they let her out again?'

'Of course; it's a temporary episode – but what about you? It's a shame that boarding school didn't work out. I've got some ideas, but first you get a cup of tea for your mother, and I'll make a few phone calls.'

'The one in Uncle Neville's room is still connected.'

From the scullery I felt reassured by the sound of Dr Eric's voice on the phone, and took a mug of tea to Ma, who was drooping on the sofa. 'I'm not quite ready to receive visitors,' she slurred.

I smiled, but then stared at the broken Lotus, whose chassis had come away from the car's body.

'I don't care what you're fucking ready for. Don't you know what you do to people? Don't you know?'

'Jeremy, Jeremy.' Dr Eric rushed in, tugged me back and kept his arms over my shoulders. 'It's sorted out. Dr Sam is taking my surgery; I was able to get Dr Flack at home. He's agreed. Now Barbara, you go and get ready. Just an overnight bag will be enough for now.' He let go of me, and spoke slowly to Ma, looking straight into her eyes: 'It would be good for you to have a few days away as a private patient at Holloway Sanatorium. There's a doctor there, Dr Flack, who you will like. He really will be able to help you.'

Ma nodded. 'I'll get ready.' She went upstairs.

He turned to me. 'I phoned your father too. Will you be all right until he gets back at lunchtime?'

'Yes.'

'I'll come back then; we'll make some plans for you both. How is he?'

'Wobbly.'

'Drinking heavily?'

'Of course.'

'I'll wait upstairs for your mother. What will you do?'

'I'll repair the Scalextric. I don't want to say goodbye when she goes. Just take her away, please.'

He went up. I surveyed the damage. Near the French windows the track had been pulled about and connections bent. I knelt down. The upturned chassis on the Lotus was beyond repair. The grandstand had collapsed and spectators scattered. The figure of Uncle Neville had been squashed but I managed to straighten his legs and set him upright. No one would ever know how Ma treated me: families like ours were beneath the radar of social workers. I looked at the pipe stand and felt brave. Perhaps I would be mentioned in dispatches. 'What shall I do now, Uncle Neville?'

'You know that I told you that when Hindus experienced a bad upset they would sit still for a long time in a guru pose with their legs crossed? It made them feel much better. I liked the way they dealt with the trials of life, and God knows they had more than their share. Sometimes they hummed, om om om om om – but if I were you, I'd not worry about that part – just sit cross-legged on the sofa and stare at that beautiful fireplace. I often did.'

'Thanks.'

I sat cross-legged on the sofa. The red and cream of the marble swirled like strawberry-ripple ice cream. 'Om... om... om... omomom... om... om...' and when I closed my eyes my mind expanded. Cosmic Consciousness? I shall definitely become a hippy. That was the way forward. I stayed in that pose for ages until an image came into my mind of Uncle Neville, dead in his Morris Minor on Chobham Common, an army revolver on his lap, and blood clotting in his head. For the rest of the morning I mended the tracks and put the spectators back in their proper places.

Just after midday Pa called out 'I'm home, Jeremy' in his confident voice, so different from the rest of him.

'Coming.'

I ran up to the hallway.

'Dr Eric told me everything; Mr Marshall knows.'

Marshall was quieter than usual and stood behind Pa. Perhaps he realised that having a mad woman as his bit on the side was not the best idea.

'I'm all right now, Mr Marshall,' Pa said. 'Thank you so much. Jeremy can take over from here.'

'All right, sir.' He took off his chauffeur's hat and squeezed its black patent peak. He walked out backwards like a weak actor leaving the stage and craving applause.

'Take this, will you, old chap.' Pa handed me two carrier bags. 'Smoked salmon in one; we'll have it in sandwiches for lunch. Scallops for supper in the other. I'll do my special with bacon; you like that, don't you?'

'Very much.'

I got behind Pa on his way to the dining room. As he lowered himself into the chair, the doorbell rang.

I answered it. 'Come in, Dr Eric,' I said.

We all sat at the table.

Dr Eric leant forward. 'Barbara has settled in. Dr Flack has met her. They got on well. I am sure he will be a good influence – but what are we going to do with you two?'

'Well, I have something to tell you first.' Pa sat upright. 'I've decided to retire; the partners' meeting today was about that. It had to come.'

'What do you mean, Geoff?'

'I'm not up to it. They were carrying a very expensive burden.'

'Do we face bankruptcy, Pa?'

'Plenty left for chocolates and blue jeans.'

And for whisky, I thought.

Pa said, 'I'll make the sandwiches, and I'm quite all right on my own.' He hobbled off.

Dr Eric told me he had almost finished building the yacht in his garden: I put up a good show of being interested. After what seemed an age, he said, 'Better check I locked the car,' and walked off.

Pa returned ten minutes later with a tray of sandwiches and wedges of lemon. It was a miracle he had made the return journey without crashing. Dr Eric came back in.

'Tuck in,' Pa said.

He poured two glasses of white burgundy and half a glass for me. We chomped away and joked as if we were prep-school friends, sitting in the copse with a bottle of Woodpecker, donuts and crisps.

Dr Eric explained the situation: 'Barbara may be away for a month,' Dr Eric said, 'and with a little luck, she will return much better.'

'I'll ask Mrs Parish to come in for a few extra hours,' Pa said.

'I can do more shopping,' I said.

'I'll be popping in regularly.' Dr Eric got up. 'No need to see me out.'

'Thanks for all the help, Eric,' Pa said.

'Pleasure. Bye.'

'Remind me to phone Mr Belsey to fix the window,' Pa said. 'We'll say I slipped. I'm going for a nap. I'm very stable today. The new pills are helping.'

'That's good.'

I was tired too and went upstairs. I lay on my bed and read *From Russia with Love*.

An hour later, Pa called up, 'Cup of tea, old chap?'

'Thanks. Be down in five minutes.'

In the dining room the tray was laid out nicely, including toast with Patum Peperium. We enjoyed the silence. From time to time Pa touched his tortoiseshell bifocals, and this was often a sign of pleasant thoughts. When he worried he usually took off his glasses and cleaned them in circular motions with the handkerchief from his top pocket.

Pa was modest but really clever: in the exams for a fellowship of the Royal Institute of Chartered Surveyors, he had won the Crawter Prize for being second out of all Commonwealth students in the Rating and Valuation paper; at thirty he became the senior partner of Gale and Power. He developed the business from one branch to six and made lots of money. What made him drink and smoke so much; why was he so disillusioned with life?

He stared out of the window, as if he too were looking for the answer. The bright light on the lawn and rock garden was cheerful, or rather would have been, without those awful net curtains. What was the point of windows if you couldn't see through them? Half an hour later I cleared away. Then I popped my head round the door, 'I'm going for a walk in Egham.'

'Good for you. You have to face your public some time.'

I put on my jean jacket and headed up Station Road. Bennett's, the little chemist, was on the other side of the level crossing, next to the garage; on the far side of the road was the station car park where the 117 bus took you to Staines, the beginning of south London, horrible and ugly, except for the Odeon, where I saw films with friends. My favourite shop was halfway along Station Road, Marge's the sweet shop, where you could buy a fantastic amount of chews, flying saucers, black jacks and sherbert dips, all for a shilling. I looked in the window, wary to enter as Marge would ask me about school. The paint was peeling off the shop front, which may once have been purplish, but had dimmed to a mud shade. The Five Boys Milk Chocolate poster was torn, and the boys, the same boy actually, although each image made a different facial expression, a story from 'Desperation' to 'Realisation (It's Fry's)'.

At the end of the road was the optician, Mr Sanders, who always wore a bow tie, and knew my father. They both liked bridge. Once a month he would collect my father in his two-tone-green Riley One-Point-Five and they would go to one of the group's houses to play (about twice a year my father hosted an evening). Mr Sanders was a short, dapper man, with red, rubbery lips and a pale complexion. Last Christmas when Ma and I passed his practice he came out: 'Isn't he growing up?' he said, appraising me. We had a brief chat and walked on. Ma said quietly, 'He's charming; not married,' and squeezed my hand. That was code for 'He's a homo.' Not that she had anything against homosexuals. 'They understand women, darling, and that is more you can say for most men.' Mr Sanders's establishment was on a second, higher level of very old stone pavement and made me think of Egham as it was, before they began to destroy its history. Egham now was only about the kind of 'progress' that made people rich by selling even more stuff that no one needed. At the top of Station Road, I turned right into the High Street. At the other end of it I went into the Parish Church grounds and sat on my favourite tomb, which always calmed me, rather like Uncle Neville's om om omming. Walking back past the primary school in School Road, I soon reached my house and stopped at the gates. A few minutes later I went through the ground-floor front door as this morning I had found a key under the sink in the scullery. I crept up the side stairs. Pa was reading *Barchester Towers* in the dining room.

'I didn't hear you come in.'

'They don't call me twinkletoes for nothing.'

'Quite so.'

'I'm going to play with my Scalextric.'

'You do that.'

'Let me know if you want help with the supper.'

'I will – isn't it peaceful? I think we all needed a break.'

Downstairs, I leant against Uncle Neville's bedroom door. 'Got the key to the house now. Was it the one you used?'

At 7.30pm Pa and I sat at either end of the dining-room table and he served the scallops, bacon, mashed potato, and salad. As he handed the plate to me, his face was drawn as if suffering from a slow puncture; our airy talk at teatime was Pa on the last of his high pressure.

He savoured a few slices of scallop: 'Delicious'; he perked up further after he sipped the white burgundy. He came fully back to life when he discussed his interest in the Civil War, and the family story that we were descended from an illegitimate child of Nell Gwynn. Well, who wasn't? I thought. It was not as if I was about to claim a lost title – 'Arise Sir Jeremy' – or inherit an ancient country estate. Pa considered that this idea of our genealogy was possible, and he did not often believe anything 'speculative'. He said, 'See those wine stains on the table?' and rubbed his finger over them, 'they could have happened at Oak House. It's a sixteenth-century building in West Bromwich, near Birmingham. The owners' family name was Turton, which was my mother's maiden name, and King Charles is known to have visited the house. The Turtons owned it for generations, and managed to swap sides in the Civil War without losing their heads.' He pressed the stain with his forefinger, and the flesh on his face looked suddenly plump, as if the family spirit had revived him. I said the story was a 'bit unlikely', and 'Where did Nell Gwynn fit in?' He did not tackle that point but 'Finally,' he said 'this Elizabethan dining table,' and moved a hand along its edge, 'in all probability did come from Oak House – my mother told me.' My third forename was 'Turton' – Jeremy Simon Turton Worman.

Pa's new-found zest did not last, and a few minutes later his face was ashen. He stared into his glass: was he imagining a different life that connected more closely to his family history, and which did not include Ma? Anyway, how did I know it was my family?

'Ma's background was more complicated than yours, Pa.'

'Definitely. Though of course one would have assumed your mother had been county since the Conquest.'

'If not before.'

'I'm going for a pee.'

Actually, a strength of Ma and Em was the ease with which they navigated their way through, and up, the English class system. Ma had gone to boarding school and spoke with received pronunciation, a lovely voice, full and well modulated without the overstress of being too cut glass; Em maintained a northern accent that could best be described as Manchester Posh. She often wore a full-length brown mink coat but was never fazed by snobs who may have thought she was not quite it: 'They should look back a few generations, Barbara; they would find a coalmine at the bottom of their money, or worse.' I think it was a genuine Lancashire quality to see through the facade of the Home Counties upper-middle class and laugh at their presumptions.

When Pa returned from the lavatory he said, 'What a relaxing evening. And by the way, I've been in touch with Mr Blundell. He's moved on from being a housemaster at

Haileybury prep school to set up a tutorial college of his own, to cater for all kinds of boys and girls. I know you always got on well with him. I have arranged for you to go to his new place in May. He doesn't think he can fit you in until then, so for now you really must have a tutor, at least a few times a week.'

'Thanks. I like those ideas. Do you mind if I go up? I'm really tired.'

'You do that, old chap. I'm turning in early too.' He looked straight at me. 'Goodnight. One more thing: I'm sorry I am so decrepit.'

'Don't worry about that. You'll get better. God bless.'

Behind his bifocals were tears.

A few days after Ma had gone to Holloway Sanatorium, Dr Eric dropped in. We sat in the dining room and agreed it was a good idea if I did not see Ma for a few weeks. Pa went into work most days, 'Lots of loose ends to tie up'. He ordered the *Guardian* for me – 'If I'm going to have a socialist for a son, I had better have an educated one' – and I enjoyed reading it. When I took the papers off the mat, the *Guardian* was always on top of *The Times*, never the other way round. Perhaps the paperboy was a socialist too.

In the evenings, Pa went to bed early and I watched television. In May, the BBC six o'clock news showed a Parisian policeman charging at students protesting against the closure of the Sorbonne. Cars smouldered on a wide avenue near the Rive Gauche. From behind a hastily built barricade of jagged wood, one young man, his blond hair flowing, a tied handkerchief covering his face, threw a stone at the riot police, dipped his hand to find a second, and flung that too. The camera was in line with our television set and the third stone went wham, straight into my dead Surrey world. These students were hurling missiles for me too. They were freedom. The camera had flashed onto a poster stuck to the wall, 'LA BEAUTÉ EST DANS LA RUE', and showing a girl chucking a brick. Only by breaking the government could we stop the capitalists killing us.

I ran down the steps into the front garden: I wanted a new start, a happy kaleidoscope world.

Pa called from the top of the steps, 'Cauliflower cheese is ready.'

'I'm going to be a revolutionary!'

'Let's have supper first. And don't scare the neighbours.'

'Okay.'

After our meal, I took the London Telephone Directory from beneath the hall table, returned to the dining room, and flipped through to find an address.

'What are you doing?'

'Looking for the Chinese embassy.'

'What on earth for?'

'They send you a copy of Chairman Mao's Red Book and a badge.'

'A badge! That's marketing. The Chinese are learning capitalism.'

'Pa, really.'

'Perhaps you'd like to go to school in China?'

'I don't speak Chinese.'

'I'm sure Chairman Mao could arrange private lessons for someone of your potential!'

For the next two weeks I had five two-hourly sessions per week with Mr Gibbons MA (Oxon), a retired teacher from Strodes (Pa had found him through a contact at the Rotary Club). I used to cycle to his bungalow in Thorpe, where his wife, a former music teacher and keen pianist, was always practising something Wagnerian as I arrived. She opened the door, always in a black dress, her wiry dark hair adrift from its bun, her glasses askew, and her face flushed, as if she had been having sex with the piano. Mr Gibbons's study was a lovely wooden outhouse at the end of a long garden. He was short and white haired with smooth pink cheeks and a gentle smile. He always wore sports jackets a little too large for him, as if he had shrunk since the time he bought them. He was lovely, and a super teacher. We did Latin, Maths, and English, and he gave me lots of interesting homework.

At weekends, Pa was driven by Dr Eric to see Ma but he did not say much to me about it, only, 'Barbara is coming on well; she will be back with us soon.' I imagined their meeting: 'Hello Barbara; I've bought you some red roses.' And Ma would say, 'They're gorgeous. How did you know?'

At the end of the third week, Dr Flack phoned Pa to say that Ma had responded well to ECT, and to her sessions with him. After their conversation Pa told me that 'Your mother will be back in about a week's time.' He looked pleased.

'I want to go and see her,' I said.

The next Friday afternoon I cycled there and left my bike for safety in the racks at Virginia Water Station, which was five minutes away from Holloway Sanatorium. I walked through the front gates and stood in the tall, ornately marbled Victorian entrance hall. It was more like an Italian cathedral than a place for the mentally ill, but then it was 'Holloway Sanatorium', which had a healing sound, unlike 'Asylum', 'Madhouse', 'Loony Bin' or 'Nuthouse'. At the reception desk they were expecting me. A white-uniformed male nurse came out of the office and led me up long corridors, which were painted light green, and hung with paintings and prints. We climbed two flights of spiral stairs. On the second floor we passed several patients: one elderly woman, well made up, and dressed in a brown two-piece, with a row of pearls to set off her outfit, made me think I was in Ma's country-house-style-hotel territory; a tall thin man in a blue woollen-dressing-gown danced by, his right arm outstretched, as if catching birds or demons.

113

His black hair was brushed to one side, and remained horizontal, like strands of stiff spaghetti.

'This is your mother's room,' the nurse said. 'If you get lost on your way back, ask anyone. Bye.'

I went in.

'Hello, darling.'

She was sitting in an armchair, reading *Vogue*.

'Hello, Ma.' I kissed her on both cheeks.

'So long since we last saw each other.' She smiled, but one side of her face remained stiff. 'I know I look a mess.'

'No, you don't.'

I stood by the window and glanced out at the little quad where a mass of daffodils swayed in the breeze.

'I will get better. Dr Flack is helping very much. He's retiring next year. He was at Shrewsbury, same school as your great-uncle Ernest.'

'Marvellous!'

'Sometimes I think how nice it would be to stay here forever. In my life I've talked to a lot of expensive experts, but Dr Flack really is the best.'

'But will you change for good?'

'Another time, Jeremy.' She crossed her legs and slammed *Vogue* on the side table.

There was a blue painting on the wall above the fireplace.

'It's a copy of Picasso's *The Guitar Player*,' she said. 'Funny choice, isn't it? But I like it. Perhaps private patients get better-quality paintings. Do you think so? Thank God for Bupa.'

'But what about the way you behave towards me?'

She looked out of the window.

Then we talked about my bike, her car, our need for an extra daily help, Ma's frustration at not having all her beauty products with her, Great Fosters, Nell Pemberton's new perm ('it's really not her'). I added snippets about Pa's great cooking, of how he was looking better and not drinking so much. I told her I was looking forward to studying again. Tittle-tattle went on for over fifteen minutes.

'Have a proper look at the quad,' she said.

'Ma. I want to talk about, you know, what happened.'

From the corridor, a woman's voice said, 'Anyone want anything?'

'Get the door, darling.'

A middle-aged lady with an evangelical smile had stopped with a double-decker trolley. It was loaded with a big pot of tea, instant coffee, milk, biscuits, homemade cakes, papers, sweets, and more.

'Thank you, Joan,' Ma said, 'this is my son, Jeremy.'

'Isn't he lovely!' She squeezed my shoulders and from close range looked into my eyes as if she could divine secrets.

'A cup of your lovely tea, please, and a digestive,' Ma said.

'Tea too, please, and may I have a piece of that chocolate cake?'

'What lovely manners,' Joan said.

I stepped back into the room for fear of further molestation.

The cakes were on the trolley's lower level and Joan bent down in her dark trousers and green V-neck jumper and cut me a slice of the chocolate one. 'I made it today.'

She arranged everything on a small tray and handed it to me. 'You two enjoy your afternoon together. See you tomorrow, Barbara.'

'You're a marvel. I'll look forward to it.'

'Bye, Jeremy.'

'Goodbye.'

Joan closed the door.

Ma and I sat on either side of the small table.

'Isn't she lovely,' Ma said.

I took my cake to the window and looked at Ma. 'Your face is still a bit numb on one side; is that from the treatment?'

'Don't show off about things you know nothing about.'

'Dr Eric told me.'

She turned away. 'You're here to cheer me up and aid my recovery.' She stared at the door. I think she was crying. A few minutes later she blew her nose and turned round.

I sat down again but we did not talk. She had managed to turn our meeting into Ma-and-Jeremy-at-a-nice-country-hotel scene. If I asked real questions, I knew she would turn against me. I traced the patterns on the rug and remembered what Ma had told me about her family. I wondered if childhood held the roots of her mental problems: her grandfather, Em's father, Isaiah Piggott, 'Sinker' Piggott, had been a door boy in the Wigan colliery, Lancashire, in the 1860s. But by the time of Queen Victoria's death in 1901, he had made a fortune as a coal and goldmine owner, mainly in India, developing a drainage system for making mines deeper. One of his sons went to Shrewsbury but not my mother's father, Arthur; he squandered his inheritance, drank heavily and was nasty to Ma. When she was eight years old he abandoned the family. Ma was only thirteen when her mother died – an illegal abortion in the back streets of Wigan. Ma and her brother, Fred, were brought up by their loving grandmother in a large house, Carlton House, at Burscough Bridge. After tea, I kissed Ma goodbye.

I found my way out and cycled home.

I let myself into Uncle Neville's front door with my new key. Pa would not notice my absence for a while. In the sitting room I om... om... ommed in front of the red marble fireplace. Uncle Neville in the lotus position became a recurring image to me when I was a student and exploring eastern mysticism.

Ma came out of Holloway Sanatorium in April, a month after my fourteenth birthday. I am not sure if she was on tranquilizers or had discovered Jesus but her smile was often strange and otherworldly.

On a damp early May Monday I got on the Green Line coach outside Record Wise in Egham High Street. It was the same route I used to take to prep school when I was a dayboy, if Ma was too busy to drive me. The coach went up Egham Hill and turned right to Englefield Green. Near the green was the lovely Georgian house of the Dexters, whose son Justin used to play with Giles and me in the holidays. I glanced down Middle Hill where the Buxton boys lived. They had been at prep school with me. In the next road were the Moncktons, whose place nestled in trees, with a long sloping roof of brown tiles. It was a fairy-tale house. Their son, Nicholas, two years above me at prep school, used to hit the biggest sixes in the inter-house cricket matches, and often won the game for our house, Dewar. He batted at number six. His father had a silver Jaguar Mark X. Would those families want to know me again? They would think I was a coward for running away from boarding school. I often thought so too. At Windsor, the coach stopped next to the King Edward VII hospital. I got off and walked for ten minutes to Mr Blundell's.

He stood in the drizzle on the porch of his bungalow. 'Hello, Jeremy. I didn't expect to see you again so soon.'

'No, well, sir.'

He smiled thinly. For a few moments I lost my bearings and was back at prep school as the nine-year-old Jeremy who would collect the weekly Latin class tests for Mr Blundell. He had short dark hair with a tight side parting. A gold strip beneath his black glass frames gave a yellow tint to his olive complexion. He looked at me. 'We're here for another three months and then we're moving to a bigger house; my new establishment will be called "The Windsor Tutorial College".' His off-white summer jacket flipped up from a squall of wind.

'That's a good name, sir.'

'You always were a charmer, Worman, though from now on of course you are Jeremy.'

'Yes, I am.'

I followed him to the side of the bungalow. Black paint peeled off as he opened a door into the large converted garage, which had become a big classroom; it extended into the back garden. In the shock of electric light I lost my bearings and we were back at school, outside the masters' common room, when my eyes focused again.

'Bonjour, jeune homme. Assez-vous, s'il vous plaît.'

'This is Jeremy Worman, Mrs Shaw. He is joining us.'

'Très bon.' She smiled warmly from her powdery face, and her short brown hair shone. 'We will have a discussion *dans quelques instants.'*

Mr Blundell stood by the door.

I sat in the far corner, next to the window that looked onto the neat garden, and scanned the room: about fifteen of us, mainly boys, different types and ages, from about ten to seventeen years old. I was not sure I would like them – too serious, not sporty, odd looking, some from different backgrounds to me. The best thing was that no one was wearing school uniform; I felt cool in my grey cords and white shirt with blue stripes. Sitting close to the teacher was an older boy, with thick brown hair and a middle parting.

Mr Blundell said, 'Sit up, Roddy. You have two resit A Levels next month.'

'It's not a school, sir; that's what you told my father.' He yawned.

'Then don't abuse the privilege.'

'I don't, sir; do I?' He flicked his long hair.

Mr Blundell gave him that special look, with a face that was motionless like a wedge of blotting paper which expanded to smother you. You could hear his silent voice: 'You horrible little person. Conform or I will destroy you.'

Roddy sighed.

'Get on with your work now,' Mr Blundell said and walked out.

Roddy winked at a girl on the other side of the room, whose dark page-boy hair bobbed as her lovely body pressed the contours of a tightly fitting green dress.

'Stop it, you two,' Mrs Shaw said, 'this is not the time for lovemaking.'

Everyone tittered. Roddy mimed hello to me.

The next few hours passed quickly. I was given exercise books, a copy of the timetable, and some English into French translation to do. Then I sat by Mrs Shaw and read it out: *'Cela est très prometteur,'* she said. We had a break: tea, coffee, biscuits and orange juice were brought in on a large tray by Mrs Blundell. Then Mr Blundell took us for English. He gave me an essay to write, 'My Future'. Eventually the clock above his desk reached 1pm.

'Lunchtime.' He looked at me. 'Did you bring sandwiches?'

'Not today, sir.'

'Is anyone going into town?'

'We are,' Roddy said.

'Will you show Jeremy a few places to get food?'

'Of course,' he said.

We got up. Roddy and the girl stood together by the coat pegs as she put on a floppy straw hat. Outside, she looked even prettier as she led us away; perhaps we would sit in the shade of the long lawn by the hollyhocks at her house as her mother brought out a cold lunch. I was sure her home would be Tudor and her parents would have owned it for ever and that her mother would say to me,

119

as she poured homemade lemonade, 'I think I met your mother...' or 'Your surname is familiar; did my husband, he's a barrister, once work with your father on a planning application...?'

We stood on the gravel entrance drive and looked at the dual carriageway. Sun had burnt off the rain haze. A red Ford Cortina's windscreen rippled with bubbly light. My eyes followed the car to the roundabout where, if it turned left towards Clewar, the driver would pass Haileybury Prep School where only six months ago I might have been scoring a try in a rugby match. I imagined the boys lined up against the fence, with masters, kitchen staff and groundsmen chanting, as Matron led the chorus: 'Worman is a coward, Worman is a coward.' The senior boys would be having dorm feasts this term.

'I like your shirt,' she said.

'Thanks.'

'Real Ben Sherman. The blue stripes are cool. I'm Carolina.'

'Hello.'

'Come on,' Roddy said, 'Let's get out of sight of Mr Puritan Man.'

They put their arms round each other and I followed them up Green Lanes, a road of large detached houses. We turned into a new subway, banked with concrete slabs, where the light shifted to dark and the puddles shone black. The new concrete was beginning to stain but there was not much graffiti, only 'Danny loves Susan' in a lurid purple love heart with a black felt-tip pen arrow and 'Chelsea Shed Boys' in bright green. It was the greenest thing there. The world was being covered in crude buildings and roads and paths. If I were Danny or Susan I should run away to some green place before it all went; if I were a skinhead Shed Boy (actually I was a Spurs fan) I would unite with other football hooligans and smash it all up. Chairman Mao put it well in his *Little Red Book*: 'The revolution and the class struggle are necessary for peasants and the Chinese people.' Well, the struggle of our working class was really the same as that of Chinese peasants.

'Are you all right?' Carolina called.

'Oh, yes; I was just thinking.'

I sat next to them on a tree trunk at the side of a patch of waste ground. Roddy was making a roll-up.

'You smoke too much.' She kicked his leg.

'I'm worried about A levels. I'm fed up with Blundell getting at us for going out – he's a Methodist, and they don't believe in sex.'

'They must reproduce,' I laughed.

'They do it with their clothes on – and their eyes shut.'

'Stop!' Carolina said. 'Don't give Jeremy the wrong impression. Mr Blundell is always nice to me.'

'Probably wants a date.'

'Roddy!'

'Well, I'm going to France after the exams to pick grapes, even if you don't.'

She kissed his cheek.

'Let's get into town.' He stood up in his sky-blue loons.

We reached the bottom of Peascod Street and stood by the traffic lights.

'So what do you want to eat?' Roddy said.

'Cornish pasty, chips; don't mind, really.'

'There's a great bakery in the new development by the car park,' Carolina said.

'Okay,' I said. 'After that I want to buy a new LP; I've got some birthday money, but you don't need to come with me.'

'Of course we will,' she said.

Roddy and I bought pasties and a coke; Carolina had a cheese and tomato roll. We chomped away as we walked up to Castle Street; outside the castle gates was a red-tuniced guardsman in a sentry box, a black bearskin on his head. On the other side of the road was the tourist shop, and down the smart little lane, Market Street, our jewellers, Harold Cox & Son. They were good for silverware too. We bought wedding presents there, and Pa sometimes got bits and pieces for Ma, and once an emerald ring. Close by was Caleys, another kind of castle for me. At the top of Peascod Street we turned left and halfway down went in to WH Smith. Carolina and Roddy browsed the books while I crossed over to the record stacks and found what I wanted, Bob Dylan's *John Wesley Harding*.

'I've got it.' I tapped Roddy on the shoulder. He was reading the first page of *In Cold Blood* by Truman Capote.

'That's an amazing opening,' he said. 'What did you get?'

I held up the cover.

'Great choice: his return album after the motorbike accident.'

'I saw it in *New Musical Express*.'

As we walked back down Peascod Street Roddy did a jig and his beige desert boots splayed out on the pavement as his loons blew in the breeze. Carolina tapped his ankle with her high-strapped brown sandals. She flicked his beads and the brim of her hat rippled. People in suits and ties, Macs and dresses, polished shoes and umbrellas, passed us on their way up the hill.

At the underpass by the same tree trunk Roddy made another roll-up. We all looked towards the Kipling Memorial Building in the distance. I knew about that place. It was now Windsor Council Offices but was once a part of the Imperial Service College, which merged with Haileybury in 1942. My most hated teacher, Mr Davidson, had been a pupil at the I.S.C. When he was on duty to take us to church, he pointed in the general direction of his old school: 'Over there was the Macaskie Block, knocked down to make way for a bloody silly dual carriageway.' This made him cross and I liked him getting upset as he was such a bully. I imagined him being demolished along with the block and screaming, 'Worman, come up to the blackboard and explain to the class how these triangles are congruent' and then, 'Ah! Ah! Ah!' as the falling plaster turned him to dust.

'You okay?' Roddy said.

'Those buildings over there were once part of my school... I can't explain.'

'Don't let the buildings look at you – you look at them.' He patted my shoulder. 'I've got to run on; I have a meeting with Blundell about my "progress". Are you coming, Carolina?'

'Do you mind?' she asked me.

'It's fine. I know my way back.'

They held hands as they walked through the tunnel

I looked across the straggly grass to the old School Room, with its broken windows, and the deserted chapel, squat and dim. The bricks were dingy, as if the repressed fears of the boys had stained them, boys who wore army uniforms from an early age, and would lead British soldiers across the wastes and glories of the Empire, brave boys who would not dare run away, but were trapped as much as Chairman Mao's beloved peasants. I had escaped but what kind of boy was I now?

I took *John Wesley Harding* from the paper bag. It was a strange cover: a clearing in a wood with one big tree behind and straggly ones all around; Dylan wore a dark cowboy-peasant jacket with a black wide-brimmed hat; on either side of him were two red-indian looking men, one in a woolly hat, the other in a strange curved-up brim of a light coloured hat, and behind him a very white old guy wearing glasses and an American civil war Union cap on his head. What a crew of misfits! The image made me so happy as none of them felt the need to conform. They did not give a shit about being 'fashionable'.

If they ever came to Windsor they would go through the ranks of soldiers and get them stoned (not that I had ever been stoned) with crazy music. All the straight housewives would throw away their shopping and go naked to have sex with butchers' boys and shop assistants from the men's department in Caleys; bank clerks would rush out from the National Provincial Bank to scatter five-pound notes. Even Prince Charles would slip out of Windsor Castle and might say, 'What's going on, you chaps? Looks like a lot of fun. Do you mind if I join in? Don't think I'll bother with that bloody investiture next year at Caernarfon Castle to be Prince of Wales. Let's all get stoned, er, man, and Ma'am, if you see what I mean... Oh well, Spike Milligan likes my jokes.'

I touched the tree trunk. I had to be back by 2.15. I did not actually know who John Wesley Harding was but he might have been a Texan outlaw, a great friend to the poor, who always went around with two pistols – a sort of Christian anarchist. A bit like John Wesley? Hadn't he started the Methodists before they got boring and wore suits and sang dirgy hymns that made you want to commit suicide or at least cut off your sexual organs?

At Mr Blundell's I leant against the door. Was Prince Charles also trapped like those boy soldiers at the Imperial Service College? Giles had told me that Charles had got fed up one day at Gordonstoun when all the boys from Bruce House threw snowballs at him. 'Fuck orff,' Charles had shouted (Giles's brother, Soames, was deputy head boy when Charles was head boy). It was not always fun to be a Royal and they did not deserve to have their heads chopped off. Prince Charles loved nature and if he met Donovan I was sure they would meditate together. Charles would be the first hippy king.

'Worman, I mean Jeremy; you aren't here to take in the balmy air. Would you mind if we started class?'

**

124

I settled at Mr Blundell's. By July I was used to the routine. Most days, I took the Green Line coach to Windsor. Roddy and Carolina were leaving at the end of term; Roddy, with luck, to do English at Sussex University, Carolina to do a foundation course at Hornsey College of Art where she had an unconditional offer. Ma was controlling her drinking and Mr Marshall had gone. He had a job as chauffeur to a director of Shell and lived in a flat in the grounds at Burnham Beeches. Dr Flack was Ma's new close male friend. She said his wife was very unstable: 'She sits at an easel all day and does oil paintings of the Kent coast; I'm surprised she hasn't drowned in all that sea – such a waste of paint.' I had made a few local friends from Strodes Grammar School. One of them, Tony Gilpin, knew a lot about motorbikes, was keen on politics, and had long dark hair; we used to talk over tea and cupcakes in The Grotto, where the Strodes boys went after school to chat and play pinball.

Throughout the next school year I worked hard. In the summer term, when I was fifteen, Mr Blundell told me I could do well in O levels next year. Ma's mental health seemed to have stabilised; she was enjoying her afternoon outings with Dr Flack; I became less afraid of her outbursts; Pa's physical decline was slower. In the holidays I spent two weeks with Giles's family at their house in Gozo.

***

I started back at Mr Blundell's at the beginning of September for a week of extra tuition before term began. He had moved to the new premises in Clarence Road. As I arrived he stood on the front-doorstep, wearing the same off-white jacket he always wore in the summer.

'Morning Jeremy.'

'Morning, sir. Have you had a good holiday?'

'We went to Weston to stay with my wife's mother.'

'Sounds lovely.'

'You go inside; I'll be with you in a minute. I'm waiting for the builders to come and complete the alterations. It's very exciting.'

'Definitely, sir.'

There were five of us doing extra tuition; four of them were working on common entrance material for their exams next year; I was the only one preparing for O levels, and Blundell gave me lots of attention as we worked on English Literature, English Language and Latin.

At the end of the intensive but enjoyable week I got home at 4pm. I took advantage of the Indian summer by lying in the garden on a lounger with a Coke and a peanut-butter sandwich. Ma had left a note on the hall table saying she had gone swimming at Great Fosters, part of her new fitness regime, 'So I can look good again in a costume if we get away to Spain at half term.' The French windows were open. I rubbed in suntan lotion; it reminded me of Uncle Neville's lavender shaving soap.

From upstairs, Pa's after-a-nap cough, more relaxed than his morning cough, moved from his bedroom to the bathroom, as his walking frame rattled like Tin-Pan-Alley. On a bad day he might shout, 'Old chap, can you give me a hand?' or 'Hurry up, can't you?' and I would dawdle before standing behind this farting decrepitude as he inched forward. There was no call today.

I flipped through adverts in *Motorcycle Mechanics*, to help prepare my pitch for getting a motorbike for my birthday next March. I wanted a 125 cc Yamaha, the biggest you could get as a learner, and not a flat-cap old-man's BSA Bantam, which Colin Duncan-Smith had suggested to Ma. Can I clinch the deal before my father dies? I thought. How bloody horrible can you get, Jeremy! I said so loudly in my head that my brain echoed. The last year had been a time of Pa seeing specialists and having more falls. There were smells in his bedroom-cum-sickroom: Bengies Balsam, Rennies, urine from the pot under the bed. The whisky regime never changed but these days it was taken with milk because, Ma said, 'It is nourishing for your father.' During the early stages of his decline I used to imagine he would be cured. But as he fell away from the person I was beginning to know, I lost patience and learnt instead to endure his disintegration. I shook my head. 'Forgive me, Mother Mary,' I whispered and lay down with the smell of fresh-mown grass near my face.

Half an hour later I ran upstairs. 'Fancy a cup of tea, Pa?'

'Lovely.'

'I'll have a quick shower first.'

After that I put on my new red Paisley shirt and blue loons to try out the look; I combed my hair back so the long strands curled behind. I carried in a tea tray, put it next to him on the dining-room table, and let *Motorcycle Mechanics* slide off close to his arm.

'Hello, old chap.'

'Are you feeling better?'

'Not noticeably.'

A Capstan was angled between his fingers. Only eighteen months ago he had walked into the dining room wearing a smart, well pressed suit, stiff collar and dark silk tie, a father with a successful job. Now his face was squashed, his red nose bulbous and his legs twiggy. He was looking at a cartoon in *Punch*.

He stared at me, 'Planning to be a popstar?'

He pushed his thumb round the cartoon's edge as if making an impression of my face. If you knew you were going to die, and were haunted by the thought of your wife's deceased ex-lover, might you not want to carry an image of something young through those dark nights? Perhaps he could even imagine that when he was dead a bright ray of me would vibrate in the blackness around him. I don't think he believed in God but this was not the time to discuss religion.

'You'll get better,' I said.

'You'll have a good life, old chap.'

127

'You've had a good life too, Pa.'

This was probably not the best thing to have said.

On the side table the silver optic of the whisky bottle was shaped like a petrol pump. He checked his watch. Not long before he could fill his tank again.

'Have you thought what you might do in life?'

'Apart from being a revolutionary?'

'If you want to talk about it.'

'I might be a barrister.'

I wanted to give him another nice thought to take into the dark.

'God knows, you can argue. Mr Blundell suggested we could try for St Paul's sixth form.'

'I want to stay with my proletarian comrades.'

'Of course; you know so many of them. How lucky they all live in rather nice houses and give good parties.'

'I'm not to blame for my unfortunate class position.'

We roared with laughter. I poured the tea and took a chocolate biscuit. He was back, as if he had found his way out of a fog, so I said, 'Could we have a look at a few really good-value motorbikes?' I leant over to flick to the right page but he stared out of the window, as if the mist had come down again.

'Pa?'

'I need to make a phonecall; it's very important.'

'But we were talking about motorbikes.'

'Motorbikes? Are you a bloody salesman? I need to phone.'

'Who?'

'Gale & Power wants my advice.'

I picked up the phone. 'Shall I dial for you?'

'I know the bloody number.'

Ma's key turned in the front door. 'I'm back.'

She stood at the dining-room door. 'What's up with you two?'

'Pa suddenly said he had to ring Gale & Power.'

The phone was on his lap.

'Well, he does have some important calls to make.' She squeezed my arm and sat down.

'Pa and I had been having a really good chat and then…'

'Is it one of the partners who wants to talk to you, Geoff?'

'Ted Turner has been in touch.'

'Shall we phone him tomorrow?'

'If you like,' he said. 'Have you had a good time?' He patted her hand. 'Motorbikes, of course. We'll get round to that once I've got rid of the pressure of work.'

On Monday the new term began officially. I stood outside, looked up at the large three-storey house and read the brand-new discreet sign on the wooden front gate, 'The Windsor Tutorial College'. In the porch of the newly painted black door, the brass letterbox and knocker gleamed. Mr Blundell must have seen me and opened the door.

'Jeremy. You're early. Well done.'

'Thank you, sir. Did you have a good weekend?'

'I went to a Methodist educational conference in London.'

'That sounds interesting.'

'We have quite a few new students this year. I would like you to make them welcome.'

'All right.'

'Go round to the side door. The whole place has been refurbished. Now go and choose yourself a locker.'

He almost smiled.

In the long thin changing room a neon strip-light glared. Every conceivable piece of wood had been painted gloss cream. I put my black briefcase in the locker and took out a pad of paper, my black Papermate pen, and a new geometry set. I went into the newly gleaming central teaching room.

'Hello, Wormie.'

'Hello Philip. How are you?'

'Very well.'

Philip Yeoman was tall and gangly with wiry dark hair.

129

'I hear there are going to be more girls this term,' he said and sat on the desk.

'Won't make any difference to you.'

'Cheeky shit.'

'Let's put a bet on it.'

A few more of the old lags came in.

'Hello, Alphonso,' we said in unison.

He was half Persian with a Jordanian stepmother but his birth mother was Italian, a countess, as he had told me last week. His thick black hair was slicked back and he wore his shirt with the top two buttons undone; suede blue sneakers, tight black trousers and a smile that had such a disproportionate effect on the goodwill of girls that it often concluded with him driving away in his Lotus Cortina on a Friday afternoon with one of them or even, once, a waitress from the Wimpy Bar.

'I'm not going to try too hard this term,' he said.

He never tried hard. He looked much older than the rest of us, as if someone had failed to remind him he should have gone to university years ago.

'Watcha.'

'Hello Five Cars,' I said.

'That name is only for my close friends.' He scuffed my head with his big, ringed hand. His father was the leading Windsor builder-cum-property speculator. Five Cars was blond, tall and thin with chiselled features and a worked-on body from press-ups and football (he played for the Slough Second Elevens). 'I'm bored here; I might join the Marines.'

Not a bad idea, I wanted to say. Last year he was prosecuted for stealing cars and siphoning petrol. 'I got done for two cars,' he told me and Philip, 'but I did five. It's fucking exciting; I'm the quickest in the trade.' It could have been Borstal but the female magistrate must have been taken by his Michael Caine bad-boy good looks, his startling blue eyes, and the appeals of an expensive barrister. So here he was, sort of on bail. Mr Blundell had to write a termly report for the magistrate. 'If I met her in the street,' he told us last term, 'I'd say "Just call me Alfie, darling", you know, after the film, *Alfie*. She'd go for it...' He went off to the changing rooms, probably to hone his lock-picking skills. The aroma of Brut hung in the air.

There was a door that led into the central corridor. Mr Blundell stood there and tried to smile. 'Gentlemen; three new students, Abid, Lakar and Rajan.'

He stretched out his arm and they walked in, three brothers in ascending orders of height and age; three Sikhs, with loose yellow turbans and broad open smiles.

'We're the Banga brothers,' the eldest said in an expensive, rather fruity English accent. 'Our London school isn't ready for us yet.'

'Well, very nice to meet you anyway,' I shook their hands. So did Philip and Alphonso. I was pleased Five Cars was out of sight picking locks as he gave a bad impression.

Mrs Blundell, who wore glasses, short hair and sensible shoes, brought in a tray: a large pot of tea, slices of lemon, cups and saucers, a bowl of sugar lumps, and a big plate of shortbread biscuits.

'Not for you, Jeremy.' She put the tray on the teacher's desk.

'Of course not, Mrs Blundell. I'll just pour for our guests, I mean the new students.'

The Banga brothers sat happily at the front, sipped their lemon tea, and devoured the biscuits with no sense of guilt at all.

Over the next half hour more new students came in, and I showed them round the three classrooms and the upstairs study rooms. After that, we congregated in the central room. Mr Blundell stood at the front.

'We are all mainly here. I am expecting one more; we are a much larger institution than before. Including part-time students there are about seventy of you.' He smiled.

'We now have a proper set of rules, which Mrs Blundell has lovingly made into booklets.' He gave a bundle of them to Philip. 'Pass round, please.' Mr Blundell's eyes swept the room. 'I expect all of you to read and inwardly digest the information.'

At the back, Gillian Bailey, who had been in the television version of *The Railway Children* and was currently in *Double Deckers*, was sitting next to Elizabeth Jeffries, daughter of Lionel Jeffries, the star of *Chitty Chitty Bang Bang.* They were nice, fun girls, not at all Darling Darling types. Charles Flint was in front of them, his lips swollen and greasy as if coated in Vaseline, or perhaps he'd used a blob of Brylcreem from his short back-and sides-black hair. He always wore a shirt, tie and sports jacket. His parents were desperate to get him back into a public school; he had special lessons in Greek upstairs with Mr Blundell; when Charles came down, his round glasses stuck to his nose as he looked over the heads of us trendy boys, as if we were unworthy of his classical thoughts. He had left Lancing under a cloud. But we were all misfits here and allowed each other the space of a few secrets.

'Now do you all have that?' Mr Blundell said and checked we had not instantly thrown the Windsor Tutorial College Guidelines into the bin.

A register was called; the subject and class lists were read out, and we went to our rooms. The new extension, a long white rectangular classroom with four wide windows, took up half of the back garden. I sat there and waited for the geography class to begin. Through the French window, the flowerbeds were sodden from last week's downpour and the bulbous white clouds fringed grey-black. A bare hollyhock hung on in the borders.

Miss Gee stood at the front. Her large round green-framed glasses jumped as she spoke and her sporty body moved with the enthusiasm of a Hockey girl (she had been captain of the Roedean team). Her face was mobile and could become serious, especially when talking about the problems for the indigenous Brazilian population. We were a mixed-age class of about fifteen students. Five of us were doing O levels.

'I'm expecting real concentration from you, Jeremy, this term.'

'So am I, Miss Gee.'

For the next fifteen minutes she sorted out the other groups, and had the two new students up in turn to sit beside her, while the five of us looked through our course book.

Mr Blundell stood at the door. 'I want to introduce the last of our new students, Leila Jaggi.'

I turned. A few boys turned. All the boys turned.

She stood in front of Mr Blundell on the lower step that led into the class: long dark hair, a short purple skirt, blue eye makeup, a lovely smile and a brown complexion. She wore a hugging white blouse. Her hair shone like the girl in the Sunsilk advert but it was her open hazel eyes that caught me: I could look into them forever. Her white plimsolls were stained off white, as if she was not obsessed with her image. She was a girl who would like muddy fields, farms and motorbikes, I thought.

'There is a place next to Jeremy,' Mr Blundell said.

'Ooh,' Philip said.

'Come and see me at lunchtime,' Mr Blundell said.

Leila sat down. 'Hello.'

'Hello.'

'Turn round class.' Miss Gee looked at Leila. 'As you are doing O level Geography, would you mind sharing Jeremy's textbook for this class?'

'Ooh,' Philip said.

'Don't be so childish, Philip,' I said.

'Don't be so childish, Philip,' Miss Gee said.

Leila's long eyelashes fell and rose.

133

'We're looking at the social and economic structure of South Africa today, aren't we, Miss Gee?'

'Very good, Jeremy.'

'It's chapter seven, I think.' I put the book between us. After Miss Gee had settled the rest of the class, she sat on a chair in front of the two long tables of O level students. She discussed the syllabus for the term: 'South Africa'; 'contour maps'; 'The geological structure of a country and its impact on the formation of a society'. I nodded encouragingly to Miss Gee but was most conscious of Leila sitting next to me: her well-shaped legs, her fragrant shampoo, the seven buttons of her blouse, two undone. Leila had become my geography lesson.

Then I went to Maths while Mr Blundell had an 'assessment chat' with Leila in his upstairs study. The Maths class was the other side of the corridor, the door ajar, and I watched as Mrs Blundell carried up a tray with shortbread biscuits on it, and two mugs of real coffee. The aroma wafted into our room where we were struggling with revision on quadrilateral equations.

At lunchtime we congregated in the main room.

'You going into town?' Philip asked.

'I'm not hungry; I might stay here.'

'Ooh.'

'Fuck off.'

I fiddled around at my locker; I took the Paper Mate biro from my geometry case and polished it on my shirt. As I watched, Leila's plimsolls came down the steps; I camouflaged myself behind a coat.

'I think this is my locker,' she said as Five Cars stood behind her.

'You've chosen the best one,' he winked.

Probably the only one he hadn't picked, I thought.

'How do you know?' She pinched his shoulder.

'Let's talk another time. I've got a meeting with Blundell. Ciao.' He went inside.

I came out from behind the coat. 'Hi, Leila. We often sit in the back garden for lunch; shall I show you?'

'Thanks.'

She took out a brown satchel from her locker and put it over her shoulder like a schoolgirl.

'This way,' I said. 'There are rugs in the shed we're allowed to use.'

As she walked round the garden path, Gillian and Elizabeth were sitting together. 'Come and join us,' Gillian called.

I got a rug and sat by them. Leila took a bite from her sandwich. She looked round. 'It's better here than being at school,' she said.

'What happened?' Gillian asked.

'It's a long story.' Leila licked a piece of cheese from her lips. She glanced at me. 'Nothing to eat?'

'I'm learning to fast.'

Gillian and Elizabeth tried to stifle their laughs. The girls were chatting happily together. After five minutes I got up: 'Need to get something from my locker.'

They didn't look up. I went into the changing room. Philip charged through the outside door.

'How did you get on?' he asked.

'My fasting is going well. I feel more spiritual already.'

'With Leila. Twit. You're behaving like a dirty old man on heat.'

'That is a tautology.'

He sat down and his long legs stretched. 'She'll have millions of boyfriends.' I picked up my geography exercise book. 'Sorry,' he added. 'I didn't mean...'

'That's okay. Of course she'll have a boyfriend, or two.'

'Or three.' He put his arm round me. 'The trouble is the older boys with cars and a bit of money will ask her out.'

From the locker I took *The Power and the Glory*. 'We've got literature, haven't we, with Blundell?'

'Yes.'

135

'I'd better check the garden rug has been put back.'

It was on the grass. The girls had gone in. I returned it to the shed and sniffed the creosote; hedge cutters on a wall hook; a spade and fork in the corner; apples on the rough wooden work top. All so lovely and natural. Pa had an appointment with another specialist next week. He was finding it hard to talk and his tongue hurt. I bit a chunk of apple. In the window's corner a spider mended its web. I felt the same comfort here as I did with Uncle Neville in his flat. I threw the apple core onto the flowerbed.

We had double English and then it was time for home.

Alphonso was standing by the changing room door. 'I've got a geography book you might want,' he said to Leila.

'Thank you but my father told me to ask Mr Blundell to order what I needed. Goodbye, Jeremy.'

'Bye, Leila.'

1 watched her all the way to the gate.

'She's quite something, isn't she?' Alphonso said.

'Too classy for you.'

'Out of your league, brother.' He pushed me and left.

November began with rain and wind. All my thoughts were tangled with my crush on Leila.

Two weeks ago, when she'd asked for a pen as we sat next to each other in History, her finger brushed, well, stayed for more than a few seconds, on the back of my hand. I couldn't tell if she was blowing hot or cold. The following week she did *not* ask if I was having sandwiches outside (I always kept a sandwich in my briefcase for such eventualities) although she went directly past me on her way to the garden. Then, two days ago, when she walked down from the bathroom, she smiled, and said, 'Hot, isn't it?' My mind was full of sex scenes, her, Blundell's shed, work bench, apples, fingers, but I mumbled, 'I'm going to get a drink of water.' Yesterday she was sitting in the

136

central room talking to Philip, well, actually laughing at one of his jokes, although they were hopeless compared to mine. They had not seen me peeping in from the corridor. 'Danny Johnson? I know him,' she said. It turned out this Johnson boy played at the Maidenhead Rugby Club with Philip in the Second XV. Although I liked Philip, it was clear he was working slyly on Leila. And what did she mean by, 'I know him?' Was Danny (shit name) her boyfriend? Had he been her boyfriend? Had she known him in a Biblical sense? I took a final peep. Philip's long thin arms stretched round the table: 'What bus do you take to Maidenhead?' I could bear no more. I tiptoed into the kitchen and asked Mrs Blundell if she needed help with the washing up.

In the afternoon I had private study in the attic room and worked on my *Hamlet* essay. At the end of the day I packed books into my briefcase.

'I wonder if you could help me?' Leila said.

'Got to rush; sorry.'

She put her knee on the bench and looked up at me.

'Tomorrow, I mean.'

'I'm behind with my *Hamlet* essay.' I felt naked and embarrassed.

She flicked my cheek.

'Hey.'

'Could you show me round Windsor at lunchtime?'

'Me?'

'You are Jeremy?'

'I know Windsor pretty well.'

'Is that yes?'

'Yes.'

We walked together to the front gate and set off in different directions.

The next morning I sat on the bus and sniffed my Chanel Pour Monsieur After Shave – not that I had shaved on this occasion. I was the first person to arrive at Mr Blundell's.

In the empty changing room I imagined Leila flicking my cheek, her finger warm and soft.

Double Physics passed like a slow-motion silent film. At break we sat around in the central room; I leant over Leila to get the sugar bowl, but she went on talking to Gillian. At the end of the History class, and before anyone asked what I was doing at lunchtime, I rushed to the changing room and sat behind a coat to remain incognito.

'Are you going into town, Wormy?' Philip shouted from the steps.

'I'm going up to the study room to finish an essay on Graham Greene.'

'What did you say?'

I came out from the camouflage. 'I've got to work.'

'Okay. You don't know what you're missing.'

He rushed off. I sat on the bench. It was obvious what Philip meant when he said, 'You don't know what you're missing.' He was going into town with Leila. She did not want to be alone with me. Leila made me feel depressed in the same way Ma did.

'There you are!'

'Leila.'

She stood at the entrance door. 'I thought we were meeting by the gate.'

'No, the changing room. Never mind. Let's go.'

We walked up Clarence Road side by side. When a couple passed us, Leila's shoulder bounced against mine. I was afraid that my thoughts and fantasies of her were badges she could read.

'What do you want to eat?' I said.

'Shall we get a sandwich; it's such a nice day?'

'Great idea.'

We went to the bakery in the shopping arcade near Peascod Street; both of us bought Cornish pasties and plastic mugs of tea. We walked on towards the river and sat in the park not far from Eton Bridge. Her dark-blue duffel

138

coat fitted snuggly; she stretched her legs in faded Levi's. I was warm in my dark-brown suede bomber jacket. We made a nice colour contrast as we sat opposite each other at either side of the wooden table. The cold sun pierced the bare branches.

'I hear your father is very ill,' she said.

'How do you know?'

'Philip told me.' Her right hand moved across the table. 'I'm sorry. It must be hard.'

'My mother and I make the best of it. Thanks for asking.'

We talked between mouthfuls of meaty pasty.

'Some boys are very shy with me while others, you know, just want to chat me up.'

'Disgraceful.'

'You're not like that.'

Her eyelashes moved up and down. Her hair swayed round her collar; two silver earrings, doves with open wings, glinted. I sipped my tea. 'You're not like that' was the same as when a girl said, 'We could be such good friends' or 'You're so sweet'. Leila was putting me off in a nice way. I was never going to kiss her.

'People always think I go out with older boys.'

'Do they?'

'Do you like me?'

'Yes.'

'I like you.' She wiped her lips. 'I think I'm going to be happy at Mr Blundell's. We've only been down south for a year.'

'Why did you come?'

'My father needed a change. He was a solicitor in Leeds, but something went wrong.'

'That's a shame.'

'He said it was racism.'

'There's a lot of it around.'

'You wise old man! Don't mention it, will you?'

'I'm mister sealed lips.'

'My mum is from Buckingham; she was pleased to be nearer her roots.' Leila got up. 'Coming?'

We squeezed each other's hand. Under the railway arch I inhaled slowly to extend the moment. Some Himalayan Buddhists hardly breathed and did not live in time. Uncle Neville told me that. The arch's roof was slimy green. If I took the train home, from Windsor and Eton Riverside Station, I walked through here, which made me sad, as if the things I had forgotten all day returned as a shroud above me. Today the slimy bricks were just bricks.

'It's lovely, isn't it?' I said.

'It's yucky. And creepy.' She pulled me forward.

Around the new shopping arcade were modern flats. The new buildings broke up my identity – the pulling down of the old destroyed part of me – as if this was the only way to be modern. I hated the idea that 'progress' meant people living in rabbit-hut flats like caged things. I would never be part of that world: it began with a 9-5 job but soon sucked you in to marriage, mortgage, and more debt. Our culture encouraged us to buy tons of things – only then did the state label us 'Human'. When I was miserable, I felt change would never stop. Each knocked-down house, with its ruined stories of love, families and jokes, dug up my inner self. My home was being uprooted in the same way. I looked at Leila. The world no longer shifted under my feet.

'Come on,' she said, 'we'll be late.'

I put my arm round her and pulled her towards me. We faced each other. I took my arm away.

'It's all right,' she said.

We rushed back and took off our coats in the changing room.

'You've got a crumb on your lip.' She stroked it off with her finger, and then kissed me, soft and sweet on my lips.

'See you later,' she said and went to class.

Leila Jaggi had kissed me. All the boys in the world wanted to kiss Leila. She had chosen me. The vibrations of her lips on mine kept repeating; they sent messages through all the nerves of my body; when they ceased, I closed my eyes and she kissed me again... It was my first proper kiss. I licked my lips. The next class was Maths although it could have been Dutch or Astrology for all I cared. I had found the one subject that mattered.

At the end of the day I waited outside.

'We must keep it secret,' she whispered, 'for now.' She looked down the road. 'Oh God, my father's come to collect me. You'd better go.'

I walked away like a guilty schoolboy.

The start of December was bright.

At lunchtimes, if I was lucky, I smuggled Leila away from the two chief locusts, Alphonso and Philip. Fortunately, Five Cars was involved in extra-college activities with 'two of the dirtiest girls in Windsor'. Amazing. His toxic cloud of Brut must have drugged them. One Friday lunchtime Leila and I were sitting in the Wimpy Bar in Peascod Street. She'd only ordered a strawberry milk shake, but tucked into my chips, part of a double Wimpy cheeseburger deal. 'My father is being horrible,' she said. 'I can't tell you about it now. It will be all right soon.'

'How soon.'

'Not long. But my father is suspicious.'

A tall well-built boy walked in; he was about eighteen years old, with a grotty teddy-boy haircut, a swanky black jacket, quite well cut, grey drainpipe trousers and black suede winklepickers; he was good-looking, I suppose, in a gypsy sort of way; Ma would call him 'rough trade', and he bloody well winked at Leila. She gave him a quick smile.

'It's the easiest way to get rid of boys like that.'

On the last day of term, at the end of Geography, she put a card under my exercise book. I ran upstairs to the private-study room and tore open the envelope. On the front there was a polar bear, dressed as Father Christmas, smoking a joint. Did she smoke joints? And with whom? Inside, in big letters: 'Trust Me xxx. Leila.' I read it twenty times. It was like being kissed by her all over again.

On Monday, the week before Christmas, Giles and I pinned two targets to the old apple tree at the end of his garden. It was a cold day with blue sky and frost-still air. I lay on the rug he'd brought out and rubbed my hands to ensure a supple trigger finger. I fired off four pellets from my .177 BSA air rifle and then adjusted the telescopic sights. I had cleaned the barrel the previous day and oiled the mechanism. Giles lay down next to me and I shuffled further to my side of the rug. His family had a good policy of making things last and keeping old objects forever, although it must have been embarrassing for Giles as he rode around Egham on a black bone shaker of a bike, which was surely not far from the Penny Farthing era. He had a .22, a German one, possibly one of the first made, as the barrel was gnarled, like an oak tree, except the knots were pitted rust. It could explode at any minute, backfire or shoot a pellet out of the side. Before he aimed I always tried to cover my head discreetly as I did not wish to appear rude.

'Fancy a bet on our competition, Giles?'

'You're so bloody cocky, Worm.'

'In terms of equipment it is the Modern versus the Ancient World.'

'You cheeky bugger!'

He pushed me aside, dug me in the ribs, and forced his knees onto my shoulders.

'Submit!' he said.

I was not equal to the twenty-four hour Gordonstoun fitness-training regime.

'I submit.'

We turned back to the matter in hand.

Twenty minutes later I was the clear winner: three bull's eyes (ten points each); two in the white (nine points each), two in the red (eight points each) etc. I did not have many outside the furthest white ring (5 points). Giles would have won if the apple tree had been the target.

'Well tried,' I said.

He looked at his gun. 'It is a bit past it. I'm getting a new one for Christmas.'

'That's good. If you hand in that one to the Army they will dispose of it safely.'

'Ha, ha.'

He took his gun back to the shed.

I lay on my back in the crisp day and my mind freed itself in the expansive blue sky: in the fields on the road to Prune Hill, I imagined Mrs Caddy's prize-winning Jersey cows, their gleaming bodies huddled for warmth and their breath smoky in the frozen air. Inside her farmhouse she would have arranged the holly above the range, and a clump of mistletoe from the middle beam, tied with green and red ribbon. She never changed the routine. Two years ago, Pa and I visited her just before Christmas. She thanked him for his advice about a planning matter. 'The best sloe gin I ever drink,' he said as he toasted her. It was the last time Pa and I had been out together.

It's a great day,' Giles said, 'Why don't we go for a bike ride before lunch?'

'Let's.'

'I'm really sorry about your father.'

'Thanks.'

After our ride to Thorpe, I went home. Ma was in the kitchen, stirring brandy cherries in a glass jar.

'Perfect for Christmas, darling, with my meringues and whipped cream. Try one. Slurp it off the spoon.'

I did. 'Delicious.'

'We'll make it a great day.'

'Suppose so.'

This was the Boadicea Ma who took away your fears; if only she had a focus for her courage she would not despair and drink. But she was not a Women's Institute sort of person, and 'if I take up riding again I will think of Neville. He was so happy on a horse'. If not riding or flower arranging, what else could she do? I wondered.

We had not noticed Pa rattling up the corridor towards the kitchen with his walking frame. 'We'll have a lovely time on Christmas Day,' he said. 'I'm looking forward to wearing my smoking jacket again.'

His tongue was swollen and his speech slurred. He bent forward.

'Steady, Pa.'

His last word, 'again', came out in slow drips, as if he wanted it to last. The black velvet smoking jacket had been his father's and he always wore it on Christmas Day.

'Old chap, there are two bottles of vintage champagne in the workshop; could you fish them out?'

I looked down, as he sometimes dribbled, and I did not want to embarrass him. If the pain was bad at night, Ma was allowed to give him extra spoonfuls of the morphine mixture.

'Yes, Pa. Of course.'

I ran up and found the Krug in a dusty corner; they were the last of the case, in a solid wooden box, with the bottles wrapped in straw containers. I held them carefully as I walked down. I stopped on the landing to listen: 'Your Christmas puddings always were the best, Barbara; I'll make the brandy butter'; 'When are Chilvers delivering the turkey?'

These were the traces of memory he wished to leave. I went to the kitchen. 'Here's the Krug, Pa.'

'Put it straight in the fridge.'

He turned to Ma. 'In the New Year, you need to see our stockbroker. Charles is very good; be guided by him.'

'I will; I promise.'

'Just going to sort out a few things,' I said.

I tiptoed downstairs. Uncle Neville's old sitting room felt damp. The curtains were drawn, the foxes and riders in an endless dance. I stroked the thick material, to make the horsemen come alive under my touch, and blow their horn, 'Tally Ho!' but the images were faded. And I felt like that fox cub being chased into a hole. The curtains smelt stale too and, as I gently tugged, they tore. 'Oh, bugger.' I stood on a chair and unhooked them so the run of hunter and hunted came to ground on the carpet; I did the same with the curtains at the other side of the French windows. Soon the floor was like the undulations of a hunting field.

'Jeremy! What are you doing?'

Ma stood in the doorway.

'I didn't think you would mind... I'm sorry.'

She stared at the tangled heap. 'So much better. Well done. This room has become a sepulchre to Neville.'

'What's a sepulchre exactly?'

'Think of Jesus, darling, those sort of times – a memorial place for the dead.'

'Actually for a dead body?'

'Let's not split hairs.'

'Thanks, Ma. Sometimes when I was in this room, I felt the ghost of Uncle Neville as if he didn't really want to leave us.'

'Leave you, do you mean?'

'Oh, Ma.'

'When I look in that mirror I see Neville, and remember the good times; but that is past, Jeremy; you have to say goodbye, so you can enjoy what is to come.'

'I liked the past as it was, with Uncle Neville here. What if you don't think the future will be up to much?'

'Then you've been blocked – I can't tell you how much I have learnt from David, I mean Dr Flack – he's so wise but still full of energy.' She checked her hair in the mirror above the mantelpiece. 'You need a girlfriend, darling.

You could phone Clare; she was keen on you, and she's so pretty, if rather forward for her age.' Ma flicked her head. 'And love affairs always remind you how magical life is.'

'Could Uncle Neville be my father?'

'Good Lord, darling, no.'

In the mirror she watched me watching her.

'But you can't be sure?'

'Oh, darling, I can. Uncle Neville was my lover, but only after you were born. At that point, your father and I agreed that we were happier without that side of our relationship.'

'Truly?'

'Truly, truly, darling.' She walked across the room. 'I swear it on Neville's rack of pipes.'

'That's sacrilegious, Ma.'

'Would you have liked Uncle Neville to have been your father?'

'No. Yes, I think I would.'

She hugged me. 'Geoff is a really good man; you are lucky he is your father.'

'Why?'

'Because you are what you are – a young man with great potential – and your father is part of the reason for that.'

'You're right.'

'I am. Now, what shall we do with the curtains?'

'Salvation Army jumble sale?'

'Yes.'

'I'll put them under the stairs for now.'

'Good boy. Lunch at 1pm sharp; I have to go to Caleys for a few extras.' She turned back to the mirror. 'Sometimes I wonder what would have happened if...'

'If what?'

'Candy Cope took me loop-the-looping in his plane.'

'Who was he?'

'Heir to the Liverpool tobacco manufacturer, Cope Bros & Son; he rode with my local hunt in south Lancashire; he was very keen on me.'

'And?'

'He proposed marriage, but his eyes were too close together, so I declined.'

'Do you regret it?'

'Not for a minute. See you at lunch.' She went back upstairs.

I folded the curtains and dragged them to the utility room where they took their place with broken walking sticks, old raincoats, muddy boots, empty pickling jars, ancient tins of food and cobwebs. As I opened Uncle Neville's bedroom door it creaked. In the grey light his large bed dominated the room. I pulled off the bedclothes.

'Goodbye, Uncle Neville.'

I sat in the blue velvet corner chair. How would I feel when I looked at my father's empty bed? It was not sensible to rely on families, least of all fathers. Uncle Neville was dead through suicide; Pa would soon be dead through decay. John and Yoko had been in bed for peace at the Amsterdam Hilton earlier this year. Posters in their bedroom said 'Hair Peace' and 'Bed Peace'. The event was called a 'Happening', which was live art made political. If we all spent half a day in bed, staying in one place, vibrating peace – that's how real change would begin. I imagined Uncle Neville's cavalry-twill trousers hanging neatly over the back and his brown brogues tucked underneath. His clothes and shoes were lovely, but dated like his ideas.

I stood up. 'You're in the past, Uncle Neville – and perhaps that is the happiest place for you – but I'm going forward.'

Ten minutes later Ma called out, 'Lunch.'

'I'm going to be a revolutionary hippy, Uncle Neville; hope you don't mind.' I patted the bedhead.

I went up to the dining room door. They were laughing.

'But what does it matter now, Barbara.'

'I was telling your father he should give up smoking.'

'And go to your mother's health farm, Liphook, in the New Year.'

'It was an idea, Geoff.'

'I'd be bad for business; they'd pay me to leave.'

'We could do with the extra money, Pa; you're always saying that.'

There were parts of the day when he was lively as if a new engine had been put in and, however grotty his bodywork, he revved like a Ferrari. He took loads of pills, and when the right combination kicked in, vroom.

'Get the champagne, will you, Jeeves?'

'Yes.' I went to the kitchen and came back with the Krug. 'May I open it?'

'Of course, old chap.'

'I'll bring in lunch,' Ma said.

Three old Victorian flute glasses, which had belonged to his parents, were on the table. I put the white linen napkin over the bottle, prised out the cork and, as the bubbles fizzed, poured with my left hand.

'Perfect,' Pa said.

Through the hatch Ma handed me plates of smoked salmon and scrambled eggs.

When we were seated, Pa raised his glass: 'To Jeremy, for doing so well at his new college.'

'A girlfriend, Geoff; that would complete his reintegration.'

'I've not come out of Borstal.'

Pa sipped. 'That really is good.' He turned to Ma, 'And girlfriends aren't always reliable. I'll get the Lea & Perrins.'

As he went up the corridor, Ma whispered, 'Check he's all right.'

I stood behind him as he passed the kitchen and opened the front door. 'Fatty smell in the kitchen.' He stood on the porch and looked down the steps.

'What on earth is that?'

'What, Pa?'

'Who's bloody well left that there?'

I stood in front of him.

'A motorbike!'

'It's yours, old chap. A second-hand Yamaha 125; John Watson, the partner in our Shepperton office, found it for me at a motorbike shop there.'

'And you drove it back.'

'Funnily enough, no. They delivered it last week and it was camouflaged in the back of the garage. Your mother wheeled it out earlier. I'll show you the documents after lunch; you can practise in the drive until March; have you applied for your licence?'

'I will do in January. Thanks so much.'

'My pleasure. Now let's get back to our champagne lunch.'

We sat at the table and tucked in.

'Spurs are doing well this season,' I said.

'Perhaps you'll drive me to Bedford in the New Year, Barbara; I'd like to see my old family home, take a look around Bedford Modern School and the old boat club.'

'You really should try a day at Liphook; homeopathic cures can work magic.'

'I'm a little beyond magic.'

We had seconds of smoked salmon. The next course was Stilton, which Ma gouged out from the middle of a big cheese. It was Pa's favourite, which we had delivered once a year from a farm in Leicestershire.

'Owh,' he winced. 'Too strong.' He spat it out into his white handkerchief and the creamy, blue-veined shades mixed with blood. He put the hankie in his pocket and drank an inch of champagne. 'That's better.' He smiled from his ashen face, and his speech slurred. The temporary energy charge was draining from him.

'Soon be time for your rest, Geoff.'

149

The phone rang. Ma jumped up. Perhaps Dr Flack was taking her for an afternoon drive. She rushed to the hallway phone.

'It's for you darling. A girl. She sounds lovely. Lisa, is it?'

'Leila.'

Five minutes later I sat down.

'Well, come on, Jeremy.'

'Come on what?'

'Oh, men. Your girlfriend; has she dumped you?'

'No. She is not a girlfriend.'

'She had such a pert voice; she must be terribly pretty.'

'Don't fish, Ma.'

'How exciting!'

'Please.'

'A motorbike and a girlfriend. Is Leila an English name?'

'Barbara! Don't tease.' Pa slumped in his chair.

'You need a rest, Geoff.'

'Not until our final toast to my revolutionary well-bred son.'

I looked from one parent to the other through the diffused light of the cut glass: Pa's grey cheek expanded and seemed to crack into boils; Ma's face was like Marilyn Monroe on a poster for cigarettes. But when she put down her champagne, she had her witch look on. My parents' mobile faces never settled into people I could rely on.

'Very little for pudding,' she said.

'I'll have a lie down,' Pa said.

He hobbled off and I followed him. 'Thanks for the motorbike. Brilliant,' I said when he was safely on his bed.

'Think nothing of it. Could you get me a fresh handkerchief?'

'Of course.'

I took one from the top drawer.

He held the white hankie between his clasped hands as he lay with his head supported by two bolster pillows.

I tiptoed to the door and turned. He was very still. As I stepped into the corridor he was already asleep.

I cleared the table and helped Ma to wash up.

'After Caleys, I'm going on to the Wyatts in Virginia Water: they asked me for tea. Do you remember their daughter, Mary, from Miss Fish's?'

'Yes.'

'People are being so kind. Must get ready.'

She went to her bedroom and I sat in the dining room. The empty Krug was in the middle of the table and the debris of our luxury food was scattered. Leila had said we could go out properly and she would explain it all next term. Her voice was lovely, and our conversation so relaxed, it was almost as nice as kissing her. Last night I had practised kissing on my bedroom mirror, trying to get the shape of my lips just right. It confused me and I decided kissing should be treated without theory.

The Christmas holidays were happy most of the time. Tony Gilpin came round on New Year's Day. We pushed the Yamaha into the front; he demonstrated how to use the clutch; to tighten the chain; to lubricate the throttle. Ma came out with slices of Christmas cake.

'Happy 1970, Mrs Worman.' He gave her an Alphonso-like smile.

'And to you, Tony. Your long hair suits you; do they allow it at Strodes?'

'Not really.'

'So narrow minded.'

He stood up; he was tall, dark and solid; his faded blue jean jacket and worn black jeans made him look like a roadie for a minor rock group.

'Are you letting Jeremy come to the Isle of Wight Festival this year?'

'His father isn't keen.'

'My big sister, Sandie, will go with us. You could join us too.' He smiled again.

151

'I'm far too old.'

'You're just right,' he said.

Yuk.

At 8.15 on the first day of the new term, Leila was waiting in the changing rooms. We said nothing but sat next to each other on the bench and hugged. She was wearing a black mini skirt. Her cream cardigan was soft as I stroked her back.

'My parents aren't getting on well; they might split up.'

'And my dad is dying.'

'Isn't life horrible.'

She cried on my shoulder. Her blue mascara smeared and I gave her my handkerchief. We looked into each other's eyes and the buzzing in my mind stopped. I held her shoulders. We moved forwards and our lips touched; we kissed slowly and the space dissolved until we were thrusting against the coat racks as she guided my left hand to her breast.

'Stop; we must stop,' she said.

I backed away. 'Are we going out now?'

'Yes, yes.'

There were footsteps outside and we went into the main room. It felt different. And so did I. 'Why couldn't we have gone out before?' I whispered.

'My dad was keeping a curfew on me; I'd got into trouble in Leeds; late-night parties; underage drinking. You know the sort of thing. I'm more settled now.'

What sort of thing exactly I wanted to ask but Alphonso came in with his smile hanging out. Luckily, he was on other business and did not dawdle.

I held her hand. 'Come on; let's go and talk before class.'

'Where?'

'Outside the garden in the back lane.'

I led her out and at the gate checked that Blundell wasn't at his study window searching for examples of

'Immorality', his new hot topic. The gravel lane, between two rows of houses, was lined with straggly plants and dark, creosoted potting-sheds.

'This is nice,' she said.

'Someone's left a football around.' I passed it to her.

'I don't like bloody football.' She kicked it away, with her toe, and it flew into a neighbour's garden. 'My little brother, Freddie, is always playing the stupid game.'

'Sorry.'

She came over to me. 'I've upset you. Ah, my little Tiddles.'

'Tiddles?'

'Yes, Jeremy; you're very cute. Tiddles.' She kissed me quickly.

'I'd prefer to be handsome if you don't mind.'

'That too.'

'Come on. Let's not bother with college; Brighton for a few days?'

'We could go the pictures on Wednesday. My dad has a meeting.'

'Great.'

We turned round and walked in.

A pattern was set: we would have lunch on our own in Windsor; we would go to the pictures and fondle each other, although the usherette always showed us to seats far from the back row; after college we would canoodle along the Thames, though it was too cold, and public, to explore each other for long. We talked and talked. I did not want to take her home; I was embarrassed by Pa, when people did not know him. And we couldn't go to hers: Leila said, 'My parents quarrel too much; you can't come back yet – but wait until they go away with my brother for the weekend.'

At home I rode my motorbike around the drive; the two-stroke whine must have annoyed the neighbours. By the end of February I was an expert rider. The second of March was my birthday and I rode the Yamaha to Windsor and parked in the lane behind the college. At break-time Leila handed me a card when no one was looking. I read it in the private-study room: *Parents and brother going to grandparents next weekend. Come over on Friday night? Love, Leila xx*

When college finished on Friday I grabbed the overnight bag from my locker, ran to my bike, and used expander straps to secure it on the rear rack. I set off and took the back roads to Maidenhead. I knew my way around there, as Ma and I had often taken this route as we drove to picnics at Bisham, or perhaps lunch at The Compleat Angler in Marlow. In the cold air I sensed the fallow fields, the old hedgerows, the grass and soil, as the landscape in which I was most at home. Leila's house was on the Marlow road. Ten minutes later I found it but as I was early I drove into Furze Platt and had coffee in a greasy spoon. I had told my parents I was staying the weekend at Philip's. I parked at the back of her terraced Victorian house and walked down the garden path. She opened the back door. 'Hello. I've just got in.'

We stood in the large scruffy kitchen. On the walls were a French Impressionist poster of a bridge over a river, a flower calendar, and an electric clock. In the alcove was a boiler, with black coat hooks on either side where a jumble of coats hung.

Leila tugged the shoulders of my black Barbour motorbike jacket. 'What do you want to do?'

'Well...'

'You're a dirty old man, Tiddles. I'll make you a coffee and then I'm going to shower.'

I sat at the oblong breakfast table, covered with a red shiny tablecloth. I watched her put on the kettle and grind the coffee beans; I closed my eyes and from her sounds made a map of us in my head: we were walking round her house, making love on the sofa, putting on music.

'You think too much, Tiddles.'

'What?'

'You didn't even hear me say, 'How many sugar lumps? Your face was so sad. Do you get depressed a lot?'

'No.'

'Liar.'

She put the cafetiere in front of me and sat on my knee. I stroked her leg.

'No! I'm going to have a shower.'

On the table there was a letter addressed to her with 'Pinewood Studios' on the front.

Twenty minutes later she came down in a sky-blue silk kaftan.

'You look lovely.'

'Do you like fish?' She flipped back my hair. 'Isn't it funny how little we know about other people, even though we see them a lot?'

'I often think that. I like fish.'

'I don't really know my dad; nor does my mum.'

'I don't know my mother.'

She turned on Radio One and the DJ played Rod Stewart's 'Maggie May'.

She danced in front of the boiler, using her hands like paddles above her head, but I couldn't take my eyes off her swaying hips.

'You should join Pan's People.'

'I'm too short – anyway, they're tarts.'

'They are not.'

'Fancy them all, do you?'

'Not quite. Why are Pinewood writing to you?'

'A producer is going to show me round. My dad knows him and I think I'd like to work for the BBC one day.'

'You never told me.'

'We're not married, Tiddles.'

'I like being with you.'

'Me too. I'll put the salmon in the oven. Mum left it; savoury rice as well; green salad.'

I took the bottle of Strongbow from my bag. 'Shall I light the candles?'

'Yes.'

I poured two glasses. We stood up and kissed. Through the silky material I felt all her nakedness.

'Salmon first,' she said.

'Cheers.' We chinked our glasses.

We ate at the kitchen table in candlelight.

After that she gave me a tour of the house.

'That's our sitting room.' She opened the door and the space stretched towards the garden; a sun lounge had been attached. The room at the front was her father's study. 'It's a mess,' she said, 'and he hasn't even brought all his books from Leeds yet.' The old mahogany stairs, with thick twiddly balusters, rose steeply and I followed her up. 'This is the middle floor; my parents' bedroom, and the rear one is our spare room.' I followed her to the third floor. 'That's my smelly brother's bedroom – and this one is mine.'

On the dark green door was a brass sun figure with its rays splayed out. A smell of joss sticks wafted out from inside.

'Patchouli,' she said, 'my favourite. Do you like it?'

'I love it.'

Under the sloping pine ceiling her bed nestled. The walls were yellow; in the deep-blue alcove was a dressing table on which three linked mirrors were hung with necklaces, beads and bracelets; small Indian rosewood boxes were stuffed with jewellery which dripped over the sides; tie-dye T-shirts hung from hangers around the room. There was a vivid red Paisley bed cover.

'I much prefer The Beatles,' I said, glancing at The Rolling Stones poster above her bed.

I closed the door and drew the blue velvet curtains.

'I'll have a shower,' I said.

'Okay.'

Outside the room I shivered and put on the landing light.

Ten minutes later I ran back with a cream towel round me.

Leila was combing her hair at the dressing table and dropped the kaftan from her shoulders, which settled on her waist. I stroked her neck; she turned and undid my towel. I covered my genitals with my hands. She gently pulled them apart as we watched our bodies in the mirror. We aroused each other as we glanced at our reflections. 'Like this,' she said, and guided my fingers up and down her clitoris, while she rubbed my cock. I watched the pleasure in her face and lips, and realised I must have been doing it all right, so went on stroking her. As we touched and kissed each other's bodies our desires rose. Leila's luscious moans drove us both to orgasm. We slipped under the bed covers and with our arms tight round each other fell asleep.

On waking, I pulled back the curtains and saw clouds speed across the moon. Leila's house was at the edge of the suburban world. On the left, at the brow of the hill, after the secondary school, the pasture fields opened out into meadows and woods. I wanted to be a hippy and bring back the lost things. A Himalayan Buddhist said you had to let yourself get lost before you could truly find yourself.

'You're thinking too hard again,' she said.

'I love you, Leila.'

'I love you, Tiddles.'

'Are you sure your parents won't be back until Sunday?'

'Sunday afternoon. I'm certain.'

We drank the rest of the cider. She lit another joss stick and put Leonard Cohen's *Songs from a Room* on the small record player in the corner. We lay down and faced each other as I traced my future in her eyes.

'I'm on the pill now.'

We pressed together. Her body smelt like earth in spring.

Quite early the next morning there was noise from downstairs.

'Leila; where are you?'

157

'Oh, God.'

Feet ran up the stairs. The door opened.

'Oh my, oh my – you really are your father's daughter.' Her mother peered over us like Cruella de Vil.

'It's not like that – how dare you.'

'And who are you?' Her mother moved to the end of the bed.

I sat up. 'I'm Jeremy. Hello, Mrs Jaggi.'

She was tall with long dark hair, cream slacks and a blue blouse; pale-skinned, in contrast to Leila's dusky complexion. She gripped the bedpost and sat down on Leila's side.

'This isn't how I wanted to tell you but your father has gone back to Leeds for a month – he says he wants time to think. Oh, Leila.' She burst into tears.

'You drove him away – poor Daddy.'

'The moment we're gone you get into bed with a boy.'

'I don't blame Daddy having a girlfriend.'

'You little bitch.'

'Where's Freddie – have you dumped him too?'

'He's staying on for a few days with my parents.'

Leila pulled the blanket up to her chin. I folded my arms.

'You two get dressed and meet me in the kitchen.' She slammed the door.

I held Leila as she sobbed.

Ten minutes later we sat at the breakfast table as Mrs Jaggi clattered pots in the sink.

'You can't even wash up, can you?'

Mrs Jaggi stood at the kitchen table and held the empty salmon dish with her yellow rubber gloves.

'What are we going to do, Mummy?'

'I will have to talk to your parents, Jeremy.'

'Please don't; my father is dying; it won't help at all.'

'Oh.'

'Jeremy has done so much to help me survive the quarrels with you and Daddy.'

158

'Leila, we are going to Buckingham for a few days.' Mrs Jaggi stroked her brow. 'You must get ready. And you, Jeremy, will have to go home.'

'Of course.' I wanted to say more but knew that retreat was my only option.

'You're not going to split us up, Mummy.'

We ran back upstairs; I quickly put things in my bag and sat on the bed as Leila assessed the clothes in her wardrobe. She took a suitcase from under the bed.

'Phone me tonight if you can,' I said.

'Of course I will. I love you.'

'I love you.'

'Here.' She scribbled down her grandparents' number. We hugged.

Downstairs, I stood at the back door. 'Goodbye.'

'Goodbye Jeremy.'

Leila waved from her bedroom window as I drove off slowly.

When I arrived home at lunchtime, Pa was in the dining-room nibbling his food.

'Your mother is having lunch with the Duncan-Smiths. Did you have a good time?' He pushed aside his ham salad.

'Very nice, thanks. I'll make a sandwich and then get on with my homework.'

'All right, old chap.'

I read *Hamlet* all afternoon in preparation for my A levels. That evening I stayed in my bedroom and tried to write a history essay about the English Civil War. By 8pm Leila had not phoned. I dialled her number on the upstairs line.

'Is Leila there, please.'

'She's not available,' said an old man's voice.

'It's Jeremy here.'

The phone was put down.

On Monday Leila was not at college; nor on Tuesday. She did not phone. Where was she? On Tuesday evening I phoned again. It was picked up but no one spoke.

'It's Jeremy,' I said.

The line went dead.

On Wednesday morning I arrived early at college and sat in the changing room. Students passed through but not Leila. At the last moment, just before class, on the steps, Mr Blundell appeared.

'Come to my study, please.'

'Yes, sir.'

I followed him up.

'Leila!'

She was wearing a green trouser suit.

Mr Blundell stood in front of his desk. He turned to Leila and gave her his special look. 'I had a conversation with Mrs Jaggi about you two. I hope you are both ashamed? You, Leila, are not yet sixteen.'

'I am next month.'

'That is not the point.'

He looked out of the study window at the dead garden and then turned to me.

'Your attitude, Jeremy, has been going downhill for some time.'

He stared with his coldest face so I had to meet his look or it would take me over and I would see myself as he saw me.

'I'm not at all ashamed, sir.'

'Don't be insolent. I suppose you have made your bed so you must lie in it.'

'That's horrible, Mr Blundell,' Leila said.

He opened a folder and looked at our records.

'So you were hoping to stay on and do A levels, Jeremy?'

'Perhaps.'

'Perhaps not. I think you would be happier elsewhere.'

'I agree.'

He flipped over to Leila's record sheet. 'Your mother tells me you are both moving to Buckingham for a few weeks.'

'No, no.'

She gripped my hand.

'You and Jeremy must desist from this disgusting behaviour.' He stood at the door like The Grim Reaper. 'Now go and join Geography. You are a bad influence on the other students.'

We sat at the back of the class and Miss Gee glanced at us.

At lunchtime we left at once.

'Come on; I want to show you something,' I said.

We turned into Alma Road.

'Where are we going?'

I did not answer as we rushed to the underpass and sat on a tree stump where Carolina and Roddy had held hands.

'This is a lucky spot,' I said.

'You're a lucky spot, Tiddles.'

'We mustn't split up.'

'Never.'

The subway graffiti had spread like ivy. Half an hour later we walked back to college.

On Sunday evening Leila phoned, and I spoke to her from the upstairs phone. 'I'm in Buckingham – they told me it was only for a few weeks, but I think we're staying here for good.' She took the phone away from her ear and screamed: 'You bastards! I hate you; I hate you all.' Another voice, her mother's, said, 'Give that to me, Leila; I'll speak to Jeremy.'

'Hello, Mrs Jaggi. Are you well?'

'When we're settled you must come and see us. Goodbye for now.'

'Jeremy!... Jeremy...!'

Dead brrs...

'Was that Leila, darling?' Ma called up.

'Yes.'

'I can't wait to meet her. I know she'll be ravishing.'

I lay on my bed and cried. Then I beat up the pillow.

The next day Leila was not in college. At midday I was called to Mr Blundell's study. Another man stood up.

'I'm Veda Jaggi, Leila's father.'

'How do you do, Mr Jaggi.'

We shook hands.

'Jeremy, I am sorry for these complications.'

He gave me a dazzling smile as he touched the knot of his black tie with yellow spots. 'As you know, things have not been good between Mrs Jaggi and myself.'

'I was supporting Leila, Mr Jaggi.'

'That's as it may be, but Leila needs a time of calm; no interruptions – and she is only fifteen.' His eyes flared like snakes.

'She's sixteen next month. I want to see her and she wants to see me.'

'You will, in good time – but she won't be returning here.'

'May I go back to class now, sir?'

Mr Blundell nodded. 'You will soon realise this is for the best.'

Mr Jaggi put out his hand: 'I have enjoyed meeting you.'

I sidestepped past him.

At home during the next few months we moved to the next stage of Pa's decline. A male nurse came twice a week and gave him bed baths. Ma was less volatile and helped Pa like a dedicated Florence Nightingale. She bustled about: ointment for his bed sores; cocktails of pills administered at precisely the right times; homemade soups. She had a mission and it suited her. She would often ask, 'Go and see if your father needs anything.' We worked well as a team.

During April and May spring blossomed in the thickening grass and wild flowers over Runnymede. I felt the presence of Leila everywhere. 'Oh, Tiddles': I used to look round in the changing rooms and expected her to jump out from behind the coats and go 'Boo'. At college all ears were open to Leila Jaggi rumours. Was she pregnant; had her parents split up; had she and Jeremy been caught having sex in the shed; was she still in England?

Overhearing these speculations helped to objectify my pain. When I was alone the loss of Leila almost sank me. What kept me going for the rest of the term was working intensely for the six O levels I was taking in June.

One evening as I was clearing away Ma fumbled and dropped a dish. 'Bugger,' she said and her face flushed. I bent down to help and smelt whisky.

When I had put away the dishes, I went downstairs, sat on the sofa and ommed as I watched the fireplace. After a while I got up and laughed. I looked at Uncle Neville's pipes. The early evening sun was setting and the diffuse light softened the walls. This room was no longer my cocoon with a missing father figure in its midst: I was not yearning for the past but peering into the future. The space was not looking at me – I stared at it.

'God bless, Uncle Neville.'

I shut the door and went upstairs.

***

On a Thursday afternoon in late July I sat by Pa's bed and read him an article from *The Times*, about the discovery of oil in the north sea.

'That could be good for Britain,' he said.

'More bloody motorways, Pa. Would you like a cup of tea?'

'I would.'

I made a pot and poured Pa's into a beaker, mixed it with milk, and blew on it until it was a drinkable heat.

He sucked it through a metal straw.

Ten minutes later the doorbell rang.

'Lovely to see you.' Ma said.

'You too, Mrs Worman. You're looking lovely.'

'Tony. You're a very obvious flatterer – but don't stop. Jeremy is with his father; come and say hello to them.'

Tony stood at Pa's bedroom door, swarthy in brown cowboy boots and a black leather jacket. 'Afternoon, Mr Worman. I'm getting excited about the Isle of Wight festival.'

'God knows why.' Pa laughed. 'But Jeremy deserves it; I hope he doesn't get lost in all the pot smoke.'

It was such a lively sentence, as if the best Pa was back, but then he grimaced and lay back on his pillow.

'We'll look after Jeremy,' Tony said.

'Is that okay, Pa?'

'Yes, all right.'

Tony gave me the thumbs up. 'Shall we change the air filter on your Yamaha?' he said.

***

A month later, at 8am on the Saturday of August Bank Holiday, Ma opened the front door.

'Hello, Mrs Worman. Are you coming with us then?'

'Tony! I'm far too old.'

'Not at all. You'd love it.'

She turned to me: 'You must eat properly when you're camping. My home-cooked ham in your sandwiches may help.' She handed me a silver-foil package, which I put in the rucksack. Tony licked the lips of his dark moon face. They glanced at each other.

'Bye, darling. Be careful. There has been a lot of trouble since the festival began on Wednesday.'

'Only if you read the *Daily Mail*, Ma.'

We headed off. At Egham Station, Tony's big sister, Sandie, was waiting at the end of the platform in her muddy-green Parka. She merged with the drab morning, which spread flat light across the tracks to the boggy recreation ground where the grey metallic swings hung

164

limp. Two small cooking pots jangled from the outside of my rucksack.

'Hello boys.' She smiled. 'I've got to bring you two back safe and sound so remember who's in charge.'

She was strongly built, medium height, with thick dark hair which flowed out on either side of her hood. She was like an enthusiastic girl-guide leader. In October she was starting the second year of a geography degree at Manchester University.

The train arrived and we had the single compartment to ourselves. What would happen to Ma until I got back? Sandie took a *New Musical Express* from her inside pocket and read the caption beneath a photo of Jethro Tull: 'Jethro is looking forward to the Isle of Wight'. He was my favourite rock-folk star, as I watched him play his anarchic, shaman-like flute on *Top of the Pops*, with his body curled up like a cobra in front of his group.

At the other side of Staines, the tentacles of London had extended their reach. Some fields were still there but the fences were rotting; a few horses and donkeys looked withered and flea-bitten. An old plough was red-brown from coruscated rust; next to that, a wrecked once-cream Austin A40 had its bonnet bent upwards. In between this urban-country confusion were well-tended allotments, where an old man in a flat cap and a black belt round his thick waist bent down to cut flowers. Perhaps no one had told him the landscape had changed (was his wife inside their bungalow watching the 1953 Coronation on a tiny television in an endless loop)? Disused railway sidings were scattered with long grass, wheat and yellow flowers between the sleepers. London never stopped its urban colonisation. By the time we got to Clapham Junction it was hard to remember my country world.

We soon arrived at Waterloo. The ticket collector clipped our tickets, and mumbled incomprehensibly, as if he had taken speech lessons from the announcers of the Waterloo tannoy system. We traipsed along the concourse to the low-number platforms from where the Southampton trains departed. I did not know Tony well, and Sandie not at all. I wanted to go home. The festival site would probably be as boggy as the recreation ground. The cartoon cinema was at the end of the station, where Ma and I would often finish our London shopping day. I remembered when I was eleven, just after my birthday, and we sat together in the dark, cosy cinema.

Our train was at platform 2. It was a corridor train and we found a compartment to ourselves. Half an hour later we ate our sandwiches and passed round a bottle of Strongbow. I kept seeing Ma in the landscape: coming out from behind a bush in a pink silk dress, blowing me a kiss; then in front of a tree with her rage face on, no make-up, and a stained white dressing-gown. 'Love and hate are the same, love and hate are the same,' strummed the wheels. I shut my eyes and when I looked out again it was Leila who blew me a kiss.

It did not take long to reach Southampton and we walked the short distance to the Isle of Wight ferry, which was already loading. On board, we sat outside at the bow end. Tony went off to buy snacks. Sea spray freshened the deck. The hippy passengers were dressed variously, in flowery shirts, loons, platform boots, headbands, kaftans, swirly scarves and big hats. I had on an ex-Army greatcoat and Levi's but my blue shirt was dull and my hair too short. The hippies rippled through groups of polished-shoes-and-moustached men whose blue-rinsed wives gripped their handbags.

When we got off the ferry, taxis, cars and coaches collected the straight people. The festival crowd, in scattered groups, talked loudly, 'Yeah, buses over there to the site,' and 'Not far to hitch' and 'Man, everyone will give you a lift'. Eventually we jumped on a scruffy single-decker bus, which took ages to get to the site. When we arrived, it looked like a First World War battle scene: the grass had been moulded into squelchy mud and there were gaps in the perimeter fence where it had been knocked down. There was a kind of entrance gate but no officials. We got into the festival for free.

We followed Sandie. I wanted to go home. She grabbed my hand and when I looked up a few minutes later, Wow! A floating sea of flags, sleeping bags, a kaleidoscope of colours, reds, mauves, greens, balloons, and smells, patchouli and cannabis. We put down a groundsheet, and made our encampment of back packs, Calor Gaz stoves, plates, cups and sleeping bags. All around us people cheered. 'Where's Wally?' I heard for the first time and soon realised it was the motto of the festival. The stage was stacked on either side with rickety speakers piled so high that I feared the noise would topple them. We were a long way back. In the afternoon sound technicians were testing the equipment, which crackled a lot. It was clear that there would be no live music for a while.

The site was a mass of cheerful refugees and I was younger than most of them. 'Going for a wander,' I said. In an adjoining field, there were queues for the primitive lavatories. Next to them was a tent of tarot-card readers. There were food stalls and meditation areas. I bought a veggie burger from a hairy hippy who was almost lost in the barbecue's smoke; next to him, a woman could read your aura for a pound. At the first aid tent a screaming girl was carried in by her boyfriend. 'Bad trip,' he whispered as he stroked her heavily ringed hand. Sun emerged from the fast-moving clouds and the site became brilliant: people stretched out far into the distance, shirtless, some braless, laughing, lazy, free. I went back to Sandie. Tony was about twenty yards away, sprawled on a tartan rug, getting to know a girl in an orange tie-dye cowgirl skirt. He waved me away with the back of his hand.

As night darkened on the curvy hills, bonfires lit up, and some puffed smoke signals. We were pioneers, leaving our so-called homes, flats and families to start again as a new tribe. The sound system started working and John

Sebastian played but went on too long. Joni Mitchell's 'Chelsea Morning' filled me with such happiness and 'Woodstock' spoke straight to me: 'I'm going to camp out on the land / I'm going to try and get my soul free'. Someone jumped on stage and made a speech against the 'capitalist festival', but Joni calmed the audience and finished her set. Her live voice was even better than on a record.

The Doors and Melanie were my favourites of the other live acts on Saturday. Very late, I drifted in and out of sweet phases of sleep. On Sunday morning we made sausage and beans for breakfast. The sun came up by 11am, it was warm and the rest of the day passed dreamily.

That evening, Jethro Tull came on with pagan abandon and playing a flute. He was wearing yellow trousers and a sort of sporran. 'Nothing is Easy' was fantastic. Later, Jimi Hendrix was memorable, not because I loved his music, although his guitar work was amazing, but because he looked so alive as he played the strings with his teeth in the drizzle, flipping his guitar and stretching its thin leads. Most of all I loved Leonard Cohen. 'Bird on the Wire' was the song Leila and I had listened to that night in her room. I had lost her but she was a messenger for all that my life could become. I brushed away a tear. Cohen was my guru. He was a western version of a Himalayan Buddhist. He was a mystic revolutionary. I think Uncle Neville could have been like that too if he had not felt such a failure. When Cohen came on stage there were aggressive shouts from some of the audience about the rip-off of the festival, and so on. Cohen began by talking to them, and he looked up at those on the hill and asked if they would light matches so he could see them. Fifteen minutes later there were hundreds of tiny flames up there, and I felt I was one of those flames too. In the beautiful 'Famous Blue Raincoat', the central character left the city as she 'tried to get clear' by seeking spiritual freedom in the desert – did she ever find it?

The dawn began to rise and soon after that we left. Tony and Sandie were staying with an aunt in Ryde.

On the train to Waterloo, I imagined the moving wave of people on the hill, glimpsed in all those lit matches. I missed Leila so much but Cohen gave me hope that love would one day come again for me. In the years ahead I often despaired at the lack of vision in left-wing politics, as if hard-edged confrontation had replaced a deeper imaginative impetus, but my hope revived when I saw in my mind the hillside of lit matches at the Isle of Wight Festival.

I returned from the Isle of Wight in the early afternoon, opened the front door, and was conscious of Pa's degeneration, as if his bed sores, boils and bruised limbs were giving off a whiff that seeped from his flesh. I took off my rucksack and felt tenderness, not fear, about his coming death. I put my ear close to his door and could hear his strained breathing. Memories of his kindness came back: presents to me from his business trips, Neapolitan chocolates or toy cars for instance or the discussions we had about rises in pocket money: 'You must make a good argument for it, old chap,' he would say as I sat next to him at the dining-room table. When I was six, he had brought me a toy steering wheel with a rubber suction pad that pressed on to the dashboard on the passenger side of his Alvis and I remembered Pa driving to his office in Egham, with me driving keenly beside him. 'That's the way, old chap,' he would encourage, 'but slow down when we pass a policeman...'

I had grown used to my collapsed idea of him, alcoholic and discreetly senile. In contrast, I had found Uncle Neville's death more distressing because I loved him, although I was too young then to put a name to it. I loved too Pa's gentle kindness, and his wit. But he was dissolving as my father and that made me angry.

I listened for sounds of Ma, but there were none. Perhaps she was sleeping off a lunchtime booze session. My stomach tensed. Which Ma would I meet today? The hallway looked different, with its speckled green carpet, mirror and dark side table with a black telephone on it; our number was Egham 2009; until 1967 it had been Egham 9. Now it was less personal, which was how I felt about this house. It was not a home.

I stood outside his bedroom door.

'I'm back, Pa. Do you want anything?'

He coughed. 'No thank you, old chap. Tell me all about it later.'

'Where's Ma?'

'She's having lunch at the Duncan-Smiths; don't worry, she's all right.'

'Good.'

I sniffed my blue duffle coat, which smelt of bonfires and outdoors.

'I'm going to have a bath, Pa. See you later.'

'Look forward to it.'

After my deep Badedas bath I stood naked and steaming in the hallway. I was pine fresh like a Bavarian forest. Pa was still in bed and Ma had not returned. In my bedroom I put on jeans and a blue shirt. I sat on my bed and felt depressed and claustrophobic, as if I was being smothered by a younger Jeremy, from whom I needed to detach myself, as I had been able to do that in the few days at the festival.

I went down to Uncle Neville's sitting room and opened the French windows. 'Time for an om, Uncle Neville.' I sat cross legged on the floor in front of the fireplace and ommed for several minutes.

'Darling. How are you?'

'Ma!'

She stood at the door. 'Are you practising cosmic consciousness?' She dangled her sunglasses over my head.

'You don't know about that sort of thing.'

'I'm totally with it, Jeremy.' She stroked my hair. 'It's gone fairer in the sun.'

I got up and stretched my legs.

'Sit next to me on the sofa. There is something I must tell you.' She patted the seat and I sat down.

'Geoff is in a worse state than we realised.' She squeezed my hand. 'He has several degenerative illnesses, and, yes, premature senility is one of them, which must be horrible for you, darling.'

'Get on with it, Ma.'

'He's got cancer too, of the tongue, and who knows where else.'

'You mean...'

'They see no reason for further investigation.'

'How long?'

'Three to six months.' She put her arm round me. 'Our duty is to make that time as easy for Pa as we can.'

'I've had such horrible thoughts about him. I'm sorry.'

'Not your fault. Lightning would have struck me down on several occasions if the litany of my bad thoughts had been revealed.'

'Will he go to hospital?'

'I want to get enough help here so he does not have to.'

'I'll do anything.'

'I know you will.' She patted my arm. 'We're having cold salmon for supper with potato salad; I'll start getting it ready. We'll talk again later – and you must tell me all about your adventures. There was a picture of Jimi Hendrix in the *Daily Mail*. He looked terrifying. When he bit his guitar it made me think of a black Dracula. I hope they weren't all like him.'

'You're funny.'

She shut the door.

'Well, Uncle Neville; I could do with some courage now.'

***

Mr Blundell had phoned Ma a few weeks previously and said he was prepared to take me back for A levels (I had passed 6 O levels with good grades). 'We can overlook other matters; everyone makes mistakes and I am sure Jeremy has learnt from it.' Ma told me she wanted to tell Blundell that my relationship with Leila was not a mistake, and probably did me a lot of good, but thought better of it.

Looking back at my relationship with Leila, I have often wondered what became of her. After me, she went out with a good friend of mine; a year after that, she phoned me to say she wanted to go out again with me. Having only just got over the pain of our broken love affair, I could not risk it in case she left me. I can only say that without the relationship with Leila I am not sure I would have thought life worth continuing. She saved me.

Blundell was starting a discrete sixth-form group and I would be one of the first of the intake (there were six of us). I was going to take English, History, and British Constitution when they could find someone to teach it. The other option for me was Brooklands Technical College in Weybridge. I liked that idea but because so much was going on at home I decided to stay with Mr Methodist Blundell. Perhaps someone at college would have news about Leila.

Many of the old crowd had moved on: to everyone's surprise, Five Cars had passed five O levels with good grades and had started at Welbeck College, a military boarding school, to do his A levels, a sort of foundation course before going on to Sandhurst, and then joining one of the Army technical regiments (I wondered how much it cost his father to bribe the examiners). Alphonso must have finally realised he was getting old and was going to study Economics at university in New York; Philip had gone to work for an insurance company in the City; the Banga brothers had become boarders at a public school somewhere in the west country.

I arrived early on the first morning. Mr Blundell was sitting at his desk in the main classroom, flicking through a pile of papers.

'So you're back,' he said.

I was nonplussed by the obviousness of this.

'Come on; I'll show you what's been done.'

I followed him to the third floor. He had converted two large rooms into airy, light classrooms; a third, small attic room had been made into a mini kitchen.

'What do you think, Jeremy?'

What I thought was that he must be bloody well making loads of money from us, but I said, 'Lovely, sir. I'm very pleased to be back. Thank you.'

'Make yourself a coffee. I must go and welcome the others. By the way, your hair is okay for now, but you won't let it get much longer, will you?'

'Of course not.'

'Good. Very good.'

He smiled, which I always found a little alarming, as if he had to make a special effort to use the muscles at the side of his face. It seemed to hurt him, as if they were straining from lack of use. It was a relief when his mouth snapped back into its tight letterbox shape. He was wearing a light summer off-white jacket, and it could have been the same one he wore the first time I had seen him at Haileybury Prep School. He clearly did not spend much on clothes.

The next month at college was straightforward: ordering new books, getting to grips with *Mrs Dalloway*, and reading Christopher Hill on the English Civil War. The gender mix was balanced: three boys and three girls. One of them, Lucy Herbert, had long blonde hair, a plummy voice and wore black mini skirts at the top of her elegant legs. She was sharp, clever and wanted to be a fashion journalist; she liked to make fun of her large, eccentric family who lived in Winkfield. Apparently she had been asked to leave Benenden and I wanted to find out why. The college side of my life took my mind off the challenges at home.

When I arrived home one afternoon in late October Ma was hunched over the stove, as she ladled out soup into an orange Tupperware beaker.

'Pa will love this, darling. Fish soup, whizzed up in the liquidizer. No salt so it won't irritate his tongue.'

'Smells lovely.'

'His new bed arrived today from the cottage hospital. So kind of Dr Eric to arrange it for us. The porters even took away the old bed. He won't fall out again now.'

'That's good. It was difficult getting him back into bed last week.'

'He could so easily break a bone or two.' Ma wiped her brow, and whispered, 'He was furious this morning when I explained about the new bed – "I don't need a bloody cot," he said, "tell them to cancel it".'

'Was he okay once it had arrived?'

'Oh, yes. He sat in the corner chair and told them how to construct it. His mind can still be so sharp.'

She put a round green tray next to the cooker. There were two cream dahlias on the draining board, which she placed in a thin blue pottery vase and put that in the middle of the tray, the beaker next to it, and a white linen napkin at the side.

She turned the wedding ring on her finger. 'Don't get too upset by Pa, will you?'

'Bit late now.'

I picked up the tray.

I knocked on his door but there was no response.

'Pa?'

He was curled up in his double-sided bed-cum-cot. All the vertical poles were white and one side could lift up like moveable bars of a prison. Last year when I was visiting Ma at Holloway Sanatorium, I had peeked into one of the secure wards, and all the beds were like this. As the outdoor light shot a few bright arrows through the chinks in his dark-green velvet curtains, his drawn face, and the stubbly hairs on his chin, made me think of a plucked chicken.

'Pa?'

His legs unbent; he turned onto his back as his thin arms gripped the bed poles; veins protruded above his wrists, which looked as if they could snap like matchstick men. He squeezed the bars tight.

'Want a hand?'

'No... no... no thank you.'

I put the tray on the table by his bed, and then pumped his bolster pillow, and rearranged the others which supported his head. I lay the napkin across his chest and handed him the beaker. I put in the soup spoon and stirred.

'That's probably the right heat now.'

'Thank you, old chap.'

He sipped. 'Umm, delicious.'

'Fish soup, Pa.'

'Barbara always made a lovely one.'

It was as if he knew he was already in the past tense. He put aside *The Times:* 'Just read a fascinating article about boundary changes. Every government tries to alter them for electoral advantage – remember that!' His head sank into the pillow, a half-smile on his face. His drug-induced consciousness seemed a pleasant space to be. Death would be a release for him. He sat up and supped from the beaker.

'Lovely.' I smiled and watched. Ma and I were doing all we could to keep him alive, which lessened our guilt.

'Do you mind if I open the curtains, Pa?'

'Good idea.'

Pellucid autumn light filled the stale room.

'It used to be my favourite time of year,' he said.

If you knew the end was close, did it sharpen your senses? I wondered.

'That's enough.' He handed me the beaker.

He rested his hands on either side of the bed. 'At least I'm bloody safe in here.'

'You are.'

'I'm a hopeless old wreck. Take a look at that photograph album on the floor.'

It was their wedding photographs at Knutsford Parish Church in Cheshire; Pa looked sleek and confident in his morning suit, shining shoes and white carnation. A young man with prospects. Where on his life's journey did despair take over? Why? I was sure that Ma had never loved him, but he had loved her.

'You looked very happy, Pa.'

'I was.' His left hand stroked the gleaming white bars. I put down the album.

I wished he would ask me how I would be when he was gone. Did he not care or was he afraid that I did not care? His skin was brittle like an egg's shell. He pointed to the photograph of his parents on the corner table.

'Bring it over will you, old chap.'

I handed him the large silver-frame.

'That was in our garden in Bedford.'

'It's lovely.'

My grandparents looked so kindly in their summer garden: 'Pop Worman', in a rich houndstooth suit, holding a pipe; granny in a loose blue-and-white cotton frock, her hair in a bun. I tiptoed to the window. Mrs Timms walked past, dressed in a two-piece burgundy suit, and a hat with a feather. She was probably on her way to watch Peter sing something in the Eton College choir.

Pa lay back and clasped the photograph.

'God bless, Pa,' I whispered and picked up the tray.

The next morning I woke with a start – 'Jeremy, Jeremy!'

I put on my jeans and ran down.

'Ambulance, darling – now,' she called from Pa's bedroom.

I stood at the door. Pa was on his side; his eyes half open.

'Geoff, Geoff.' She knelt by the bed.

I knelt beside her.

Pa's left hand poked through the white bars. I touched it. Stiff, cold. 'I think...'

'Don't be silly.' She put her fingers round his wrist. 'You're right. Nothing, no pulse. Phone Dr Eric. No need for an ambulance.'

Twenty minutes later I opened the front door and Dr Eric ran in. He put the doctor's bag on the floor and lifted Pa's wrist. Then he took out his stethoscope and pressed it gently to Pa's chest. 'I'm so sorry; Geoff has gone.'

He gently uncurled Pa's fingers and put the photograph on the table.

The undertakers, Lovetts, were a great support. Nigel Lovett, the director, took personal responsibility for the funeral. 'I greatly admire the work your father did for the Rotary Club,' he told me when Ma and I visited his premises in Englefield Green to choose Pa's coffin. He sat behind a large highly polished mahogany desk, its top covered with red leather and embossed in gold around the edges, and leant across to show us a coffin catalogue, which Ma flicked through. 'We must have some brass, don't you think, Mr Lovett, but not too much, and a dark-wood coffin of course.' She directed him with the same confidence she showed to assistants in the Caleys hat department.

'Quite right, Mrs Worman,' he said, and suggested a coffin on page fourteen.

'That's the one!'

The following Tuesday was wet and there were about fifty people at a crematorium chapel in Englefield Green where the vicar of Egham Parish Church led the service. As Pa's coffin disappeared from sight through the curtains to be burnt by the intense flames I had a joyful feeling that he was at peace at last.

***

On a Sunday morning a month later, after the feverish activity following Pa's death had subsided, Ma and I sat at

178

either end of the dining room table with fresh coffee and wholemeal toast.

'We must look after ourselves better, darling. Put some honey on your toast.'

'But we've always eaten pretty well.'

'Pretty well is not good enough. You and I must think organic.'

'You sound like a hippy.'

'I'm serious.' She sipped her freshly squeezed orange juice. 'I can't promise how things will be financially, but while you're still at home we're going wholefood, to extend our lives by at least ten years.'

'But on your trip to London last week, you ordered all that delicious food from Fortnum's.'

'I'm still upset; I need a little comfort. Stern measures would be no good for us in the short term. Geoff would not want us to scrimp. He was marvellous like that.'

'Here's to you, Pa.' I raised my coffee cup towards heaven.

'Jeremy, really.'

The next six months was a period of surprising calm. My studies were going well and Mr Blundell and I had come to an understanding: I kept my hair shortish and my political opinions discreet. Pa's bedroom was redecorated and the odours of illness and death began to dissolve. For all Ma's financial anxieties (and she warned me on a weekly basis, 'I may have to sell the house, the MGB, my rings, the mink coat, and the sable stole'), we lived as well as ever. In the spring, Bill Cranham planted out the annuals and said, 'This year I want it really special; I'm doing this for Mr Worman.'

'What a lovely idea,' Ma said and looked away guiltily.

On a late April Sunday morning at breakfast – croissants, stawberries, cereals, goat's cheese, coffee – Ma said, 'Darling, I have an announcement: I'm going away for a year on a world trip. Pa's stockbroker, Charles Bentley, do

179

you remember him, has offered me a little financial relief. As you know I had a meeting with him last week in his City office. As he put it, he wanted to "recharge Geoffrey's portfolio – too full of sleepy duds" – so I said, "Go ahead. How can I help?" To cut a long story short, he is selling lots of the boring shares and wondered if £7,500 would be helpful for me to "have a little fun". I could have hugged him; actually, I did on the way out. His secretary laughed. I will buy you a car. How will you cope without me, poor little boy, and only just seventeen?'

'The car will help. What sort?'

'Merry's has found me a lovely little Fiat 600D for you; I knew I could trust them; such a reliable garage. And from the lessons I have given you on the Wentworth Estate, it's clear you're a natural driver, like me. You must never take out the MGB. I've also arranged for professional driving lessons. And Bill Cranham will sit with you when your car arrives, in order to give you extra practice.'

'Thanks, Ma. That is really kind of you.'

'Shall we celebrate tonight with a glass of champagne? I bought dressed crab as a treat. We've had such a tough time.'

At the end of July, Ma flew from Heathrow to Florida to stay with an old friend from boarding school, Joan Turner, who had married an American lawyer. This was Ma's first stop on her world trip; after that she planned to stay with Uncle Fred in Australia for a few months. Having passed my driving test first time, I took her to the airport in my blue Fiat.

At the start of term, I felt alone. I missed the old crowd, and now it was only me and James Frampton left in the so-called A-level set. We had nothing in common, and his dark matted hair and black shirt gave him a haunted look; I was sure he would rather not be here, especially with me. On Monday morning of the second week, I got in early and knocked on Blundell's study door.

'Come in.'

'Mr Blundell, I don't think this is going to work; there is no longer an A level group; I've decided to leave.'

'Sit down, Jeremy.' His beige summer jacket looked duller than ever. 'That is a rather hasty decision. Have you have discussed this with your mother? What will you do? And there is the question of fees for the term.'

'My mother phoned last night from Florida. She agrees with me, and I think any question of fees would be unfair in the circumstances, sir.'

'The rules for payment are clear. One term's notice must be given.'

'But that assumes I was going to have the kind of A level class you promised.'

He stood up, and so did I. 'Circumstances changed. I was not responsible for that.' We shook hands. 'And let me know how you get on.' He closed the diary on his desk.

'I will, sir.'

We both knew I wouldn't.

As I collected my books from the glossy white classroom, some of the fun incidents with the old crowd came into my mind; now they were gone, it felt merely that I was leaving a dentist's waiting-room. Blundell never pursued his fees.

At home, I sat on the porch of Uncle Neville's sitting room as the puffy grey sky pressed on my thoughts, and the breeze shook our shaky brown garden fence, which kept us nicely separated from all the other large suburban houses – if only a raging wind would tear down all these dead fucking fences and expose the squalid little secrets of my neighbours, which they kept in check like the tightly mown lawns of their mausoleum houses. Inside, I sat cross-legged, ommed for some minutes and on opening my eyes felt buddha calm: Ma was gone and there was nothing to fear from her violent outbursts, nor did I feel guilty about my negative feelings towards Pa, and my need for Uncle Neville had passed. I was free. I had some money so did not need to get a job for a while. Mrs Roberts, who was the husband of our handyman-cum-decorator, came in three times a week to cook my supper, Mrs Parish twice a week to clean the house. For the rest of the time I looked after myself and, due to my alcoholic parents, I was used to that. I'm sure that Ma would have agreed with me about leaving Blundell's had I spoken to her.

The next month was pleasant as I rearranged my bedroom and turned Uncle Neville's sitting room into my study for writing poems, and fervently reading Robert Pirsig's *Zen and the Art of Motorcycle Maintenance*, and lots of Virginia Woolf. But I was beginning to get bored; my only regular social contact was with the sixth-form boys from Strodes in the Station Road café to play pool. On a Wednesday morning towards the end of October, I walked up the high street and into Record Wise to flick through the massed ranks of LPs for inspiration. The shop was quiet and the owner, Adam Rolfe, came over, 'How's life treating you, Jeremy?' Tall, dark and thin, with an easy smile, he was wearing one of his trademark floppy jumpers, a sky-blue one today, which had a hole in the elbow, as if he had been living as a beatnik in a Soho jazz club since the 1950s and forgotten times had changed. I explained my situation. 'Are you looking for something to do?'

'Suppose I am, really.'

'I need help in the shop; you know the scene pretty well. I'll pay you cash, all right?'

'Fine.'

On the morning of my first day at work, I had dressed carefully, blue ironed loons, cream shirt, blue platform boots, finishing off with my new Mr Kipper red psychedelic tie.

'You'll be good for business!' he said and gave me practical exercises in using the till. It took a few days to get to grips with it, and to work out the order of the record-storage system. I enjoyed the banter with customers. An added bonus was the number of lovely girls who came in, often sixth formers after school, and I realised with a bulging ache how nice it would be to have a girlfriend. It was easy to slip into the rhythm of work here, and the weeks flowed by. At the beginning of December, at the end of the day, in the back office of the shop, Adam opened a bottle of chilled Muscadet and poured us both a large glass. 'You've done well,' he said, 'bet you'd like more money.'

'I deserve it!'

'You do. I want you to run my tiny shop in Staines until the lease runs out in February, and I'll give you an extra fiver a week.'

On Saturdays, Egham Record Wise was always run by Gary, and after meeting Adam there at 10am, we set off for Staines in Adam's worn Mercedes estate. He parked behind the shop and we went in through the back entrance.

'Morning Lizzie,' he said to the young woman at the counter. 'She's off to Spain tomorrow for nine months before she goes to university.' We introduced ourselves, while he bustled about, tidying up the record racks. After twenty minutes, Adam said, 'Got to go; Lizzie will explain the system, and give you the keys for Monday. You don't mind, do you?' After he'd gone, Lizzie said, 'Adam gets away with what he can; I bet he's not paying you for today?' She was right, but I enjoyed my day in the shop.

On Monday morning I felt very grown up as I opened the shop at 9 o'clock, made a coffee and sat by the till, but after twenty minutes, I realised there was not going to be a rush of shoppers. Adam had told me, 'Fill the shop with music.' I enjoyed my solitude in this cosy little place. Record sleeves were pressed to the windows, and the main collections arranged in sections – Rock, Folk, Jazz, Musicals, etc. – down two long aisles. There was hardly any classical music. I put on Al Stewart's *Bedsitter Images*, followed by tracks from the Doors and Joni Mitchell and then Nick Drake's *Bryter Later* (my first introduction to the wonderful Drake). At 11, my first customer came in, an older guy, long straight hair, blond going grey, with lined eyes; jeans and a purple shirt hung on him unwillingly. 'I'm looking for a John Mayall, perhaps a compilation,' he said to me, exhaling beer and cigarettes.

'There's a small blues section in the corner.' As he thumbed through it, I watched in case he was tempted to put an LP under his voluminous shirt. But he found what he wanted and paid. There was a trickle of customers throughout the day, and that set up a pattern for the weeks ahead; the pace did not quicken much as Christmas grew close. As stock was low, I had to order records from Adam in Egham, who would drop them off in the evening. There was plenty of time to make an inventory of all the records, and of 'fixtures and fittings' as Adam wanted that too; part of me enjoyed creating clarity and order, but another me felt anxious as this little job was yet one more thing in my life coming to an end. My sense of isolation was compounded by the steady flow of people who passed the shop: young, old, bearded, bald, sexy, scary, rich, poor, but they all had families, friends, lovers and places to belong.

The *Evening Mail*, a local paper based in Slough, came through the letterbox every evening. On the day before we closed for Christmas, I was flicking through it and noticed an ad: 'Great Career Opportunities: Tele-Ad Sales at the *Evening Mail*'. On a whim, I sent off for an application form. The Yeomans asked me for Christmas Day, which was lovely but also sad as I realised what a happy family was really like.

After Christmas, the shop was quiet. I filled in the *Evening Mail* application form; two weeks later I was interviewed in Slough and offered a job as 'trainee tele-ads salesman' to begin next week. Adam let me off the last week, but paid me for it, telling me he was grateful for helping him out.

On a January Monday in 1972 I drove to Slough in my blue Fiat 600 and parked in the *Evening Mail* car park, which was full of light-blue Volkswagen Beetles sales' reps cars.

The manager, David Reynolds, a cheerful, youngish man, well-built if a little rotund, wore a flowery red tie with his dark suit, and introduced me 'to the team': they looked up, mainly women, from the rows of long desks under neon lights where they sat by telephones waiting for people to phone in with classified ads; the more senior ones were busy phoning local businesses to sell advertising space. For the next two weeks, in a smaller 'conference room' on the next floor up, three of us were trained by different members of the senior sales team in the mechanics of the job: how to take down classified ads clearly; how to follow up for payment; the specialist areas of expertise we could develop (motoring; business; sport; births and deaths etc.). The promise of bonuses for high sales enticed us. One part of me resented being here, as it was nothing I would ever want to do in the future. When I parked each day and saw the sales reps drive out, there was a lump of dread in my stomach at the fear of being trapped here for ever. In the third week, the ebullient David Reynolds took me into his office: 'You've done well.' He raised his arm in my direction and I noticed a big blackboard behind him with long red arrows of sales figures – motoring, local businesses, sports' clubs – pointing skywards like rockets of hope and progression. 'We have a special assignment for you; we want you to be the receptionist-cum-tele-ads salesman at our small Staines branch; it would just be you and two or three journos who work in the back office.'

On the Wednesday morning of the next week, I met David at 8am outside the tiny Evening Mail office just off the High Street in Staines. 'I've bought us breakfast,' he said. Inside, we munched bacon rolls and sipped coffee from plastic mugs. 'Do you think you'll go to university one day?' he asked.

'Perhaps.'

He gave me a big-brotherish look, and I glanced away, not wanting him to see any personal stories behind my mask.

'I did an English degree at Bristol and now I'm on a Thompson management training course; it's very good; I want to get into oil eventually.' I smiled enthusiastically but could imagine nothing worse than a Thompson Management Training Course. 'Any problems, get in touch. Full-speed ahead!' His purple flower tie waved in the breeze as he left. I sat at the desk and checked the drawers. There were plenty of tele-ads dockets for all those customers who were going to rush through the door to place expensive ads, I don't think. Half an hour later, a man peered over the desk.

'So you're our new front of house.' He smiled. 'I'm Geoff Ward, one of the journalists who work here.' He had a Beatle-mop haircut and his shoulders were rather high, which made his neck appear short, but his smart loons and grey herringbone linen jacket were cool, and he made me think of a pop journalist. 'Make yourself at home,' he said and went into the small back area of the open-plan space, where he made a phone call and read his 'copy' to a typist at the other end of the line. The process was interesting in its precision (Geoff often checked if she had got the word down accurately or placed the comma in the right place); interesting too in its aliveness – this would be in tonight's paper – and that thought excited me. During the next month I enjoyed the range of people who came to place an ad, to complain about something in the paper, to moan about the non-delivery of the *Evening Mail* to their house or office, to see a journalist, to ask my advice about the best way to sell something. The journalists didn't take much notice of me but they were pleasant and amusing; Colin Irwin came into the office most days; he was keen on folk music; Chris Goffey was a less frequent visitor (his special interest was cars). Staines was being redeveloped and it was like being in the midst of a slow, endless building site. On Monday at the beginning of July, I made a coffee for Geoff and put it on his desk.

'Ever thought of being a journalist?' he said.

'I certainly want to be a writer.'

'Why not do your A levels and then you might have a chance to do the journalism course in Cardiff, which is a really good one?'

'That's a great idea, Geoff.'

I went back to my desk and phoned David Reynolds who said he would discuss my idea 'higher up the line'.

The next morning, David phoned me back: 'CJ thought it was an interesting idea and would support it. He'll give you a good reference. Well done, Jeremy!' Yippee, I thought. I wrote a letter at once thanking David and the *Evening Mail* for giving me such excellent training, and for this new possibility in the future etc. I finished working at the *Evening Mail* at the end of July. In August, a perky Ma returned from her world trip: 'I almost married a lawyer in Florida, Max Paul, Jewish of course, but I didn't mind that a bit. He was keen, twice divorced, affable and good looking in a Mediterranean sort of way. But I woke up one morning and realised I could never live with all those yellow shirts. And that, darling, was that.' In the middle of August, I spent two lovely weeks with Giles and his family at their house in Gozo.

***

In September 1971 I enrolled on a one-year intensive A level course at Brooklands Technical College in Weybridge. Ma was in a stable condition and, anyway, she went away for weeks on end, visiting friends all over the country. During my first term I had a girlfriend, Mathilda, which lasted until Christmas. But something inside me was going wrong: I did not like studying anymore, and didn't really connect with my fellow students. Fears and doubts from the past infiltrated me and I began to smoke cannabis heavily, often alone in my bedroom. I carried on at college, but only just. In July 1973 I passed two A levels with poor grades. The thing I felt most was of not wanting to join the conventional world; it seemed now that it was another Jeremy who had worked at the *Evening Mail* where, for the first time, I was able to imagine some kind of future ahead. Actually, I went through with my application for a journalist training course and after waiting for a few weeks I was accepted, but declined the offer. I was looking for something else; I had lost confidence too. It could be seen as the biggest mistake of my life but I have never regretted it. For whatever reasons it was not the right time to do that course. For the next two years I drifted: temporary driving jobs for firms around Heathrow, working on the door of a Windsor folk club, bar work in a pub near Marlow. I also lived for five months with two acquaintances who were at university in Aberystwyth. I couldn't settle on anything as if I was being constantly driven away from thinking too deeply about my depression. I had to do something more positive. In October 1974, aged twenty, I began a philosophy degree at the Polytechnic of North London.

For the first year I stayed in a Tufnell Park bedsit, the one Giles Summerhays had lived in during his first year at London University's Royal Veterinary College in Camden. He had moved into a larger flat near the college's field station in Hertfordshire. His old room was dingy, did not seem to have been redecorated since the 1950s, and smelt of cats. The philosophy department at the polytechnic was situated in Kentish Town, in what had once been a mental institution. On my first day there, in the airy library on the first floor, I read the noticeboard. The Students' Union, which was essentially a branch of the SWP (Socialist Workers' Party) had organised a talk by Paul Foot, 'The Crisis of Capitalism: The Way Forward', which was taking place later that day in the large hall at the central location of the Polytechnic of North London in the Holloway Road. That evening I walked there from Tufnell Park through the dusty, dirty streets of north-east London. The hall was already quite full and I sat towards the back. Foot, with his remarkably posh accent, gave a clever, amusing speech amid cheers, and some heckling from the IMG (International Marxist Group). And the first question was from Colin of the IMG: 'We totally reject your analysis of...' but the rest of the question was drowned out by boos from the larger SWP contingent. Foot answered whatever the question was, to be greeted with a further round of loud cheers. I got up and stood by the side wall in order to see better. I scanned the first four rows of seats, which were filled by the SWP High Command, serious politicos, whose gestures and utterances seemed to me cold, abstract ideas that spouted out like manifestos. In a moment of clarity I knew this could never be my kind of revolution – it was all head and no heart. I trudged back dejectedly and bought a shish kebab in the Kentish Town Road, which I munched on my way to my bedsit. Reflecting on my life, I felt completely lost.

My philosophy classes were quite interesting, and well taught. But I knew after the first month that this was not the course, the college or the city for me. I could never be at home here, but where was home? Certainly not from where I'd come. I phoned Ma occasionally but it was as if I was someone she had once known as her son, but who had now moved out of her life. I soldiered on with my course, determined not to give up on anything else. Christmas was spent with Ma: she was well behaved and I put on a show of cheerfulness. The spring and summer term were more endurable as I had accepted my temporary fate, of having to stick with the degree; taking breaks in Aberystwyth to stay with friends kept alive my hippy hopes.

That summer I hitchhiked around Ireland for a month with Dave Smith, an old friend from Egham. After a few days in Galway, we took the ferry to Inishmore, the largest of the Aran islands. The weather was blue and hot and the bare limestone rocks bleached white in the sun reminded me of my holiday in Gozo with Giles's family. Dave and I camped in a remote part of Aran for three days and I loved the vagabond freedom. Every step took me further away from any anxieties about Ma. We met Lorrie, who was hitching on his own, and spent a great day together, smoking his grass, making barbecues, swimming. He told us about a huge squat in Hornsey Rise 'where the action was happening'. Throughout my life, whenever I have looked back on that time in Aran, I am aware that it solidified my counter-culture inclinations: I really never would join the rat race. This was no longer adolescent posturing but a fact at the deepest level of my being. But I also knew I had to take a leap into a new future.

On a blustery August day the 14 bus dropped me at the foot
of Hornsey Rise. My black loons were sodden at the ends
and the dampness of my sky-blue corduroy jacket made me
shiver. A Mott the Hoople track, 'All the Young Dudes',
floated from a corner shop; the sound vibrated above the
outside table of red and green peppers, aubergines, celery
and tomatoes. Raindrops scattered on watermelons.

Garlic and kebab smells drifted from a Turkish cafe. I
leant against the door and inhaled the aroma. I had missed
lunch and was tempted to go in. But there was a summer
fair at the squats and I did not want to be late. I pulled
out the wet notepaper on which I had scrawled rough
directions: Three blocks. Walk up Hazellville Road. Can't
miss them.

I set off and my heart raced as I wondered what I was
going to find. The warm sun between clouds made my
clothes steam. Ranked up the hill were the three London
County Council blocks: Ritchie House, Goldie House,
Welby House. A barbed-wire perimeter fence erected by
the council had been torn down and strips of colourful
material hung along its length as if an Apache raiding
party had attacked a cowboy encampment. The entrance
to Welby House was blocked by bags of old clothes, broken
fridges and smashed-up cars. Banners flapped over the
corridor wall outside the flats on the third floor:

'Don't Dump Rubbish!'

'Order your organic vegetables.'

'Stay Cosmic!'

'Hornsey Rising Yippee!'

The smell of homemade bread guided me through the
entrance gates. Folk music, a sort of Incredible String
Band discord, was coming from the other side of the block.
I adjusted my rucksack and stood by a wooden stall, where

girls in rustic skirts, and hairy men, were cutting up bread and cheese. Behind them was a noticeboard: 'Contribute If You Can'. I handed over some change and a fair-haired girl gave me a thick sandwich. I touched her wrist and a bracelet of silver stars glinted from the sun's rays. I smiled and blushed. This was where I wanted to be.

Along the incline of the steep Hazellville Road a column of trees led towards a T junction at the top of the rise; the connecting road was also lined with greenery. It felt like London and the country at the same time. I stared at the glossy leaves until a child's scream made me jump: all the terrors evoked by Ma returned and I felt sick. I wish I had screamed back at her. I kicked a stone into the gutter.

The music guided me past tables about 'Drugs Advice', 'Organic Vegetables', 'News from Copenhagen', 'How to Set Up a Commune'. I wandered to the centre of the communal garden, decorated with anarchist flags and psychedelic bunting. I looked up at the three floors of Welby House: jagged glass in some windows but most were unbroken. On this thundery day many flats had their lights on; some rooms showed off colourful lampshades while others had only bare bulbs. On the third floor I noticed a full bookcase, with one row of Penguin Modern Classics, while in the next-door flat the far wall was painted a lurid gloss purple. My farmer-style brown-leather boots were leaking through the elastic sides. I trudged back to the sandwich stall and next to that was a small table and an Australian man sat behind it: 'You looking for a squat?'

'It's just for me.'

His stubbly chin jutted forward from a fair-skinned wrinkly face as blond hair hung in corkscrews from a tan-leather bush hat. He wore loose-fitting black jeans and a cream cheesecloth shirt; he had the ballsy confidence of an Aussie and I bet he was a surfer when young.

'You a student?' he said.

'What's wrong with that?'

'Want somewhere cheap to live?'

'I believe in squatting.'

'Why?' Two rows of shell beads were tight round his neck; his Adam's apple protruded like a fat lizard about to jump. He opened a yellow folder. 'Fill that in.' He handed me a form.

'It's like applying for a council house,' I said.

He laughed and his even teeth were bleach white. 'A few of us are trying to control the kind of people living here; it's the largest squat in Europe. We're looking for commitment.'

'I am too.'

'Want a tea?'

'Thanks. No sugar.'

He went off to get it.

The late-afternoon sun intensified the shadows. A group of mucky kids were holding hands as they turned in a circle. Behind them a ginger-bearded man was playing a silver-metal slide guitar; to his right a short man with a withered arm, wearing a checked lumberjack coat, jived to the music; nearby, three Hells Angels sat on a tree trunk and passed round a bottle of Captain Morgan. Folk meandered around. I felt lost too and saw the chasm between my former world and this, as the rural-style roads of the Wentworth Estate came into my mind, and the people I knew then – were they my real tribe? No, Jeremy, no, I repeated like a mantra.

My interviewer plonked a white mug in front of me. 'I'm Steve. Fill in the form then, while you drink your tea.'

The form had five short sections. The last, 'Special Skills', was the most difficult. After a few minutes I handed him the single sheet of paper. He read it quickly.

'You're interested in organic farming?'

'*A Blueprint for Survival* is a brilliant book.'

'Ever seen the magazine *Street Farmer*?'

'No.'

'It's about making the city greener, ploughing up the streets to grow crops, ecological houses, that sort of thing.'

'I'd like to see a copy.'

'I want to grow vegetables on a patch near here. I could do with some help.'

'I will.'

A fuzzy-haired man tapped Steve on the shoulder.

'Watcha, Pete.'

'We must keep out those Hells Angels,' Pete said in a Glaswegian accent. He was tall with a goaty beard, a red spotty scarf and a tangle of dark curly hair.

Steve looked at me: 'Pity you don't have a few friends who could move in with you. A place for one is tricky.'

'It will take a few weeks, that's all.'

They got up and moved away.

To their right, I noticed a stripped-pine table with a spindly banner above it, 'Tarot Readings: £1'. Sitting there was a gorgeous dark-haired girl with a silvery gypsy shawl over her shoulders.

She waved. 'I can do yours when you're ready; might bring you luck. I'm Clara.'

'Thanks.'

I wanted to walk among the oddballs first; people like me, who had jumped out of the London bog to live in fresher air. By the tree trunk The Hells Angels had been joined by a stout black-bearded man with silver rings on his fingers; at his feet was an Alsatian which he held on a brown-leather leash.

Steve and Pete came back again: 'Apart from an interest in organic farming, any other skills?' Pete said.

'I've got a minivan.'

'For collecting supplies? We could use it for that?'

'Of course.'

They nodded.

'Come on,' Steve said to me.

I picked up my rucksack and followed him across the grass. As we went up three flights of urine-scented stairs to the top floor our feet twanged on the concrete like an out-of-tune guitar. There were about ten flats with kitchen windows that looked on to the shared open corridor. No broken panes. The doors and window frames of one flat were painted in the bright primary colours of a Steiner kindergarten. We stopped at the far end outside a gloss-grey front door.

'This is it.' Steve took out a bunch of keys from his side pocket. 'I think it will be to your liking, sir; it's a maisonette; you must find a few people to move in with you.'

'I will.'

He bent down, undid a padlock and turned the Yale. As the door opened, heavy feet ran up the stairs behind us. A barking Alsatian reared its head.

'What the fuck you doing?' its owner said.

'Hello, Mick,' Steve said.

'That place was lined up for a few of my mates.'

The dog and Mick advanced. Steve, over six feet tall and well built, faced them.

'Sorry, Mick, but you know we're trying to make the system work better.'

'What fucking system?'

Mick flicked the leash. The Alsatian dribbled through sharp teeth.

'Apologies for the confusion,' Steve said.

Mick rubbed his mouth and saliva stuck to his lips. He pointed at me: 'Who's that little tosser?'

'I'm Jeremy. Hello.' I stood behind Steve.

Steve put his arm on Mick's shoulder and they looked over the balcony.

'We want you to join the Allocation Committee. Got time for that?' Steve said.

'Join you middle-class wankers?'

'You need a bigger flat for you and that lovely dog.'

'Lucy is a bit cramped, ain't yer girl?' he agreed, stroking her ears.

'I'll drop in and see you tonight,' Steve said.

'Make sure you fucking do.' Mick clenched his fist. 'Then I'll sit on your poncey location committee.'

Mick farted and walked off with Lucy.

I followed Steve in.

There was a kitchen to the left with cream cupboards and a gas cooker; to the right, a tight staircase and on the middle step a Barbie doll in a torn pink-chiffon ball-gown. Straight ahead was a large living room, bare except for a blue-velvet armchair.

'We can find you some tables and chairs.' Steve sat down. 'The last guy who lived here restored furniture; he left in a hurry.'

I opened the wide window that looked on to the square. The cheerful crowd was beginning to disperse. I liked the idea of us all sharing a dream of the future, but how did I know it was the same dream as we all seemed so different from one another?

Steve stood up. 'Got to go. Gas and electricity are on. Welcome aboard.' He shook my hand. 'You really do have a minivan?'

'Of course I do.'

'This place is in good shape; even the plumbing looks new.' Steve glanced at a shiny pipe going through the ceiling. 'Next month I'm going to Machynlleth to visit the National Centre for Alternative Technology. May give us some ideas.'

'That's a fancy name.'

'Guess it's just a few shacks for now, but they have plenty of land.' He stood by the door. 'That cute girl, Clara, who gave you a nice smile – her so-called boyfriend, Danny, plays in a rock band. He's mean. They're always quarrelling. Watch out.'

'Thanks for the warning.'

'I'll be in touch soon.'

'Okay.'

I saw him out and clicked the Yale's catch into the lock position. His can-do attitude made me feel more confident about squatting here. I dragged my rucksack into the living room and sat down. The brown-flecked carpet reminded me of our hallway in Egham and it felt a long way from there to here.

Almost dark. There was chanting from the block at the other side of the square, 'Hari Krishna, Hari Krishna, Hari Krishna, Krishna Hari...' I expected to see a crocodile file of believers weaving across the grass, making jerky dance movements as they sang but there was nobody. The sound of tambourines was coming from a ground-floor flat. Inside, in candlelight, was a group of Krishna followers, dancing round the living room. It was a good omen as we needed a spiritual revolution, and the Krishnas were a sign of hope. On the floor above that one an older man in black shorts was using a weight-lifting bar, raising it high above his head, then down to the back of his shoulders, and up again. The top of his head was bald but he had shiny black hair at the sides and a thin pencil moustache. In other flats I watched people's shadows. There were many tatty curtains. It was a shame that Clara had not read my tarot cards, but I knew she was the kind of girl who would flirt and frustrate me, and she had a mean boyfriend. This line of thinking made me want to see Leila again, but she was long gone, and anyway love can make you so sad. In the flat beneath me someone was playing America's 'Ventura Highway' – the perfect hippy war cry. Nixon had been impeached and anything was possible, which I believed in my head but not in my heart.

I turned on the bare-bulb ceiling light. Upstairs, there were three rooms, the smallest of which Ma would have called a utility room. The largest was a bedroom, and the curtains had motifs of the Flower Pot men, the BBC children's television programme that used to be on *Watch with Mother*. So was this the child's bedroom and the parents slept next door? Why had the furniture restorer

197

who last lived here not taken them down? Or did he have a daughter? I did not want to sleep upstairs tonight. I checked out the bathroom: the lavatory flushed, the taps worked and the lime green bath and sink were clean.

Feeling hungry, I sauntered down the hill to the kebab cafe, where I sat in the corner. They brought me over a large lamb shish kebab, salads, a lager. The atmosphere was warm and dimly lit; old Turkish men sat with small dark coffees and smoked as they played cards or backgammon. On the wall, a large framed photograph of General Ataturk, the founder of modern Turkey, looked down magisterially on their games; the men chatted in their own language as if Turkish cafe life had been transported complete to Hornsey Rise. Occasionally they glanced at me. Half-an-hour later they called out 'Goodbye' as I left.

Back at my flat, I unhitched the sleeping bag from my rucksack, laid it out on the floor, and got in. I took out a Cadbury's fruit-and-nut bar and a bottle of Strongbow. I propped myself against the far wall and pulled out Marcuse's *One Dimensional Man* from the inside pocket of my jacket. Everything I needed was in that book. It was a Bible to me: his analysis of society, and his libertarian vision of the way forward, spoke truth. The best thing about Marcuse was the way in which he combined the psychoanalytic and the political. That was the kind of politics in which I believed. Marcuse and R.D. Laing were my heroes. The flickering lights around the square kept me company until I fell asleep.

For the next two weeks I prepared for my second year at college: I renewed my library books, bought a copy of Wittgenstein's *Philosophical Investigations* from Dillons in Malet Street, finished an essay on Kant that I should have done last term. I tried to persuade fellow students to move in with me, but they already had places to live. The best thing was my new realisation: college no longer mattered. My life was centred at Welby House and in the belief that my poems were getting better: Edward Thomas, the Imagist poets, W.H. Auden and Leonard Cohen were motivating my work. I had begun to send off a few poems to magazines. I put up posters in the living room: Frank Zappa sitting on a lavatory; John and Yoko in bed; Picasso's Guitar Player. Steve and Pete gave me two tables, chairs, a mattress and crockery.

At the weekend I picked up my minivan from Egham and filled it with gardening tools from the potting shed. Ma promised to come to Hornsey Rise when I was settled: 'I've never been in a squat before; how exciting.' I tried to find out more about the organisation of Welby House, but there seemed to be little structure. Steve's initiative of an Allocation Committee was a new venture, and the other blocks, Goldie and Ritchie, did not have one. I filled in a form to join the new Ecology Party, and in the twilight walked down the hill to post it, but what was the point: how could we change a world as far gone as this? The next evening, as I returned from a walk to Highgate Cemetery, three guys, a sheen on their clothes from encrusted dirt and grease, were breaking into a flat on the second floor. I looked down into the entrance yard where Mick and his dog Lucy were coming out of their new ground-floor pad. 'What's fucking going on?' Mick shouted. 'Someone is getting in!' I shouted, 'second floor.' Mick and Lucy charged up and the culprits fled. An hour later, Pete and I put a new padlock on the door of that flat.

'Been to the Railway Tavern?' Pete asked.

'No.'

'Now's your chance.'

'I'll get some cash and come to your place.'

Ten minutes later we set off and walked fast up Sunnyside Road as the trees blew in the bustling wind. Inside the pub an open coal fire blazed and the bar was busy with a selection of freaky-looking people. On the walls, the vivid posters of 1950s British Rail holiday travel shone down at us: 'Midland Railway Tourist Resorts'; 'Camping Coaches in England and Scotland'; 'Cross with us to the

Continent'; 'Winter Sports Expresses'. Perhaps the former pub customers had moved on to such happy places.

'It's like a bloody club in here,' Pete said, 'we've scared off all the straights. What you having?'

'Pint of Guinness, please.'

'Get that down you,' Pete said.

'Cheers.'

He tapped me on the shoulder. 'See that crazy little fellow in the corner, jigging around; he sells the best dope. Come on; I'll introduce you to the Candyman.'

'What's his real name?'

'Haven't a bloody clue.'

We walked over. The Candyman was making floaty movements in time to Steeleye Span's 'All Things are Quite Silent' as the LP played on the Sony hi-fi system in the corner. He bowed to us. 'Gentlemen, I had a feeling you would visit tonight. Vibrations, you know.' He looked at Pete. 'Who's your friend?'

'This is Jeremy; he's cool.'

'Sit down, sit down. Mine's a pint of Newcastle Brown.' He looked at me.

'Yes, of course.' I went off to buy it.

As I came back with the opened bottle, I had a good look at him. He was not prepossessing: about 5ft 4 inches tall, long mousy hair, round National Health specs. His checked cowboy coat smelt of fried breakfasts; his blue jeans were shapeless. He looked like a damaged scarecrow but his smile was radiant. I sat down as he was gesticulating to Pete about 'a need for the Blakean vision, man.' His withered arm hung from his coat jacket, adding to his vulnerability.

'Tell me a bit about yourself, Jeremy.'

I gave him an edited version of my life. He nodded sagely as I spoke about my wish to write more poetry and advised me that Ginsberg was the man. When I asked him to tell me about himself, he said, 'One day, if we know each other better.' After five minutes he got up and bopped to Curved Air's *Air Conditioning.* There was an energy, a mood about him, the like of which I had never known; his smile was a glorious thing, which expressed all the emblems he seemed to revere – the Isle of Wight Festival, San Francisco, Martin Luther King, Gandhi, Jefferson Airplane – as if they were all Free Lovers and Free Love was the natural state of humanity. Pete and I chatted with the Candyman for an hour and as we got up to leave, the Candyman said to me, 'Come and see me if you want something.' He scribbled his address on a scrap of paper and gave it to me. 'You're on the list.' He tapped his nose and the hand of his bad arm was turned up like a claw. I walked back with Pete and we said a boozy goodnight on the landing.

It was a dry, windy September afternoon and dust was everywhere: clouds of it as builders dumped rubble bags into a skip close to a demolished house on Whiston Road; mini piles of grit-dust in the roadside gutters; a thousand specks in the sun's rays; dust as the London Plane trees shook off their polluted veneer; a light sweeping dust that stung my eyes. It was worst on Archway Road towards Highgate where the mechanical cavalry charge of vehicles fumed up and down the hill. Although Welby House was an unlikely sanctuary, it became mine. I believed that all kinds of experiments in living could happen here – ecological, philosophical, artistic, sexual – and that people like me could remake our broken lives. It was not that Welby, or Goldie, or Ritchie, were especially hedonistic, drug-crazed places, although an article in the *Evening Standard* had described the squatters of Hornsey Rise in those terms. On the contrary, there was a tinge of puritan earnestness in most of us as we grappled to find an alternative way to live outside a ruined, capitalist world. In the middle of September Steve returned from the alternative technology place in Wales.

It was Wednesday morning and I had arranged to meet him at the vegetable patch. I put on my scruffy working clothes, made wholemeal toast with peanut butter and honey, and sat by the living-room window, scanning the square: any odd-looking characters hanging around? Shouts or screams? Usually there were just a few people going for cafe breakfasts, or even to work, while most were probably still in bed. It was not a get-up-and-go environment. I put the pickaxe over my shoulder, held the shovel in my hand and stepped into the corridor like a character from the cover of the Grateful Dead's *Working Man's Dead*. Who said all hippies were lazy? People had fallen into this place for all kinds of reasons: what most of us had in common was a sense of being dispossessed. We did not want the world on offer – 'Economic Progress'. England was a treadmill of consumerism; soon there would be no countryside and we would all die from spiritual and environmental asphyxiation. What was the point of living in a world like that? I hoped we could bring about a peaceful revolution. Or did I? Perhaps my real desire was for all I had lost, and not for some utopian idea in the future, which felt less utopian by the day. Or maybe I was helping to connect a true sense of history so that the future would become an egalitarian model of the past I most loved.

From a nearby flat, the one painted in Steiner colours, a loud male voice was singing 'Tiptoe through the Tulips' in Tiny Tim style. The singer was Milo, a professional clown, who lived there with his partner and two kids. I ran down the three flights of stairs and inhaled the new-age air. As I reached the vegetable patch, Steve was digging manure into the soil. He reminded me that a younger guy, Robbie, who had a few problems, was coming to help today. I gave Steve the minivan keys and he set off to buy more compost.

Next to the vegetable patch was a three-metre strip of concrete. I was going to make a herb garden. I lifted the pickaxe in a high arc and as it came down it splintered the surface. After several minutes my determined hits revealed the tarry under-filling, and beneath that shingle stones and then a layer of clay and after that a darker, fertile seam. I returned to breaking up the concrete and before long my arms and shoulders ached. I lay on the damp ground and watched numerous residents walk back and forth to the local shops on Hazellville Road for bread, milk, tobacco and so on. Some were dressed like bohemian vagabonds, while others wore smart casual clothes. One man had on a dark-blue suit, white shirt, flowery tie. His shoes were black polished lace-ups and he sauntered down the hill with Hampstead ease. Behind him, the Candyman had an army-surplus rucksack over his shoulders, and his withered arm flapped as he walked.

I sat up and rubbed my calf muscles.

'Hello.'

I turned.

'I'm Clara. I was doing tarot readings last month.'

'I remember.'

'You never came back for yours.'

'I was too busy.'

'You might have discovered something.'

'I'm Jeremy.'

'I know.'

She looked at me with her teasing dark eyes.

Faded blue jeans were slinky on her hips and a black V-neck jumper showed off her breasts. Her white flip-flops were worn and her feet tanned. She had medium-length brown hair with a middle parting and fringe, Sandie Shaw style. Her full mouth was soft and a pale complexion emphasised red lips.

'Steve said you're a poet.'

'I had a poem in a magazine last month.'

If I had made an Identikit picture of a girl I most fancied it would have been Clara but she was older, more sophisticated, and had a mean boyfriend.

'I'm making a herb garden.'

'That's a good idea.' She gave me an Are-you-asking-me-out-for-a-drink-smile?

She stood up. 'Got to go. I'm doing my artwork today.' She flicked her right foot behind the left ankle.

'Good luck with it.'

I watched her until she was out of sight.

For the next hour I smashed up concrete.

'Hello,' a voice said behind me.

'Robbie?'

'That's me.'

He was as thin as a Lowry figure, with a delicate face and alabaster, papier-mâché skin. He wore a purple velvet jacket and had a languid Ray-Davies-of-the-Kinks look.

'Nice to meet you, Jeremy, mate.'

'We're going to shape the boundaries of the herb garden and dig out the rest of the concrete.'

'Terrific.'

We sat on the rubble.

'Perhaps you should take off your jacket?'

'I need to get used to the world of work.' He looked round. 'Jen! How you doing?'

'Watcha, Robbie boy. See you later?'

'Hope so.'

A thin, pretty blonde girl with a Mary Quant haircut and black leather trousers gave him a big smile.

'Jen works in a unisex boutique up Camden Market.'

Robbie had perfect, unflawed complexion, which surprised me as he was a heroin addict. He was staying in Steve's flat and getting well fed; he had a sympathetic doctor and did not need to hustle for smack. I knew from Steve that Robbie had been brought up in South London children's homes but had escaped early into a life of drugs and petty crime. Something in his ironic melancholy chimed with me. He made me feel less inadequate about my own life.

204

'Let's get going.' Robbie yawned. He folded his jacket and hung it over the rubble pile. He picked up the spade and held it at different angles. 'I'm getting the idea.'

'Very stylish. But the trick is to dig it into the soil.'

'Cheeky fuck!' He laughed wheezingly. 'You've made me cough now.'

'Better have a tea break. Don't want to overdo it.'

'Funny.'

He almost fell as he made his first incision, but then dug intently, levering up the stones and jagged concrete, and throwing the big stuff onto the pile. I used the pickaxe to break up the hardcore. We worked in unison for over an hour. In the midst of the city we were bringing nature back to life. We flopped onto the grass.

'I love cabbages,' Robbie said, 'whole big fresh ones, all knobbly and gorgeous.' He looked at his watch.

'Seeing Jen in Camden?'

'Probation officer in Islington.'

'Good luck.'

I levelled the soil and checked my watch. 11.30am. I had done enough and headed off towards my flat.

Near the entrance gates Steve was talking to a man with pushed-back dark hair, post-teddy-boy style. His crisp blue jeans and white shirt had been ironed. He did not look like the kind of offbeat who lived here, but a successful builder or plumber.

'Jeremy, come and meet Ernie.'

Ernie said to Steve, 'You can't have a proper organisation until you open a communal bank account – then you have some money to do things with.'

Steve turned to me. 'Ernie used to be a shop steward in a car factory.'

'Until my wife went off with the production manager.' Ernie kicked a stone across the yard. He had the strong, agile body of a footballer, although he must have been at least thirty-five.

Steve said, 'I'm going to call a Welby House meeting next week; we can nominate a few people to open a bank account and sign the cheques.'

Ernie nodded. 'I'll get a few local councillors to support the squatters. The council should never have let this place go downhill. Let's embarrass them and they may give us short-term leases. Who knows?' He turned to me. 'I hope you'll be at the meeting, Jeremy.'

'I will.'

He walked off. I ran up the stairs. On the top corridor Glasgow Pete came out from his flat, which was the other side of Milo's. Pete shared his with two friends from back home.

'Got an idea for you: my scrap-metal business is taking off. My flatmates have given me an ultimatum – either my copper water tanks go or I do.'

'Water tanks?'

'Part of my reclamation drive. Come and see my little friends.'

In the top-floor room we examined them: eight bulbous shapes with coppery tones of different hues, each tank about 4 feet high, a foot in girth, with the top and bottom compressed into the shape of an old-fashioned wine flagon. A filler pipe was sticking out of them. The tanks were squeezed into the room like benign Daleks on an evening off.

'I know a plumber who's keen to take them; if you store them for me, I'll give you the money for one of them, a little extra for your grant.'

'Suppose so.'

We spent the next hour carrying the tanks, which were surprisingly light, from his flat to my utility room. After Pete had gone I sat in the armchair. What could I do with Ma tomorrow? Why did I ask her up here?

For the last month the only time I had seen the Candyman was when he was going somewhere, carrying a rucksack. He seemed to be gone for days on end; I never noticed him coming back. I decided to pay him a visit, read his address on the scrap of paper he had given me, put on my coat and set off. On the corner of an unlit stairwell of his block of flats a silver needle glinted. From the top-floor flat 'Mr Tambourine Man' floated out of a cracked window like a lament. Eventually someone must have heard me knocking. Locks clunked and squeaking bolts were pushed back.

'So you came.'

I brushed the collar of my brown suede jacket. A smell of incense poured from his flat: I was welcomed into a phantasmagoric seminary. An entrance hall led to a door, in front of which a red plush curtain slid smoothly on its brass rails. On one side of the corridor three mauve velvet curtains formed cubicles like confessionals. 'They're my meditation areas,' he said and led me into the living room. Another door led off from it, which he opened, and I saw a half-dressed red-haired young woman lying on three red brocade cushions.

'I'm Janey.' She stood up. 'Got to go now.' She did up the buttons of her summery, flowery dress. 'He's been giving me advice,' she said, pecking him on the cheek. He waved her out.

With his five wizard fingers he pulled a Sun Valley pouch from his back pocket, and rolled a perfect joint. 'For you, man.' Always courteous, he gave it to me to light. 'It's Leb,' he said, 'really good – that'll change yer vision, polish yer lenses.' After I had smoked his dope, the summer pavements did turn gold. The afternoon became soft and blissful; the winter sun sent long shadows across the clear day. My body felt sweet and supple. Our conversation spanned the universe and the hours passed until evening came. A milk bottle smashed on the landing: 'You fuckin' said today!' a male voice shouted. The Candyman got up and opened the front door. I listened.

'It'll be 'ere soon Geoff,' he said.

I stood in solidarity behind the Candyman and said 'Hello' to the stranger. Geoff was short, thin, with the wizened face of a speed freak. He placed his spindly hands on the Candyman's shoulder, 'I'll be back tonight.'

'Fine, man, that's fine.'

Geoff's black motorcycle jacket smelt dank. He marched away along the landing.

'You okay?' I said.

'No worries. Me and Geoff go back a long way. We understand each other.'

'I'll go then.'

When I got home I went straight to bed.

Then next morning I got up at 8.30. 'Smarten up, darling,' the mirror said as I shaved. I felt refreshed. I had dreamt of rolling in the grass with Clara.

In my bedroom I put up the rickety ironing board and plugged in the black-and-silver Morphy Richards iron. It had been here when I moved in and it had worked last week, after a few rusty dribbles of water had drained through the holes. Today, the steam puffed untainted but there was a burning smell from the colourful wires near the handle. I ironed my grey elephant cords and white Lord John shirt with a long collar. I pulled out the hot plug swiftly, got dressed and went downstairs.

My brown suede Chelsea boots were mottled with stains but, hell, what could Ma expect – I was a hippy. I stroked the thick furrows of my cords: they reminded me of the fields at the Chobham farm where Ma had milked a cow when I was a child. I remembered one late-August day, probably in 1963, when the farmer had shown us his 'special place' where 'I grow an unusual kind of barley; it's a hobby of mine'. The field had indentations like my cords. I looked round my grubby squat living room. Suddenly I felt nostalgic, wanting to be back in that world, to be the Jeremy who had stayed at public school, gone to a good university, and was going out with a girl whose father was a senior partner with a firm of solicitors in, say, Shrewsbury or Hereford. I would marry Sophie, his very attractive daughter (we were madly in love and had fantastic sex), at the ancient local church. All the men would wear morning dress. I glanced up at the 1969 John Lennon / Yoko Ono Amsterdam Hilton 'Bed-In' peace poster – 'To the revolution!' I set off and I felt almost Savile Row in the context of this place.

From the other side of the road, Clara called out, 'You're looking sharp. Going somewhere nice?'

'Not exactly. Have to rush.'

The leaves were turning soft yellow. I had arranged to meet Ma outside the Turkish cafe on Beaumont Road, assuming she made it. She had told me last week: 'I'm determined to find my way on public transport; I'd be embarrassed to ask a taxi to take me to that part of town.' But unlike, say, the floor directions of expensive department stores, tube maps and bus timetables were not her natural territory. There were few people around and certainly not Ma. I crossed the road.

'Darling, it's me.' An emerald-ringed finger pointed from the opened window of a black cab.

The taxi stopped.

'I thought this would be the safest way,' she said.

'Quite right. You can't walk for twenty paces around here without being mugged.'

'That's what I feared.'

'It was a joke, Ma.'

The cabby jumped out and opened the door for her. An emblem of Home-Counties style stepped into one of the poorer boroughs of London: well-cut black slacks, dark-green silk blouse, short beige jacket and tartan beret. Red toenails glowed in brown leather sandals.

'Such an interesting drive, John.' She gave him a five-pound note.

He touched his dark crew-cut hair, which contrasted with his ocean-blue polo shirt, and shook Ma's hand. 'Enjoy your adventure, Madam.'

A Spurs pendant swayed on the dashboard as he drove off. Ma and I looked at each other.

'Well, what do you wear when you're visiting your son in a down-at-heel area?'

'You look perfect.'

'You haven't kissed me yet.'

I did.

'Fresh coffee back at the flat, and I've planned lunch.'

'Perhaps you could get together a team to tidy the place?' she said when we reached the entrance gates to Welby House.

I marshalled her quickly across the yard without bumping into anyone I knew. Fortunately the stairs had been recently washed with disinfectant and she followed me but said nothing. She went into the living room and sat on the blue armchair. 'Very airy space. Will you get a few friends to live with you?'

'I've tried. Welby House seems to frighten them off. Traitors!'

'You'll find someone; I'm sure you will.'

'I'll go and make the coffee.'

She got up and looked out of the window. A few minutes later I carried in the old pewter tray from Egham, and two matching cups and saucers, Staffordshire bone china, unchipped, which I had bought last week from the PDSA's second-hand shop in Islington. I poured from the cafetiere.

'Help yourself to the baklavas,' I said.

She nibbled one. 'Lovely. I'm pleased you haven't given up all the pleasures of the good life.'

'Why would I?'

'I thought you squatter types rejected everything.'

'Turkish cakes are allowed.'

She put down her plate. 'I was thinking of travelling again, Jeremy; I might stay with people I haven't seen for years.' She stood in the middle of the room. 'I don't know how you ended up here.'

210

'I didn't want to live a Surrey sort of life anymore.'

Her gaze peeled off my squatting dreams and exposed my fears. How could I have any vision of my own if she did not approve it? Was my real terror not that I had rejected her but that she had rejected me? I saw this place through her eyes: the torn section of flock wallpaper around the chipped door; the semi repainted living room, in a special-offer Dulux Sage Green, from the hardware shop on Holloway Road; the loose floorboards; the stained carpet.

Where's the bathroom, darling?'

'Up the stairs; first door on the right.'

What could I trust if she was not in my life?

Ma came back from the bathroom. 'I forgot to give you the champagne; let's have it now; it's still quite chilled.' She took it out of her Liberty-print bag.

I got two glasses from the kitchen, rubbed them with the drying-up towel, and rushed back. She pushed out the cork, which bounced off the ceiling, and filled our glasses.

'To your new life,' she said.

'Smoked salmon and scrambled eggs for lunch.'

The stale smell of the flat followed me to the kitchen. How had I landed up here? Why did I want Ma to see this place? Was I trying to shock her? Was I saying, 'Just look how much I have rejected your fucking pretentious Surrey world?' Five minutes later I carried in two plates.

'Voila.'

We sat at the table and talked about family things, which seemed to come from a distant world. The champagne intensified my sense of disjuncture.

'We're going to grow organic vegetables and sell them,' I said.

'Here?'

'Yes.'

'How sweet.'

'It's not "sweet"; it's changing the way we think about the city. Do you want to see the vegetable patch?'

'I know what vegetable patches look like, darling.'

211

After lunch we looked out at the square.

'Come home for a few months if you want.'

'I like it here.'

'Do you mind if I pop off? I'll get a cab to Simpson's; I need a new outfit for the autumn.'

'If we walk to Archway Road, you'll find one more easily.'

'No. I feel quite safe. It's not as rough as I expected; if I need help I'm sure the natives will be charming.' She picked up her bag. 'Thanks for showing me your experiment in living. Come and see me soon.'

'I will.'

We kissed and she left. As the door shut, I felt terribly alone and wanted to hear her voice again. I recalled that day years ago at Miss Fish's when she was late collecting me. I had been looking out for her at the small landing window and pictured her face but could no longer hear her voice. The silence made a void in which I was nothing. Then I saw her face again, and heard different voices speak from her mouth, but none of them was hers. It was as if she no longer existed. Perhaps she had found another voice with which to speak to a boy just like me.

Twenty minutes later Pete knocked on the door. 'Want to come for a meal tomorrow night?' My flatmates are away for a few days and I've asked some neighbours.'

'Love to. Thanks.'

'Good. See you then.'

The postman arrived and handed me a postcard: pictures of Devon scenes on the front, and written on the back: 'Bloody noisy sheep around here...' It was from Giles, who was doing a placement with a vet near Barnstable. It was lovely to hear from him, but the distance between his world and mine frightened me. I tucked the card into my back pocket.

As I walked into Pete's flat the next evening he handed me a joint. The fluid waves of Ravi Shankar's music filled the place.

'Can't say I'm crazy about it but the others like it,' Pete said. 'It's Van Morrison next.'

I went into the living room. A small group was huddled around the sofa. Robbie was sitting alone on the window ledge.

'You okay?' I said.

His hands shook as he looked outside; his blue velvet trousers had a tear on the back leg. As we talked about Spurs' prospects this season he perked up. From the kitchen there was a strong aromatic smell. Ten minutes later Pete carried in a large earthenware pot with a pointy top. The four people I did not know said hello. We sat in a circle on the floor as the spicy steam from the rich, soupy sauce floated round us.

'My speciality,' Pete said.

He dolloped a large spoonful of couscous on the plates and passed them round. We helped ourselves to the lamb stew, which had in it bits of pickled lemon. With its earthy Moroccan flavours, the savoury sauce was different from anything I had eaten before. As candlelight flickered on the pot, I asked the Italian man next to me what he was doing in London. 'Resting out for a while.' His bearded Italian friend gave him a cautionary glance. When we had finished, Pete told us stories about when he was working at a whisky distillery near Glasgow 'but as I was stoned every morning I took early retirement for fear of falling in a vat and ending up as a drop in someone's glass'. A cross-eyed anarchist, Johnno, with a large, balding head and a cut-glass accent, talked about 'the gr-e-a-a-a-t challenge of forming collectives'. Ian, a thin, sour-faced Scot, a secondary-school teacher and People's Revolutionary Party activist, told the anarchist he was 'being simplistic'. Bella, a freaky psychiatric nurse, was training to be a Laingian therapist at the Tavistock Centre. Robbie looked at me with the saddest eyes I had ever seen.

After dinner we shared a hookah and drank mint tea. Ian's voice rose to a high-pitched whine as he quarrelled about the 'inadequacy of Johnno's overview' and the inevitability of 'a real Marxist workers' revolution'. Johnno poked him in the ribs; Ian grew more angry. I could imagine Ian, after the revolution, as a kind of witch-hunter general, chairing a committee which interrogated those whose views were considered 'deviant'. Bella moved next to me, sat cross-legged and rocked slightly. 'You got a girlfriend?' she asked. I smiled into her dark eyes and said 'not at the moment'. She asked if I was 'engaged with feminist issues'.

'What do you mean by engaged?'

'Can't men ever answer a straight question?' She almost spat at me.

I edged away, and could not believe these people were part of my revolution. Robbie was scraping his fingers down the window, Pete went into the kitchen. Outside, glass smashed. I ran on to the balcony. Five members of a motorbike gang, with 'Hells Demons' sewn into the back of their denim jackets, got off their bikes and stood outside a ground-floor flat. One of them took a sledgehammer from the pack bag strung over the rear seat, then broke down a front door. They dragged out a small, terrified man.

'Shit. They came back!' Pete said. 'Perhaps we should try to stop them.'

No one responded.

'Surely we can do something?' I said to Pete.

'I don't think so; they'll go soon.' He lowered his head.

In the yard, The Hells Demons circled the man and kicked him to the floor. After a while they lost interest as the man writhed, blood trickling from his nose. I felt guilty we had done nothing. 'Don't you think,' I asked Ian, 'that it would have been worth trying to stop them?'

'That would have been a very adolescent response.'

Outside, the man crawled over the threshold of his flat, and shut what was left of the door. We helped Pete clear away and then we all left. Back at my place I sat in the living room and read *One Dimensional Man* in order to keep my vision alive.

CHAPTER EIGHT
CLARA

By November, over two months since moving in, I began to wonder if Hornsey Rise would work out, although there were some optimistic signs, for example: Steve organised a 'Green Meeting' at his flat. Someone involved with the magazine *Street Farmer*, I think that was the name, came up from Bristol to talk about 'Ecology in the City'. There were about fifteen people at the gathering. However, the desire to change the way people thought about living in the inner city did not translate into Hornsey Risers signing up to work on the vegetable patch.

At its best I loved the diversity of this place. The three blocks of flats had been built in 1927 on the site of a former orphanage. Among the people living here were students, left-wing intellectuals, a group of Italians whom I suspected of being on the fringe of the Red Brigade, ex-soldiers, junkies, anarchists from Paris, acid heads, families, mental-health victims, rent boys, a few professional people, teenagers past the age of foster care, a former boxer. There were conflicts but most of the time we had a tolerant respect for one another: we shared a subconscious unity against the council, the police, and all those who did not want us here. It was those most 'committed' (the heavy politicos) who seemed to me the most divisive.

I felt less burdened by an alcoholic mother and my shame at being a drop-out public schoolboy: Hornsey Rise was a creative scrapheap, a peculiar kind of home for those either thrown out by, or fighting against, a corrupt society. Living close to Highgate Hill, on the edge of inner-city London, I felt I was also living close to the edge of our broken culture, and enjoyed the frisson this gave me. However, in the last week there had been a significant turn for the worse. Too many of the new people were heroin dealers, thieves, chronic alcoholics, while many of the good folk were leaving.

Clara was still here and I was tormented by desire. She and a group of friends, including her boyfriend, Danny, had two flats in Welby. There seemed to be about three girls who lived there regularly and two guys; numerous other people used to stay over for weekend-long parties. She liked teasing me: 'It's not too late for a Tarot reading, Jeremy'; 'Can I take a few photos of you for a collage I'm making?' What was the point of encouraging her? It would just lead to trouble. Even if we had sex, I would not be her only lover, and that would make me jealous and insecure.

The next morning at the vegetable patch, I said to Steve, 'I think the herbs will sell well next year.'

'Yeah, I'm sure. Look.' His desert-boot heels squelched into the earth. 'I'm going to do a three-month course at the alternative technology place in Machynlleth, learn more about basic green housing... I'm sorry.'

'What for?' I stood up.

'Too many negative forces here.' He stared at the ground. 'The allocation committee is a bloody farce – I haven't seen Ernie for over a week – and I think he's gone off with the communal money he should have banked.'

'How much?'

'£100. Everything we had collected from contributions.' He put his hands over his face. 'Oh, shit.'

'It's not your fault. Will you be coming back?'

He looked down at his boots. 'And I don't think the council will budge. There will be a mass eviction next spring.'

'Let's go to the cafe.'

'Okay.'

After our brunch, I spent the rest of the day cleaning the flat. In the evening, I stared out at the squalor. I was dreading Christmas. Where would I go? Who would I spend it with? The next morning, after a muesli breakfast, I stood in the corridor and looked down at the yard.

I jumped as Pete's voice rasped at me. 'There's a party tonight at The Railway Tavern.'

'I'm not in the mood.'

'You will be, posh sassenach.' He grabbed my shoulder. 'Clara will be there.'

'So what? She's still going out with Scowly Face. No chance for me.'

'You'd be good for her; I'm sure she fancies you.'

'She flirts with me; that's all.'

'She's doing too many drugs. Help her.'

'I'm not a social worker.'

Pete sometimes worked as a roadie for Danny's group so he knew what was going on between Danny and Clara.

Pete and I looked over the balcony.

'It's a bit grim but you should have seen the Gorbals.'

'Christ, is that Robbie?'

A dishevelled boy with a sunken face and a stained velvet jacket walked towards the stairs.

'And that's his girlfriend, Jen, with him.' Pete lowered his head.

'The blonde girl who worked in a Camden Market boutique? Shit.' I did not recognise her at first: the once bobbed hair was a mass of greasy rats' tails and her black leather jeans were discoloured and torn. There were purplish boils on her cheeks. Robbie and Jen were holding hands as they went up the stairs.

'I can't believe it,' I said.

'You've had a sheltered life. Don't dwell on them. They're using a lot of smack.'

'What went wrong with this place?'

A trail of once white sheets, knotted and torn, snaked from a skip. The brightest things in the yard were the two heavily chromed motorbikes of Steve and Rich, the Hells Angels who were now living in a flat on the first floor. It seemed that Mick had become the allocation officer and given them a place. Their bikes were lovely: a Triumph Bonneville with a burgundy tank and side panels; a chopper-style Norton with a featherbed frame and a big pre-unit 650cc engine. I had bumped into the bikers yesterday in the corridor and we had a chat. Rich worked in a motorbike shop on the Holloway Road and said if I was ever looking for a bike he would help me out. I liked him. (The Hells Demons never came back. We only had Angels now.)

For the rest of the day I worked on an essay about Utilitarianism. At 8pm, Pete knocked on my door. 'Let's go,' he said.

The wind and rain buffeted us as we set off and my charity shop black umbrella flipped inside out and so I threw it in the hedge. The pub was snug and boozy as we huddled near the open fire with pints of Guinness. Pete shook his dark-blue donkey jacket which submerged his small frame; his head rose up from the collar as he scanned the room. His gimlet eyes knew who to avoid: 'Watch out for Len. If he offers you speed, don't take it.' I hung up my greatcoat and tucked in my green Paisley shirt. At the edge of the disco floor, as the DJ played Bowie's 'Rebel, Rebel', Clara stood in her blue silk top and black jeans. I followed Pete over to her.

'Hello, Jeremy; written any more poems?' She glanced at Danny who was sitting at the bar. 'He's going to a gig.'

'Is he,' I said nonchalantly.

Pete went to chat to a friend at the bar.

Clara and I sat in the comfy chairs at the edge of the disco floor as the DJ took a break. We talked about our favourite groups: 'I don't like Velvet Underground,' she said, 'too dangerous. They make me think the craziest things. Nico is frightening but she's hooked me. I love The Doors.' She held a vodka and tonic in both hands. 'I really want to get back to art college next year.' I did not like to ask why she had left, or what had happened, and let her lead me to the bar to meet two of her friends, arty girls in long floaty skirts and sequinned blouses. I flicked my long fair hair behind my ears. Danny called 'Bye' from the door and gave me an ugly look.

Clara and I went back to our seats with a second round of drinks, which I bought. She went to the Ladies and came back with her eyes and lips made up again. As she walked towards me she twirled, a flick of the hips, arms rising on either side of her head, the Indian leather sandals turned at different angles, as if this was the first move to a Curved Air track. It would have looked show-offy if most girls had tried it.

'Sorry. It just comes over me.' She squeezed my wrist.

'Where's your girlfriend?'

'I don't have one.'

'That tall snooty girl with a bob I saw you with in Hornsey last week.'

'Belinda? She's a friend.'

'Oh.'

Pete sparked around the pub like the court jester.

In the hubbub I told Clara things I did not usually speak of: wanting to find a steady girlfriend again, hating my philosophy degree, and wanting to write.

'If there's something you have to do – you must!' She squeezed my hand quickly.

'I'm going to try.'

She went to the Ladies again and came back very smiley. Had she taken speed?

'Fancy a bop?' she said.

'Okay.'

We danced to The Small Faces, and then to Neil Young's 'Till the Morning Comes', a slower tempo; the other couples got close to each other but we kept a distance. The floor was sticky and the chairs and tables had been stacked up around the room. The big speakers on either side of the fireplace boomed; the DJ, wearing a red flowery shirt and a Plasticine smile, sat at his corner turntable when the music stopped abruptly; he got onto his knees and fiddled with a plug lead.

In the quiet I recalled the voluntary work I had done for a week last year at Holloway Sanatorium when I helped to arrange a party. As I watched the patients dance they seemed disembodied as if a part of them was searching for a home they had lost. They were in a vast grey space: signposts had been knocked down, or perhaps new ones had been put up in the night. We were all vulnerable. Five years ago my mother had ended up in Holloway Sanatorium having ECT treatment. I wanted to understand mental illness because who could tell if it would strike me? The music started again.

'You look so sad,' Clara said. 'I've got a great Thai-grass joint in my bag.' She tickled the back of my neck.

I followed her into the garden. It had stopped raining and the air was fragrant from the vegetation. She put her hand into a brown-leather shoulder bag and took out a perfectly rolled torpedo joint.

'Here; you have it,' she said.

I took a few pulls and waves of pleasure rippled through me. I gave it to her; she toped and flicked off the ash. I was bursting to say one of the sentences in my head. 'Shall we meet again to discuss writing or art?' No, not that one. 'If you ever want a second opinion on your painting.' No. 'Would you mind reading some of my poems?' Definitely not. 'Danny is a complete shit. You'd be much happier with me.' Yes. Yes. We passed the joint back and forth.

'I don't always get on with Danny,' she said.

That must be a sign, I thought. We went woozily back in, our thighs touching as we squeezed through the door.

'See you later.' She went off to chat to a few people.

I sat at a table on my own. Everyone was talking and I wished I had Pete next to me. The frothy swell of Guinness at the bottom of my glass bubbled... I adjusted my watch... I drained my drink... I brushed imaginary dust from my shirt... On the flock wallpaper a patch of damp had turned a red rose to rust... An *Evening News* was folded on a corner chair. Each minute felt like an hour.

221

'Fancy another bop?' Clara said.

On the disco floor we twirled to 'Waterloo Sunset'. People looked at us. Yes, I thought, this is my new girlfriend, Clara; aren't we a great couple? I instinctively ran my finger up her spine; she giggled, and I realised what I had done. The DJ put on Leonard Cohen's 'Suzanne', and we all turned into tragic mystics, but not so tragic for me because Clara put her arms round me, and her body flexed into the shape of mine. I was able to shuffle us to the corner where we clinched.

'That was nice.' She squeezed my shoulder.

'Yes.'

'Oh, no.' She looked over at the bar.

'You coming or what?' Danny marched towards us. 'The gig was cancelled. Big party on in Islington.'

She looked at me, at him.

'Well?'

'Of course I'm coming, Danny.'

He grabbed her hand.

'Take care, Jeremy,' she said. 'We're all moving to a new place in Stoke Newington tomorrow.'

Once they had gone, I slipped out and returned to Welby House. Inside, I put the Yale into lock position. For the last month I had kept on the lights in the hallway and kitchen to deter break-ins. I made Turkish coffee on the hissy two-ring gas stove and took it upstairs. I put a little yellow cup and saucer, and a bag of liquorice fudge, next to my mattress. I lay down and thought again about returning to Egham. I looked at my patterned shirt hanging over the door: I loved psychedelic hippy clothes, but in my mind now all the kaleidoscopic colours of shirts, headbands and scarves were running into a muddy splurge. The curtains were open and lights from other flats, and the glow of the streetlamps up to Hornsey Rise, shimmered on the walls. This space belonged to no one and I was just another temporary occupant. The next morning I decided to go back to Egham for a break and set off early in my minivan.

Ma was taking a pint of milk off the doorstep as I drove up.

'You could clean it, darling.' She tapped the bonnet.

I jumped out. 'Might put holes in the rust.'

'Your old banger is bad news for property prices; I may have to sell the house.'

'Hello, Ma.'

Our creosoted front fence had three panels missing. Weeds spread between the paving slabs.

'You look tired. New girlfriend?'

'Ma! We aren't all obsessed with romance.'

Her green check skirt and cream blouse were Ma in get-on-with-it mode, yet her fair lightly permed hair, subtle make up and red lips hinted at her daredevil spirit.

'Come in.' She smiled.

It was a different smile, not the usual one which said, 'I know you are mature but you are still my little boy.' No, this was a smile for a grown-up. It was the kind of look she gave to attractive men.

'Shall I make you a cooked breakfast?'

'Yes please.'

Since Uncle Neville had left the flat, over ten years ago, we sometimes had tenants living on the ground floor. These short-term residents were usually junior officers from the REME base near Chobham Common. At present the flat was empty so we used the main front door and not the steps that led up the side of the house. Standing at the door of Neville's old sitting room, my memories of him were wispy. Perhaps he was my real father, as Ma viewed truth as an option to be used for her convenience, and may have lied; actually, I was fairly sure that Pa was my father, even if sometimes I guiltily wished he had not been.

In the dining-room the varnished wooden floor was dark and the painted old-pine cupboards chipped. I could strip the floorboards, repaint the woodwork and polish the terracotta tiles in the kitchen-cum-scullery. Ma and I could help each other. Why didn't I leave college, get a job and pay rent? I could start writing properly and ask Clara to live with me. Would Ma let me drive the MGB?

'Breakfast, darling,' she called.

I ran up.

'You're at the head of the table.' She stretched out her arm: 'Chilvers bacon and pork sausages, fried bread, tomatoes and mushrooms.'

'Lovely.'

She smiled victoriously and poured the tea. 'I thought you'd prefer a mug.'

'Because I'm a squatter?'

'Ha, ha. More toast if you want it.'

Sitting in my father's chair, I glanced to the left and saw the whisky bottle with the silver optic ready for action. I chewed the sausage slowly and the taste mixed with his sickly old man's smells.

'I must get another bottle of Lea & Perrins,' Ma said.

'Umn.'

'This will be rather an odd Christmas. I might see Mary Maynard; she is coming down from Lancashire, with her very attractive daughter, Diana, who is training as an estate agent in Chester. Or was. Do you remember Diana?'

'Vaguely. What a horrible job.'

'It all blew up last week.' Ma buttered her toast. 'Apparently she spent too much time sitting on her attractive boss's knee.'

'Might help her career.'

'Not anymore.' His wife found them, well saw them – rather naked – in the office after work.'

'Ah.'

'Mary has a property-tycoon friend in Richmond who may help Diana. Mary and Diana are staying with him for Christmas.'

'Sounds hopeful.'

I finished the fried bread.

She opened the *Daily Mail*. 'I suppose you'll want the *Guardian*?'

'And the *Morning Star*!'

'The *Guardian* is quite far enough.'

Ma read out an article about the trade unions destroying Britain, and how only an Enoch Powell-type politician could restore our national identity.

'You don't need to be a hippy any more to get away from me; I've changed.' She looked at the floor. 'We must stick together, darling.'

'Great breakfast. Thanks.'

Ma got up and took my plate to the kitchen.

'More tea on its way,' she said.

'Okay.'

I was grown up; Ma had come through her breakdowns. She might let me redecorate the house. I opened the drinks cupboard in the corner: shelves of various cut-glasses, sherry, whisky, liqueur, red and white wine; colourful Bavarian hock glasses; tumblers. One shelf was devoted to drinks. I checked the floor for empties. None. Excellent.

I went for a walk around Egham.

The week before Christmas was pleasant and uneventful. I enjoyed the everyday calm of life here: walking to Prune Hill, having a chat with Marge in the sweet shop, and buying rump steak for supper from Chilvers. 'Hello, wormy,' John the butcher said, who had known me since I was five years old, 'It must be nice for Mrs Worman to have you back again.' I almost began to feel I belonged in Egham. All my squat-tension fears – break-ins, fights, quarrels, arrests – gave way to the dulcet sounds of milkman, postman and paperboy. The only reason for returning would be to go out with Clara. Whatever happened, I saw a new life ahead. 'You've got so handy,' Ma said as I mended the lavatory seat and screwed back the towel rail.

On Christmas Eve Ma and I went to the carol service at Egham parish church. When we came back we ate home-cooked ham and salad in the dining room. I opened the champagne. She lit the silver candelabra. As the flames danced in the draught from the open fire, I felt I was floating, and that each candle was a member of my family. Ma was beautiful in the delicate glow, her makeup like an alpine slope of melting shades. After supper she picked up a black box from the corner of the room.

'What are you doing?' I said.

'Your father left me poorer than I realised.'

'Perhaps he didn't anticipate the needs of a duchess.'

'I am in a constant state of economy; I even pay my Caleys bill monthly.'

She dug her hand into the box. 'I was worried I had lost a big cheque – oh, thank goodness!' She waved the cheque. 'It's the one from the Imperial Tobacco shares that Charles sold for me last week. Thank God for smokers.'

'By the way, weren't you giving up smoking?'

'I've cut down.'

'Good.'

'Thank you, Inspector Puritan. It's Christmas. A toast to your dead father.' She stood up.

'Why *my dead father*? Why not *your dead husband*?'

'How morbid.'

'Couldn't you just say: *a toast to your father*? Or *to my husband*?'

'You're terribly precise, Jeremy. Your father – note not "dead father" – would admire that.'

Our laughter made us wobble and we put down the 1930s cut-glass coupé champagne glasses before we spilt the precious liquid. Our bellies hurt. We blew our noses.

'Liberace, darling. We must.'

'Mustn't.'

'Please.'

In the sitting room I put *Christmas at Liberace's* on the radiogram, and kept open the interconnecting door so we could enjoy the maestro's rendering of 'Tannenbaum'.

'Good boy. Geoff would want us to be happy.' She dried her eyes. 'To your father.'

I raised my glass. I remembered some interesting conversations I had had with him, and his dry sense of humour, but these memories raised no deep emotions. I felt sad for my father, not because I loved him, but that I could not. I left Ma with her box and made a pot of tea to take up to bed.

She called out, 'I've found another cheque! Rio Tinto. Dividends. What lovely people.'

I opened the dining-room door: 'Goodnight.'

Liberace's 'Star Bright' serenaded me up the stairs.

The next morning we had toast and tea.

'We must pull a cracker,' Ma said.

'It's too early.'

'You poor old man.'

She picked up one of the large silver-spangled Christmas crackers. We tugged it and Ma took out a trinket, joke and hat. We pulled a second and I got the same. Memories of happy childhood Christmases poured out, times with no undertow of dread, but pure white like the pillowcase Ma used to fill with presents for my stocking. It was impossible to say when the darker feelings had begun. I held the end of the broken cracker and imagined holding Clara's hand. I longed for a festive season with her.

'You must wear your hat, darling.'

She put on her yellow crown and I put on my red one.

'That goes so well with your shirt. Now we'll be happy all day. You'll see.' She looked at her watch. 'I must get moving.'

On her way to the kitchen Ma sang 'The first Nöel the Angel did Say' and the top notes cracked – 'I can't sing anymore.' She stamped her foot.

I looked at the whisky bottle. Last night it was a quarter full but that bottle had been replaced by a new one. I took off my paper hat.

'Shall I peel the sprouts?' I called.

She pushed open the serving hatch. 'Bit late to offer help now – just make those bloody champagne cocktails.'

'We had champagne last night.'

'Are you trying to spoil my fun?'

I got up and took two sugar lumps from the bowl, dropped them in our glasses, squirted on a few drops of Angostura, a little brandy, and filled up with champagne.

She came into the room with her hat askew.

'Well done.' She swigged. 'Drink up, darling. Get in the right spirit now and we'll be set up.'

I sipped.

'I'll take mine back with me. Christmas is such a trial. Chin chin.'

I listened as she zipped around the kitchen. 'What are you doing?' I said.

She did not answer.

Five minutes later she came back: 'Roast potatoes done.'

Ma clicked the lighter on the mantelpiece, then sat in Pa's chair. In profile, her head was slightly raised, the right arm outstretched with the cigarette poised, as if she was waiting to be photographed by Cecil Beaton. It was only 11am but we were close to the tipping point. Two outcomes were possible: if I made her a coffee, and brought it in on a tray with a piece of fruitcake, she might, after that, return to the kitchen and say something like: 'Lovely to have you home, darling' – and the threat of the storm would be over. The other outcome was that the demon Ma would take over.

'Top up my champagne, will you? Cooking is therapeutic; you should try it.'

'Very funny. I think I'll go for a quick walk. I need a bit of fresh air. Give me an appetite.' I had to get out before we started quarrelling.

Outside, the damp grey weather sapped any idea that a saviour would bother to be born on such a mediocre day. I walked round the block. In the houses decorations glowed. On the pavements children played with their new bikes. A boy at number 27 was dressed up in a cowboy outfit, pistols in his two-gun holster. Along the road cars arrived and guests got out. Oh, Happy Families! I went on to Prune Hill and glanced at the woodland to the south where I often used to walk along the sunken drover's track. I liked the idea of spending Christmas Day in the meadow beyond, but I turned round and went home.

'I'm back, Ma. What can I do?'

The slow-cooking turkey and stuffing aromas rose from the oven.

'Ma?'

I went into the dining room and noticed the whisky was down a few more inches. I opened the sitting room door where the Christmas tree lights winked; from the record sleeve on top of the radiogram Liberace in evening dress smiled beatifically.

'Ma?'

'I'm in my bedroom,' she shouted.

I ran up.

'Just needed a rest. Stay with me, darling.'

She was sitting up, puffing a lipstick-smudged cigarette. Her yellow cracker hat was askew.

'Let me make you a coffee; piece of fruitcake?'

'Silly little boy. Do you think we're having an afternoon party?'

'Be careful!'

She flopped sideways. I knelt and stopped her falling out.

'Thank you, darling. Let's have a proper talk like we used to.'

I pulled out a whisky bottle from under the bed.

'The perfect little detective has found me out again – well, I don't care. I don't bloody care. You only think of yourself and a big Christmas lunch. Free lodgings.'

I wanted to smash my fist against the wall. I wanted to scream. I wanted to drag Ma out of bed and kick her round the room.

'No, darling, no. I'm sorry. I'll get up in half an hour.'

She dropped sideways again.

'You need to sort yourself out,' I said. I can't do it anymore. I've seen you too often like this. I'm sorry. I've had enough. I'm going back to London.'

I went downstairs and put the oven to low. The fridge was stuffed with food and I took slices of ham, hard-boiled eggs, a lettuce and a few apples; I chose a brown loaf from the bread bin; in the cupboard I found a jar of pickle, two cans of baked beans, lobster soup, a bottle of red burgundy. I crept upstairs to my bedroom and pushed some clothes into my suitcase.

'Jeremy; darling?'

I stood at her door. 'See you in a few days. I can't stand this anymore, Ma.'

'Jeremy! Selfish little bastard. Don't come back. Just don't bother.'

At the front door I listened: might she fall out of bed and break some bones? Could she vomit and choke? Perhaps she would walk round Egham in her dressing gown. She would probably not try to kill herself. Would she ever want to see me again?

The roads were quiet and it did not take long to get to Hornsey Rise. I was relieved that my flat had not been broken into. In the kitchen I filled up a plate with food; I opened the wine and the pop of the cork made me sad. 'Happy Christmas!' I called to my bloated friends in the storage room. I got under my duvet, shivered, and drank down a glass of burgundy. What on earth was I doing here? Prep school friends floated along the elegant Haileybury drive like a cavalcade. What had gone wrong with my life?

On Boxing Day I woke late and glanced outside: a grey London stretched like a giant lung of smog. At midday there was a knock at the door. I put on my jeans and ran down. 'Who's that?'

'Duke of fucking Edinburgh.'

'Come in, Pete.'

'Season's greetings to you.' He shuffled me out of the way. 'I need to check my store room; I'll tell you my plan while we're at it.' He charged up the stairs. 'I'm getting rid of all the copper water tanks next week but for now we're taking the one I promised you to Clara's new place in Stoke Newington. You should come with me.'

'I've got plans for today.'

'Don't get uppity with me, you effete sassenach. And I'll sell it for you at a later date.' Pete looked them over. 'Take your pick. It's a Christmas present.'

'I'm not choosing a bride.'

'Callous bastard.'

'I like that one.' I pointed to the corner: 'Love those dimples, perfect breasts.'

'She's my favourite too. Now come on, get dressed.'

We pushed our way through the clanking Daleks, and gently bumped my one down the stairs, through the yard and into the back of Pete's white-and-rust Ford Transit van.

'Let's go.' We set off. 'If you feel like a change of scene, I've heard there are plenty of squats in Stoke Newington, so don't worry yourself.'

Apparently the people in Clara's house were like a squatters' estate agent and they would be able to fix me up. It had become difficult to find good squats. Hackney Council, and many others, were vandalizing their own properties – smashing up lavatories and sinks, pulling out gas and electricity metres – in order to deter squatters. Pete rubbed a greasy hand on his scarf. At Archway the gearbox grated as he changed into fourth. Twenty minutes later we had reached Newington Green where the pavements were glossy from a shower of rain. In Albion Road the houses were scruffy but solid; three-storey Victorian ones on the right, two-storey terraces on the left. The bow-fronted Albion Tavern was busy, with men's faces bobbing above the frosted glass, as cigarette smoke and Irish music flowed out. The road curved as we got into Church Street and I heard singing from the candlelit St Mary's church. The yew trees swayed.

'Gone the wrong way.' Pete turned round.

Five minutes later, the Transit stopped outside her house.

'How is Clara?' I said.

'She wants to get clear of Danny and she's slowing down the drugs. She'll be all right. He's a shite.'

I opened the back of the van and we took out the tank. I hit it with the side of my fist, which made it resonate like a Buddhist bell. We stood on the doorstep of the late-Victorian house. The front garden was overgrown with high grass, rose bushes, shrubs and a smashed-up lavatory lay at the side of the door. Pete tugged the bell pull and eventually a short round man in a Jethro Tull waistcoat answered.

'Is Clara in?' Pete said.

The man shook his head and spread his arms as if to hide our view. I tried to look past him and he moved to block my sight. Clara was at the side of the corridor, thinner and her features sharper; she did up the buttons of a red Fair Isle cardigan.

'Get out of the way.' She pushed him aside.

He mumbled and went upstairs.

'Hello, Clara,' Pete said, 'this is my mate, copper water tank.'

'Hello, Jeremy.'

She turned away. I put the tank against the wall. We followed her to the kitchen.

'Danny around?' Pete asked.

'He's gone to Finsbury Park to pick up a guitar, a Les Paul or something.'

The torn linoleum was cracked and the joists shook. A single bulb shone on the greasy surfaces as she made tea-bag tea.

Don't you remember the disco? I wanted to shout.

We sat at the grubby table as she plonked two chipped white mugs in front of us.

Pete glanced up at her. 'Can you keep the tank safe for a few weeks? I'm going to get Jeremy a good price for it.'

Clara scowled. 'Suppose; I'll keep it in my room. Only two weeks.'

Pete fidgeted. 'Look, I'm sorry but I've got to go. Business. Can you manage it on your own, Jeremy? See you after.'

He got up and left.

'This way,' she said.

I followed Clara and clanked up the stairs with the tank.

'That's Danny's room,' she pointed across the corridor; 'we're lucky to have two; he does a lot of practising.'

I laid the tank next to the mattress on the floor. Richly patterned carpets had been nailed to the damp walls. A large moth-eaten Persian rug spread over the bare boards; a Victorian couch with a curved back was in the middle of the room, its red-velvet fabric torn. She switched on two lamps, lit a joss stick and closed the shutters.

'My mum wants me to go home for Dad's birthday party. The last time I was home he called me "a drug-slut princess", and Mum said nothing.' She flopped on to the couch and picked up a brown envelope. 'It's nice to see you again.' She took out a photo and handed it to me. 'It's me at the end of term in the fifth form; my mum sent it.' Her eyelids rose and fell.

233

The five girls, in short dark skirts and white blouses, were laughing and sharing a joke. The photo reminded me of being at Mr Blundell's, of an adolescent innocence before the future got you.

'Lovely,' I said.

'The headteacher asked me to leave that term.' She rubbed a hand across her face. 'I look a mess, I know.'

She did not. Faded blue jeans hugged her hips and bedraggled hair gave a just-come-off-the-surf beach look. I wanted to talk about the disco but dared not risk it. She rolled the tank into the middle of the floor.

'I think I'll draw that.'

The light glowed on her newly hennaed hair. She held the tank at one angle and then another; she stretched over it, knelt down, rubbed a smear from it with the arm of her jumper. The tank's yellow-red tinges were brought out by the lamps as she pressed her hand at one end and I held mine at the other. She got up and buffed the tank's top with a cloth.

'I can do something with that,' she said.

I sat on the sofa and the springs twanged.

'Do you...?' She held up a Thai stick.

I nodded. She rolled a joint and her fingers shook as she lit it. The rising smoke made shapes, which she punctured with her finger. She blew puffs through the inlet hole of the tank and smoke spumed from the outlet hole in rings.

'It's a lovely shape, and it's warmed up now.'

'What was it like growing up in Welwyn?' I asked.

'It's where we're going to that counts.'

'I know people who are setting up a commune near Aberystwyth.'

She gave me her Oh-you-nice-little-boy look. The front door banged open.

'Don't look so guilty; Danny won't think we've been doing it.'

234

I would not have thought Danny would have thought that. She held the tank upright and it swayed between us. A braided silver necklace glinted round her neck.

'You up there?' a growly voice said.

'Sure, Danny.'

'I'll drop round next week?' I whispered.

'Yes.' We squeezed each other's hand.

Danny stood at the door in his black leather overcoat.

'Nice to meet you again,' I said. 'Do you know any good squats going?'

'Not for you.'

'That's really helpful. Thanks.'

I got on to Church Street but did not know the area, nor how to get back to Hornsey Rise. I turned down the path of The Old Church, tried to open the door, but it was locked. In the churchyard an elderly lady in a brown woollen overcoat was kneeling by a grave and holding a bunch of white chrysanthemums. I asked if she knew the way to Hornsey Rise. 'You're a long way from there, love.' She got up. Her eyes were blotchy red behind her glasses. She gave me directions to the Holloway Road and smiled. She was made up with a lot of face powder, which reminded me of Em. 'Thanks very much,' I said. What I really wished was to go home with her and have tea and cakes in an old-fashioned room; she would tell me stories about her relations and her long life in Stoke Newington. I wanted to become her honorary nephew. An hour later I got back to my flat, made a tahini and honey sandwich, and ate in front of the living-room window. Motorbikes were revving up and there was a procession of four riding over the square; one was a trials bike and the rider was practising his skids on the wet grass, using his heel to control the turn of the bike. All the riders wore their Hells Angels denim jackets but no crash helmets, and they were laughing wildly. I admired their devil-may-care attitude.

On a wet and windy January lunchtime I decided to ask the Candyman if he fancied going to the pub. I put on my greatcoat and headed off. In the entrance to his block of flats a policeman was shouting orders. Lights were flashing on a patrol car.

'This way...'... 'Over there...'... 'Hurry up...'

Sneaking past, I began climbing the stairs when a policeman shouted: 'Stop him!' A scowling young constable grabbed my arm. I asked him what the problem was and he took a few steps back as my accent gained me brief authority.

'Out the way!' two ambulance men said as they came down with a stretcher. The patient's face was covered with a sheet but a turned-up right hand was dangling like a claw on the ground – it was the Candyman. I told the policeman I knew who it was, and gave him my details. I listened to myself speaking as if this scene was part of a film. I returned to my flat.

An hour later the doorbell rang. 'I'm Detective Sergeant Reeves.' His thinning dark hair flapped in the wind.

'Come in.'

His eyebrows rolled as he took in the dinginess of my squat. We sat on the window seat.

'So what do you know about him?' he said.

I told Sergeant Reeves all I knew about the Candyman. When I'd finished, he told me his version of the Candyman. I started shaking as if trying to repel what he was saying: 'Had no mother... bought up by Dr Barnardo's... £2000 under the floorboards... heroin... big dealer... looks like he was murdered...'

He put his hand on my shoulder: 'This is no place for you, son.'

The sun flashed shadows of leafless plane trees across the flats. The branches were like withered arms.

A week later, on Monday morning, I stayed in bed late. Apart from the horror of the Candyman's death I still felt anxious about Ma. When she had an episode like this, my stomach knotted up for weeks; I worried about what she might do or if she hated me. When she withdrew her love, I felt that, even as an adult, my life forces were draining out. At those times I believed I was a bad person, unworthy to be alive. In the night I'd had a nightmare about Ma and Clara: as I walked down a dark road, the Janus-faced image of them rotated and they were laughing at me. Which of the two should I trust? Not my mother. Clara was my future but she had to see us as a team. I walked to the Holloway Road and got a bus to Stoke Newington. My heart was pounding as I reached Clara's house. I pulled the bell then looked through the letterbox but the corridor was dark. 'Clara.'

After a few minutes she came to the door. 'Everyone is out,' she said.

The long silky black skirt hugged her as I followed upstairs.

'Chilly, isn't it.' She closed the shutters and lit the paraffin heater. 'Danny is in Camberwell, rehearsing for a gig.'

'Okay. Did you hear about the Candyman?'

'Yeah, terrible.' She looked directly at me. 'Did you think I wouldn't want to see you?'

'No. Yes.'

'I thought about you a lot.' She brushed her hair in front of a shabby 1950s green dressing table. 'Danny got this from a junk shop in Church Street.'

I sat down.

'I'm going to change; you'll see. If I don't, I might go under; I know that; you can help me.'

'I want to.'

She sat next to me and took a joint from behind her back. 'Shall we?'

'Yes.'

She lit up.

'Look what I've done to the tank. Danny's mate Joel is a welder – he made the inlet hole bigger. Didn't he do a lovely job?'

'Perfect.'

The tank lay along the floor, a sidelight at either end. She took my hand and led me over to it. I peered through a hole. An electric lead was connected to a light bulb in the roof of the tank and showed up two small clay models: a man and a woman, painted in rainbow stripes, sitting at a small table made from an egg box. She had managed to write a slogan above the heads of her models, 'Make Love Not War'. She shook the tank but the tableau stayed in place.

'I love working in miniature,' she said.

'It's great.'

'You can make some people go in there if you want.'

'They could stay for ever.'

We rested our backs against the tank.

She tapped it. 'It's like a goblet, a canister, a cooking pot, a storeship, a balloon; it can hold all our dreams.' She touched my arm. 'I'm going to stop taking drugs soon; I'll do my art instead.' She passed me a joint. 'What does the tank mean to you?'

'Not sure.' I blew smoke through the hole and covered the figures in fog.

'That's it; you're getting the idea!'

'Does Danny like your work?'

'He's into his music; don't know.'

'It suits you, having a project. You need a change.'

'Thanks, Dad.'

We worked hard as she rigged up lighting, while I replaced a broken plug. She fiddled with her camera, found a film under the bed, and took shots of the models in the tank for her portfolio. I wanted everything to happen in slow motion. I handed her the extension lead, which she wound through her fingers, and the space between us disappeared; our bodies curled round each other and we

238

kissed. We sprang apart, laughing. At the bottom end of the tank she drew a love-heart shape with a thick black felt pen, added an arrow and put two question marks inside the heart.

We sat on the bed and talked about Timothy Leary. She took a pack of tarot cards from a bedside drawer. I kissed her again and did not feel like a little boy anymore. We rolled on the bed and I stroked her nipples under the cream linen shirt. She gasped and undid the top buttons. I pushed against her warm body, but her fists hit my chest – 'Not here; not yet.'

We sat up and I held on to her bare arm.

'Let go.'

'Those are injection marks; you're using.'

'"Injection marks!" You make me laugh.'

'What did you want with me anyway?'

She sobbed.

I opened the shutters and looked into the late-afternoon dark. Turning round, I saw the room for the first time: the essential gloom of a squat, always temporary and never yours. For all its airy height, original cornices and new cream paint, the room was crumbling: the damp patch in the corner; the door with a broken top hinge; two cracked floorboards; a broken windowpane held together with a diagonal strip of putty. I saw my home in Egham too. It was also broken; temporary. Every room had a shifting carpet. The cherished things in my bedroom were just stage props. If you put your trust in any object, it disappeared in the end. From now on I was going to see every room like a theatre set. 'Cling to nothing' was a great Zen motto. But I did not want Clara to be temporary. Everything else would take its natural place around us.

She came over and put her arm on my shoulder. 'I'm going to change. That's what I wanted with you. I'm going to the clinic to find a rehab programme, have to get away from Danny.'

She was shaking. I wrote down my phone number at Egham in case I was there when she needed me.

'It was lovely, really.' She kissed me again, a long full kiss, and I squeezed her to me. 'My dole money's not come; could you lend me a fiver?'

I gave it to her, tiptoed down the stairs, and let myself out. When I got back to Welby House there was a letter from Ma.

My dearest Jeremy

Mary Maynard suggested I stay with her in Lancashire. We can walk on the moors. She still keeps a horse and I may go riding. She said I needed a proper break and that it would give you the chance to sort yourself out too. I'm setting off first thing tomorrow.

The house is all yours. You may as well come home and be comfortable. Mrs Parish will be in two mornings a week to keep the place shipshape.

I'll be in touch, darling.

Your ever loving Ma

I felt happy and relieved that she was better; more than that, she did not hate me. I was glad to leave the squat for a while. Anyway, the eviction would be coming soon; I might not be back. However, I'd learnt a lot by living there. I could reflect on all that in Egham. When Clara and I knew each other better, she could come down and stay with me. I asked Pete to keep an eye on my place and the next evening drove back to Egham. The following week was a torment: when I read, Clara's face was on the page and when I went into Egham every other girl was her. I did not go into college and wrote a letter to my tutor to say that my mother was ill.

On Friday morning I was drinking a mug of tea in the dining room. The phone rang.

'Clara? Hello.'

I looked out as the drizzle muted the winter garden; her voice lifted me far above it.

'Hope you're writing lots of poems.'

'Of course. Two full collections at least. Can I take you out to lunch tomorrow?'

'Can you afford it?'

'I've just robbed the National Provincial Bank.'

'You're funny.'

'On the corner by the Three Crowns? 1pm?'

'Yes. Can't wait.'

The next morning I arrived at Stoke Newington at 11am. I parked in Cazenove Road and walked up towards Stamford Hill, and back. I had coffee and toast in a lovely little café in Fletcher Street. Twenty minutes later I stood at the corner by The Three Crowns and checked my watch. 12.55pm... No sign of her... was I wearing the right clothes – faded blue Levis, red-checked shirt, brown leather jacket, tan Chelsea boots? 1.05pm.

'Jeremy!' She ran down Church Street. 'You look nice.'

'You too.'

She hugged me tight.

Her black boots stretched up her legs to a short brown skirt; the Paisley headband gave her a flower-child look. We walked up the High Street and into the upstairs restaurant of Gallo Nero where we sat at a window table with red-and-white tablecloths. I ordered a carafe of red wine, which came at once; we chinked glasses. The waiter returned with crusty bread and a small jug of olive oil.

'Did you go to the clinic?'

'Don't spoil things; I will. You must meet my parents one day. My dad is an engineer in an aeroplane factory and my mum is a helper in a kindergarten.' She took another gulp of wine.

It was Saturday and the restaurant was quiet. From the far corner an elderly couple smiled at us. We nibbled the bread and olives, drank, and talked about films, our

241

favourite books, football teams, 'My brother is mad about Arsenal,' she said, and 'Boxer shorts are very nice on a man.' I felt at home in restaurants as if these places were my natural lair; I was pleased to forget my hippy dreams and anxieties for a while. The spaghetti came, clam sauce for Clara, ragout for me. We wound the slithering pasta round our forks. We ate hungrily and caught each other's eyes. We gulped the wine.

'I've never met anyone quite like you,' she said, 'It's good for me.' She clasped my wrist. 'Shall we have another?'

'Why not?'

She waved the carafe at the waiter. I wanted this to be the rhythm of our days, alone in a restaurant where no one could touch us.

'Danny didn't come back last night; I know what you're thinking, but let's have a great time for now. I've got to get out of that squat. Cheers!'

Her foot rubbed my leg. We savoured our pasta. We chose zabaglione for pudding and with our long spoons gave each other a mouthful. We finished with two double espressos. I paid the bill and we left.

'We need to be somewhere where no one knows us.' She looked up and down the street.

'That's true!'

'I've got to get back soon; a man from a gallery is coming to see my portfolio; let's have a walk first.'

We headed towards Stamford Hill. At the entrance to Abney Park Cemetery she tugged my arm and we went through the Egyptian-style gates. Memorials twined with ivy and weeds, blurring natural and sacred. I imagined Edgar Allan Poe, who had been to school in Stoke Newington, strolling here when writing 'The Fall of the House of Usher'. The graveyard was as much a wild open space as a repository for genteel bones.

'We're safe now,' she said and put her arm round me. 'I love this place.'

She ran up an overgrown path and leant against a dark-red marble column whose top surface was at a forty-five degree angle. I faced her, unsure which moves to make. Clara pulled me to her and we held each other close. I stroked her thigh, and 'not here' she said, and hand-in-hand we walked into a kind of bower where tangled branches hung low from tall trees. Even in February the overgrowth was like a camouflaged tent. I felt safe, as if this was an outdoor restaurant and we could forget the world's troubles; it was an almost perfect place for winter hibernation if only we could persuade Gallo Nero to bring us a meal every day. I stood against a tree.

'Have you gone all shy?' she said.

'I have a bit.'

'Come here.'

She lay down in the thick tangle of grass. I put my lips on her neck and smelt her lovely hair. We kissed long and slowly. Her soft skin was fresh and dewy. For once we had no reason to rush and our kisses peeled off any defensive layers. I stroked between her legs. 'I'm on the pill,' she whispered. She took off her white pants; I undid my belt; she pulled down my trousers and rubbed my cock. I had waited so long for this to happen. We could not slow down now and pushed our heads into each other's shoulder to conceal our noisy shudders. Drunk and sex-drunk we lay between two gravestones.

'Wonder if they enjoyed that as much as we did,' she said. 'Do you want to go out with me then?'

'What do you think?'

'We'll do it properly when I'm free.'

We stared up at our green-shroud tepee and rearranged our clothes.

'I don't, you know, anymore; I don't fuck Danny. He's seeing someone else, I'm sure.'

'Never?'

'Last week was the last time.'

'That's not never, is it?'

'It's never from then, prickhead.'

'Well, "the last time" presumes a next time.'

'"Presumes", does it, "presumes". Fuck you!'

I got up and cut across a tangled space between the footpaths.

'Stop, you silly boy!'

'Piss off.'

I tripped over a grave. She stood above me and laughed. I was ready for more sex; I was sex-mad for her.

'When next?' I asked.

'I will finish with Danny. I'll phone. Soon. Promise. Got to go.'

We hugged. I watched her slip out of sight.

I was not going to live again at my squat as I could not cope any more with the heaviness of life there. But I kept travelling up to spend a day each week at college for a lecture or tutorial. My academic work was going better and I was less worried about the second-year exams. For the next two months Clara and I saw each once a week too, after finishing at college, which was often in the early afternoon. We once met at her squat, another time in a friend's room round the corner, but usually we went to cafes, pubs, parks, Hackney Marshes, often ending up in the cemetery. Stories she told about herself were indeterminate: she was going to a rehab appointment, or had gone, or was on a waiting list; her father was a doctor, and not an engineer, but she did not like to talk about it; they lived outside Welwyn, 'St Albans really'. And Danny? He was moving out, then he was not; he was 'the most evil person' or 'he's had his problems' or 'I don't have anything to do with him'.

One day in March we took the 73 bus for a lunchtime drink at the King's Head in Islington. The dark lines beneath her eyes had gone. Sitting on the top deck she told me, 'The first session went well with the counsellor.' She flicked an appointment card at me. 'I'm getting there; I told you.'

You'll have to come and spend a night in Egham soon.'

That thought filled me with joy: me and Clara setting out on our journey of life. I could meet her parents; she could go on a shopping trip with Ma. And if Ma went on a world cruise she might meet someone she really liked and never come back to England, or only to pack up. Then Clara and I could make Egham our home. We would rent rooms to Holloway College students. Ma might even have a heart attack. Everything would be mine, including the MGB.

We jumped off the 73 and rushed into the pub. It was quiet and Clara peeped into the little theatre at the back. I followed and we stood at the open entrance door. A young actress was rehearsing, sitting in an armchair, her legs crossed, smoking an imaginary cigarette, as the director called: 'Get the angle right, darling.' She moved the fag to the other side of her mouth. 'That's better, and flick off the ash.' Clara was transfixed.

'Help me to be something,' she said.

We sat by the open fire, drank pints of bitter and shared a homemade burger. Clara cancelled our next meeting. I hated going up to college and to Stoke Newington as London became a black hole, a place from which Clara and I had to escape. For the first time I was objective: I had to know what she was going to do about Danny; what had been exciting about our secret meetings now felt sordid.

The beginning of April was warm, bright, and ideal for outdoor sex. We met in the late-afternoon at Stoke Newington library at the side of Daniel Defoe's gravestone, which was on display in the entrance hall. Clara was wearing a long black skirt and her favourite Fair Isle jumper; she was lightly made up with a flash of green eyeliner. Her skin gleamed.

'How are your sessions going with the counsellor?' I put my arm round her.

'I'm getting sorted out.' She shook herself free.

'Come and stay in Egham.'

'I hate mothers.'

'That makes two of us. Ma is in Lancashire; I told you that.'

She was biting her lips and her eyes darted everywhere. I dragged her past The Three Crowns. 'Let's have a proper chat, without the booze.' I tugged her arm and we reached Cazenove Road.

I pointed at number 10, whose trade name, 'Madame Lillie', a former corsetry shop, was painted above the double-fronted shop. 'Paul Wright lives there; he's a sculptor and knows all about art schools. He's fellow of Sculpture at Aberystwyth but he's often here. I met him last year in Aber when I was staying for the weekend with a friend of mine. We can talk to Paul about anything.' As I rang the bell, Clara wandered off up the road of torn-bark London plane trees. I knocked louder but she was getting further away. I caught her up and eventually we reached Stamford Hill Road.

'We've got to talk,' I said.

'Get off.'

She rushed across and headed for Hackney Marshes. I caught her up again; she started to cry. We walked into Springfield Park arm-in-arm and I wanted to say I love you, but instead led her through the landscaped park, down the steep path towards Hackney Marshes where the Anglo Saxons had made a settlement. It was dusk and the neon lights had gone on in Walthamstow.

'You can't go on like this,' I said.

We lay down on the cold marshes and stared at the sky.

'Danny is an addict; he got me on to drugs.'

Her face was still at last. She rubbed dead wheat stalks between her fingers. We were numbed by the cold and lay on our backs like effigies for a while.

'I've got to get back.'

The lights came on in the flats and houses on the hill. We walked through the park and crossed Stamford Hill. When we reached Madame Lillie she said, 'I want to meet your friend soon; when I'm sorted out.' Paul was not really a friend yet but I liked the idea that he might become one. As we passed The Jolly Butchers she shivered and her fingers twitched. 'There are things I've got to do. Trust me.'

'What do you mean?'

She clasped me. 'I need £5; I must get free of these people. Please.'

I gave her a five-pound note.

'I'll phone soon. I'll miss you.'

She ran off towards Church Street, and I followed at a distance. She went into the Three Crowns, while I stood on the opposite side of the road in the entrance to William Patten School. I could make out shadowy figures in the pub; Clara was gesticulating to a black guy. She looked up and I turned away. When I glanced again she was getting into the passenger seat of a green Zodiac parked outside the pub.

For the next three days I stayed in Egham and walked a lot – only then did my thoughts stop. Clara did not phone. On the fourth day I drove to Stoke Newington and banged on her door but no one answered; I climbed over the locked gate at the side of the house and looked through the kitchen window; her Fair Isle jumper was hanging over a chair. From the other side of the road I watched her house for an hour but no one came or went. Why had I never got the address of her parents? I did not really know anyone she knew to ask, except for Pete, but he was busy and elusive these days. I walked fast through Clissold Park and took the back route to the High Street where, in Gallo Nero, I saw Clara.

'A table, sir.'

It wasn't her.

'Not today, thank you.'

I went into The Three Crowns as one of the regulars might know where she was. I bought a pint of Guinness and stood in the middle of the big dark space, as the drinkers and dealers huddled at the edges. I was halfway through my drink when a guy in a Rasta-colours woolly hat came through the door.

'Hello, Isaac.'

He was a wise funny old greybeard who played the clarinet in a jazz ensemble on a Friday night. Clara had taken me here a few times to listen to some really good bands. She knew the scene well and Isaac liked her. He came over to me.

'I'm looking for Clara.'

'Thought you might be. Let's go over there.'

We sat at a table in the corner.

'She was here the other night and she looked bad. She told me she was going to stay with her parents and I said she should do that.' He gripped my hand. 'Don't worry; it's the best thing. She explained the situation; she'll be in touch with you; she really likes you, man.' He spoke without drama.

'Thanks. I'll wait until I hear something.'

I bought him a large rum and rushed out. I did not want to go back to Egham before I had found out something more about Clara. But if I was not there, how could she contact me? I ran to Cazenove Road where I had parked; I decided to see if Pete was in. He might know something. Yes, he would definitely know. Perhaps Clara might even be there.

I drove fast to Hornsey Rise and parked in Sunnyside Road. I ran into Welby House and up the three flights of stairs.

'Pete!'

He was opening the door as I got there.

'Jeremy. I tried to phone.'

248

'Well, I'm here now.'

'I was at Clara's last night... they found her... overdose... she was dead. I'm so sorry.' Pete guided me to his living room.

'The others at Clara's place have left the squat, afraid of the police.'

'What about her parents?'

'No one could find an address book. And no one has ever met them.'

I looked out of the window.

'I'll make us a brew,' Pete said.

Outside, one of the of the Hells Angels was riding over the square practising his skids in the twilight. It was the same landscape as when I had first come here; yet now there were no children in the green square; their laughter and games had made me feel that dreams could become reality. As I looked at more broken windows and dark unoccupied flats it was clear that many others had moved on to try again.

I survived. Almost forty-five years later here I am in the early spring garden of my Hackney home where Nicola and I have lived for thirty-five years.

Hornsey Rise was a time of turmoil and confusion, and this vision of hell was made far worse by smoking a lot of cannabis. Hornsey Rise was always in flux and there was never any sense of security, only of impending disaster. People you thought you could trust turned out to be dishonest. I did not take my second-year philosophy exams at the Polytechnic of North London as I felt such hopelessness and futility about my life. After briefly squatting again in London with my good friend Dave Smith, and a few others, I retreated to Reading where I signed on the dole for a while and rented a room in a large student house. Here I met my future wife, Nicola, who was living in another flat of the house. At a house party I read her tarot cards... I stopped smoking cannabis, and in September 1978 Nicola and I came to London, where we rented a room at 'Madame Lillie', the house and studio of Paul Wright, in Stoke Newington. I began the last year of my philosophy degree, which I completed in June 1979.

Ma had been in a nursing home for the last few years of her life. We had come to a truce. There were still too many unanswered questions about why she treated me as she did in her blackest moods but it was not worth churning all that up again. Anyway, we had strong affinities, for instance a sense of fun, an interest in the opposite sex and fast cars. Strangely, I think I learnt compassion from Ma. Her concern for other people, especially for those going through hard times, was genuine.

Even with her failing memory, she still charmed. It was not uncommon for strangers to come over to us in a restaurant and say, 'Is that your mother; isn't she beautiful', or some other flattering accolade. She would turn her head, and smile. Ma had smoked for most of her life, and must have been pickled in alcohol, yet her complexion was radiant and her features even better defined with age. She gave off an aura of a benign old dowager, and all kinds of people were attracted by it. By instinct and inclination she was an actress. I do not think I ever really knew the real Barbara Ursula Worman née Piggott, and nor did she.

On the other hand, I hear her voice now as she looks up from a cheery party in hell (heaven would have bored her): 'Darling, I knew exactly who I was. You are the one who has struggled with his identity. Cheers.' She puts down her champagne glass and a devotee lights her Sobranie Black Russian.

My life has been driven by the need to write, to make sense of the world, to make sense of myself. I have succeeded a little. But I knew that the source of inspiration, of hope and terror, of issues deep within me, had not been sufficiently analysed. The surfaces of my life, for example, an English degree at Birkbeck, graduate research at Cambridge, teaching in various institutions, bohemian art activities, marriage, a late-in-the day and lovely daughter, Myfanwy, have been layers of paint over a structure that needed fundamental attention. The writing of this book has given me the chance to address those matters.

It is strange to be as old as I am yet going forward with a young man's vigour. I pick up the glass of chilled Pecorino Terre di Chieti. I feel I am on a raised plateau, where there is space and time to imagine the future. I am no longer ashamed of myself. I carry my story not as a burden but an inspiration. Cheers, Jeremy. Cheers, Ma.

Acknowledgements

I am grateful for the support and encouragement of Blake Morrison in writing this book. The advice of my literary agent, Christopher Sinclair-Stevenson, has been invaluable. My publisher, Bernadette Jansen op de Haar, and my wife, Nicola Horton, have helped in so many ways to keep this project on track.

The Way to Hornsey Rise is an autobiographical novel, inspired by life and the author's imagination. For reasons of privacy, some names, characters, events and locations have been fictionalised.

AUTHOR

Jeremy is a writer and critic who taught English Literature to American BA students for twenty-five years at Birkbeck, University of London. He has also taught at Cambridge University and at Hackney Adult Education Institute.

He was awarded a First in English from Birkbeck, and has an MA (Distinction) in Creative and Life Writing from Goldsmiths, University of London, an M. Litt from Cambridge University and a PhD in Creative Writing from Goldsmiths (2021) where Blake Morrison was his supervisor; the examiners were Francis Spufford and Sir Jonathan Bate.

Jeremy's short-story collections, *Fragmented* (2011) and *Swimming with Diana Dors and Other Stories* (2014), were published by Cinnamon Press. His short stories and poems have been published widely in, amongst other places, *The London Magazine, Ambit, The Frogmore Papers*, the *Cork Literary Review*.

He won the 2009 Cinnamon Press short story prize and the Waterstones / *MultiStory* short story competition (2002), and was shortlisted for the Jeremy Mogford £7,500 short story Prize (2016).

He has reviewed for the *Observer,* the *Times Literary Supplement*, the *New Statesman* and many other publications.

Jeremy lives in Hackney, London.

Holland Park Press, founded in 2009, is a privately-owned independent company publishing literary fiction: novels, novellas, short stories; and poetry. The company is run by brother and sister team Arnold and Bernadette Jansen op de Haar, who publish an author not just a book. Holland Park Press specialises in finding new literary talent by accepting unsolicited manuscripts from authors all year round and by running competitions. It has been successful in giving older authors a chance to make their debut and in raising the profile of Dutch authors in translation.

To

Learn more about Jeremy Worman
Discover other interesting books
Read our blogs and news items
Find out how to submit your manuscript
Take part in one of our competitions

Visit www.hollandparkpress.co.uk

Bookshop: http://www.hollandparkpress.co.uk/books.php

Holland Park Press in the social media:

https://www.twitter.com/HollandParkPres
https://www.facebook.com/HollandParkPress
https://www.linkedin.com/company/holland-park-press
https://www.youtube.com/user/HollandParkPress
https://www.instagram.com/hollandparkpress/